He found himself watching Alisha

I sure screwed up, Carson thought. *The best laid plans...* It was all supposed to be so easy. He'd catch his poachers, she'd get her pictures....

Instead he had a woman here who was more intent on seeing poachers brought to justice than in grabbing any glory for herself. That he admired. But he couldn't understand her eagerness to put herself at risk again. Why subject herself to the same dangers? Why not let someone else, someone qualified, someone like him, take the chances? That'd been *his* plan for her...and she'd rejected it.

Obviously she was a woman of courage—or a stubborn fool.

Despite her scars, he saw rare beauty in Alisha Jamison, both inside and out. She reminded him of those exotic air-orchids, found in places you didn't expect them, straining toward the light.

She'd be an interesting woman to get to know. As a friend...and as a lover.

Dear Reader,

Because my husband was in the navy, our family had the chance to enjoy two years as residents of the state of Florida. During that time, we visited the Everglades. I was so impressed with its unique beauty that sharing it with my husband and children wasn't enough. I *had* to set a story there.

While I have remained true in my descriptions of the wildlife, landscape and Seminole history of the Everglades, I have taken certain liberties in my story.

The hotel and campgrounds I describe are fictitious and are nothing like the primitive campgrounds that exist in reality. Also, although poaching remains a problem in Florida, the efforts of the park service and conservationists have put an end to large-scale alligator poaching on public and private land.

In fact, the biggest threat to the Everglades these days isn't poachers. The real danger is the need for, and drainage of, the park's freshwater reserves to support growing populations in the large coastal cities.

Sadly, all the species I've referred to in this book as threatened or endangered really are. But efforts are being made to preserve them, so there is hope for this one-of-a-kind wilderness.

It takes a special person to not only survive in these vast wetlands but to appreciate and protect its creatures. My hero, Ranger Carson Ward, and his lady, Alisha Jamison, are two such people. I hope you enjoy their romance and share their love of the great outdoors.

Welcome to the Everglades!

Anne Marie Duquette

HER OWN RANGER
Anne Marie Duquette

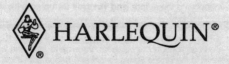

HARLEQUIN®

TORONTO • NEW YORK • LONDON
AMSTERDAM • PARIS • SYDNEY • HAMBURG
STOCKHOLM • ATHENS • TOKYO • MILAN • MADRID
PRAGUE • WARSAW • BUDAPEST • AUCKLAND

ISBN 0-373-70849-1

HER OWN RANGER

This edition published by arrangement with Harlequin Books S.A.

® and TM are trademarks of the publisher. Trademarks indicated with ® are registered in the United States Patent and Trademark Office, the Canadian Trade Marks Office and in other countries.

Visit us at www.romance.net

Printed in U.S.A.

To Donna, Bill, Luke and Jen
Who share my love for Florida

CHAPTER ONE

*June—Miccosukee Seminole Reservation,
north of Everglades National Park*

CARSON WARD, SEMINOLE-BORN and tribal-bred, sat
in the back of his private canoe, not only to steer his
passengers through the silent, unmapped waterways
but to watch for the first bullet to warn them. It
would come…and probably soon. It was only a question of when.

The poachers working the land guaranteed it. For
years now, they'd fouled the waters with the blood
of Everglades alligators, and last summer, with the
blood of Carson's father. He'd been a park ranger,
too. Ferris Ward had imbued his son with a love of
the Everglades and a sense of guardianship toward
it. A sense of justice—that was an equally important
legacy from his father.

Today was another battle in the war Carson intended to win. The poachers were clever, and as
skilled at survival as he was. But this time…

Carson's smile was deadly. *This* time, he had an
edge against the men invading his people's ancient
homeland. The three other people in his canoe

weren't the tourists they seemed to be. Instead of rangers, they were Seminoles like him—natives who knew their land as no non-tribal ranger ever could.

"Everyone okay?" Carson quietly asked in English. Those present spoke fluent Seminole, but deception was an art that required attention to detail. If they were going to *look* like tourists, they had to sound like them, too.

Sitting in the point position was Ray Weaver, cousin of thirty-six-year-old Carson and his junior by five years.

"No, I'm not okay. I feel like a damn idiot."

Carson grinned. Unlike him, Ray wasn't NPS, a ranger with the National Park Service. As a professional manager of one of the tribe's more prosperous hotel-casinos, Ray preferred tuxedos to a ranger's boots. But, like Carson, he'd grown up in these swamps. He considered the Disney World T-shirt and Mickey Mouse hat, complete with ears, an insult to his manhood, even if the baggy shirt beneath the life jacket did cover a bulletproof vest.

Carson was immovable on that point, though he wore no vest himself. He wasn't foolhardy, but his position in the rear of the canoe meant he was doing most of the steering, something he couldn't easily accomplish with a heavy bulletproof vest. Wearing one would have ensured that if the canoe upended he'd sink straight to the bottom of the Everglades. Carson preferred to take his chances.

Ray preferred same, but Carson refused to risk anyone else's life, hence Ray's present complaints.

Ray was loyal to family and fiercely loyal to Carson's late father. When he'd discovered Carson was planning this trip, Ray had insisted on coming along as reinforcement.

"If anyone from the casino saw me, I'd die of embarrassment." Ray touched the mouse ears on his ball cap and flinched. Suffering in silence wasn't his strong point. "This reeks big-time. I can't believe people actually spend money on this trash."

"Hush, or I'll make you wear the camera around your neck as well," said the older woman behind Ray. "Remember, noisy with the oars. We're all supposed to be tourists."

"I've been paddling canoes my whole life," Ray grumbled. "I don't *know* how to be noisy."

"Try," Carson insisted. "We don't want poachers thinking we're a threat."

"Fine. I'm splashing. Are you happy, Mother?"

Ray's mother, Deborah Weaver, was Carson's aunt and Ferris Ward's sister. When the poachers had killed Ferris, his widow, Mary, decided to leave the tribe's wetlands home. Ray found her a job with one of the prosperous tribal bingo halls. Mary, like Ray, detested the Everglades as much as Carson and Deborah loved them. Ray only returned for family reasons, nothing else.

Carson had stayed behind, unwilling to give up his family home or his job as a ranger. Mary repeatedly begged him to join her. He refused, vowing to stay and find his father's killers, determined to bring them to justice.

As only children, Carson and Ray looked after their aunts; Deborah was a widow, too, whose husband had died of natural causes years ago. Protection was the tribal way. Of the two mothers, traditional Seminole Deborah Weaver had always been the stronger parent, the stronger woman. She'd volunteered to accompany her nephew and son today, shrugging off their objections.

"You should've stayed home, Mother," Ray muttered, not for the first time. "We've got armed crazies out here. You could get hurt."

"Ray, I'm wearing a bulletproof vest *and* a life jacket."

"That won't keep you a hundred percent safe. Carson, why didn't you chain her to her loom?"

"I tried." Carson dodged the spray of water Deborah sent his way with a deliberate flip of the oar. "But ever since I planned this scouting party, she insisted on coming. You know that. The tourist disguise was her idea." Ignoring Ray's exaggerated groan, he said, "I couldn't shake her loose. Or her apprentice, either."

"You should have tried harder," Ray told him. "Should've told 'em both to stay home."

"I did." Carson hadn't wanted the women along, either, but Seminole women—especially Deborah—didn't take kindly to being told what to do.

"He really did," the fourth person in the canoe replied. Adoette Fisher, twenty-seven, was recently apprenticed to Deborah at the looms, although during the busy tourist season, she often worked as an operator with the tribe's prosperous airboat business. "She never listens, does she, Carson?"

The brilliant smile thrown Carson's way wasn't meant to dazzle, but to make Ray jealous. As usual, her charm failed to affect him. Carson's heart went out to Adoette.

These days, Seminoles usually made one of two choices; there were those who worked in the modern world, often in the hotel-casinos and bingo halls, and those who lived in the wetlands, following the traditional tribal ways. In the subtropical grasslands, raising cattle on the treeless savannas was part of that life. Hand-weaving colorful cloth with intricate ancient patterns was another. Seminole textiles were in demand all over the world, much like the Southwest Navaho's woven rugs.

Ray wanted nothing to do with looms or herds. He'd eagerly left the hardships of the Miccosukee Reservation wetlands—what he described as "smelly, buggy swamps"—for life in Florida's city world. Adoette, a Big Cypress Reservation Muskogee Seminole, had been born and raised in those swamps; she felt at home there. Even her Indian name, pronounced Ah-do-*ay*-tah, meant "born beneath a big tree," as indeed she'd been. Carson remembered Ray's thoughts on *that* subject.

"To think of her mother squatting under a cypress in the mud makes me sick. I don't care if I am Seminole. The practice is unsafe and outdated. No wife of mine will *ever* deliver our children that way."

A bad combination...Ray and Adoette. Neither

one wrong, neither one right. No middle ground, only trouble.

Carson knew Adoette loved Ray. Adoette had met him during her brief, disastrous try at college. When she dropped out after less than a year, she didn't return to Big Cypress. Already a skilled airboat operator and a long-time friend of the Ward family, she'd requested an apprenticeship with Deborah, moving to the open wetlands of the Miccosukee Reservation. Although she'd never admitted as much, Carson suspected the main reason she'd done it was to be closer to Ray. But Ray knew what he wanted in a wife, and a traditional Seminole wasn't it.

As for Carson, he didn't want a wife, period. Not until he'd caught the men who'd killed his father.

His vow was made as his father died in his arms last summer. Carson had begun his job with the National Park Service long before Ferris retired. Ferris himself had spent his whole life in the NPS, the federal custodian of the rare and endangered life inside Everglades National Park. All park rangers were sworn to protect it. The uniform Ferris once wore had legally empowered him to shoot any human hunters who threatened the Everglades.

Ferris's position was a unique, often solitary one, for he alone had patrolled the border between park land and Native American land until Carson was old enough to join him.

Young Carson had grown up at his father's side. Ferris had taught him to paddle a canoe, and taught him about his home. He stayed at his father's side, learning enough to make him want to become a ranger himself. The job was perfect for Carson, since only someone in his position had access to *all* the Everglades. The NPS wasn't allowed unlimited access to the five major tribal reservations, while the tribe wasn't allowed free access to the Everglades government lands. But Seminole park rangers faced no barriers. They were almost as free on the land as their ancient ancestors had been. Father and son had enjoyed the job and each other's company—until a poacher's bullet put an end to their team.

Carson had volunteered to take over the border work by himself. He continued his solitary patrol— a lone ranger—because it was the only way he'd ever find his father's killers. They'd been operating irregularly in the Everglades for the past two summers, killing gators for their hides and leaving the carcasses for scavengers to dispose of. They were careful, cautious men like himself but with more regard for money than for life. Arrests of small-time poachers had been made, but the men who'd killed his father still eluded him. Carson vowed their capture or his own death trying.

Until then, romance was out of the question. He would have welcomed a woman in his life, but his job—and now this quest—made serious courtship difficult. Carson remained solitary, grieving his father's death, and wondering if he could ever love a woman as much as he loved the Everglades. He delighted in everything about this place—its panthers, egrets, playful manatees, its cypress draped with

Spanish moss, even its snakes and those ancient dwellers, the alligators and crocodiles. The beauty of the land was his only inheritance.

In the Everglades, nature made the rules, not man. Nature determined what you ate, when you slept and the temperature when doing either. Few modern amenities existed for those in canoes.

One became a creature of the wetlands like all the others. Life continued for the fittest, the strongest, the bravest, the wisest, for male and female alike. Carson knew it wasn't right for a man to accept a woman as second-best to the land. He'd been taught family was sacred. The bond between a man and a woman should be at least as great as that between a man and his home.

Like any healthy man in his mid-thirties, he'd had his share of relationships. But, none had ever meant enough to him to give up this life. One woman, a Seminole from Big Cypress, had wanted him to move to Miami with her; that was the closest he'd ever come to marriage. It wasn't close enough.... So he accepted no women in his life except close friends, like Adoette, or kin, like Deborah. Maybe things would change once these poachers were apprehended. But until then...

"Next time, Mother, stay home," Ray was saying. "Playing tourist is bad enough. Having you watch me in this getup is insulting."

"Quiet down, Ray. Sound carries, remember?" Carson reminded his cousin.

"Yeah, Ray," Adoette added in a whisper. "Someone could be listening."

"Doubt it. I haven't seen any evidence of poaching activity here. Can't we turn around? This is a lost cause for today."

He's probably right. "Let's give it another half hour, then call it quits. We'll be home before sunset."

"Hallelujah," Ray said. "I'm starving. And I'm not providing our poachers with this target any longer." Ray snatched off the Disney World hat with such violence it landed in the back of the canoe near Carson's shoes. "There. If they want a target, it won't be these mouse ears. Let 'em aim for something else."

Carson bent over to move the hat away from his feet. "Ray, shut your—"

He was never able to complete that warning. The sound of a gun's report cracked over the water just then, the force of a bullet hitting Carson in the shoulder, knocking the air from his lungs and throwing him out of the canoe.

Adoette screamed as a second shot rang out. Ray's hoarse shout was followed by the splash of the canoe being deliberately overturned.

Carson knew his body was in shock because of the way his muscles were frozen. No pain had yet registered in his shoulder wound.

If this was a Tarzan movie, I'd be fighting the man-eating alligators.

But it wasn't a Tarzan movie. And alligators

weren't man-eaters. They only attacked prey in a certain size range; full-grown men far exceeded that range. Without oxygen, he sank like a rock in the murky waters.

Gators weren't the danger he needed to fear. Drowning was.

This is so stupid. I've been swimming all my life, and I'm drowning. I didn't even take a poacher with me.

He tried to move his arms, but could only move one. He kicked his legs, hoping to move upward, toward the surface, but couldn't. No sunlight penetrated the inky depths. His chest remained frozen in that sickening, winded condition. He had no buoyancy with empty lungs.

Damn! Time to pray. *Please, please, please…* was all he could manage. It was enough.

A hand gripped his own—a woman's, not a man's. If he could, Carson would have laughed. *Adoette, my friend, you've just paid me back for all those swimming lessons I gave you when we were kids.* Once barely able to wade without hysterics, she'd been, according to Ray, the only person in the history of the Seminole tribe afraid of water. But thanks to Carson's patience, Adoette now swam. She swam well enough for both of them.

Air! I have air! He gulped in precious oxygen as his head broke the water's surface. Carson took two more deep breaths. Only then did his eyes roll and his head fall limply onto Adoette's wet shoulder. He withdrew from the world.

CARSON AWOKE IN HIS AUNT'S chickee—the traditional summer dwelling built without walls. Deborah's was located a tactful distance for privacy from his own family chickee. His shoulder had been treated with traditional medicines and was being wrapped. It also throbbed like hell.

"Ouch! That's hurts!" He jerked in the hammock serving as his bed.

"I told them to call you a medi-chopper, but no, Mom here settled for the local rattles-and-bones man," Ray scoffed.

Adoette scolded Ray. "You'd insult your own mother and our healer? Natural plant medicine is just as good as—"

"I want the best for him, and penicillin beats swamp weeds, hands down. Not that our healer here understands English, so I'm not insulting him. Hey, cuz," Ray said, dismissing Adoette from the conversation. "How are ya?"

Ray's rough brusqueness disguised his true concern. If Carson didn't ache so much, he'd smile. The two cousins were like brothers, their close bond cemented years ago. Carson managed a faint smile, allowing Ray to relax.

"Good thing I tossed off those mouse ears and you reached for them," Ray said, "or you'd be fish food now."

Adoette shivered in horror. "How can you say that, Ray?"

"Well, it's true."

She pushed Ray aside to come closer to the hammock. "Are you okay, Carson? Does it hurt much?" She took his hand in a motion that barely swung the hammock but moved his shoulder slightly—enough to make his stomach lurch at the pain.

Carson managed to swallow a gasp. "Not much. Thanks for pulling me out, little turtle." He used her old nickname. "I owe you."

"You were the one who taught me to swim." Adoette squeezed his hand. "I hope you heal fast."

"He'd heal a lot faster if you'd stop yanking him around," Ray said. "Can't you see you're hurting him?"

Adoette started, and dropped Carson's hand. "I'm sorry," she whispered. Tears filled her eyes.

Ray, you can be such a jerk, Carson thought. *If I didn't feel so lousy, I'd kick some sense into you. Adoette only cries when you're around.*

"Lucky for you the bullet came out easily," Ray happily informed him.

"Let me see it."

"There's no need for that," Deborah fussed.

"Let me see it."

"Save your breath," Ray said. "I'm with you. I'm sending this slug to your boss at the station. If— when—we catch the poachers, the ballistics match should get them an attempted murder charge, too."

"Just guard that bullet," Carson said weakly. "So far, it's the only new evidence we have." He settled more comfortably into the hammock. "It might even match the bullet that killed my father."

"But the NPS will have to send that bullet to Miami for testing,'' Adoette pointed out. "It'll take weeks to get the results.''

"I can wait,'' Carson said. "Anyway, I should be recovered well before that. Thank God the bullet didn't do more damage.''

"Stop it, right this instant!'' Deborah interrupted them sharply. "This isn't the time or the place.''

Adoette nodded. "Deborah's right. Concentrate on getting better first. You'll be up and about soon. That really will heal quickly. Deborah says it's just a furrow.'' Adoette pointed to his shoulder. Just the nearness of her finger to his wound caused sweat to break out on his forehead. *That must be some furrow. Feels like I could drive an airboat through it.*

"I'm tired,'' he said in his native tongue.

"You two—out. He needs rest.'' Deborah placed herself between Carson and the others in a protective maternal pose.

"Thanks again, Adoette. Later, Ray.'' Carson's eyes closed. He sighed in contentment as Deborah smoothed his forehead with a gentle hand.

"I'll have Ray call your mother when he goes to work,'' she said as the tribal healer continued his ministrations. "She'd want to know.''

Carson opened his eyes again. "What will he tell her?''

"The truth—that her son is hurt.''

"She'll ask how, and Ray'll go into details. Why call her about a minor injury, anyway?''

Deborah ducked her head guiltily.

"The bullet went deep, didn't it?''

She met his eyes. "Almost right through. You could have bled to death."

I nearly drowned first. "So that's what you intend to tell my mother? You'll destroy her peace of mind—which is fragile enough as it is."

"She's afraid of losing you like she lost her husband."

"*That* is not the point."

"Death *is* the point, Carson!" Deborah's protest was so loud the healer paused over his bandaging. "Your father was killed here. Your mother left because she didn't feel safe."

"That's why the poaching has to end. This is my home. I'll protect it and our people until I draw my last breath. To ask me to do otherwise is beneath you as a tribal elder."

"I'm not just a tribal elder. I'm an aunt who loves you."

"I'm not accountable to you on this matter." He became harsh, cold, as he always did when a decision he believed in was challenged. "I forbid you to tell my mother."

"Carson, please don't make me choose. She's my brother's wife."

"Then tell her next week," Carson insisted. He closed his eyes again, feeling weak but unwilling to concede. "Otherwise she'll drag me off to some Miami hospital."

"You might be safer there."

"They have air-conditioning. I hate air-conditioning. What if I get pneumonia?"

His aunt hesitated. She, too, suffered from leaving the superheated outdoors and stepping inside chilled structures. ''It can't be that bad, or more patients would die there.''

Carson followed up his advantage. ''Who's to say they don't? Maybe 'dying of complications' is a doctors' code for freezing to death.''

Deborah frowned. ''I never heard—'' The expression on her face changed. ''Carson Ward, you are so full of it.''

Carson grinned at her capitulation.

''You make a second mother's position very hard.''

''I'm not a child who needs mothering.'' Though the hand that smoothed his hair was very welcome indeed. *Maybe I could use a woman in my life, after all. Get married and...* He pushed away the thought, brought alive in a moment of weakness. *My father's killers first.*

''You should have a family now—and you should be sending your children to the looms or the herds. Ray and Adoette, as well. Instead, I've lost your mother to the bingo hall and Ray to the casinos. I expect Adoette will get tired of waiting and join him there. You're all so unsettled. When you went over the side of the canoe...if it wasn't for Adoette...'' Her voice broke. ''You and Adoette are close, and Ray's so stubborn. She might make you a good wife.''

Carson groaned. ''First I get shot and now I have to endure matchmaking? God help me.''

"Just a thought that crossed my mind."

"Keep it there. Please, Aunt."

He flinched as the healer wrapped over a particularly painful spot. When the job was finished, Deborah brought him herbal tea with its painkilling and sleep-inducing properties.

"Drink it," she urged.

"I will, but I need you to do something for me."

"First drink the tea."

Carson downed the drink and passed her the empty mug. "I want you to contact that woman. Alisha Jamison."

Deborah looked puzzled. "Why?"

Carson moved his legs restlessly in the hammock. "You know, she's that crusading Dian Fossey type. She and her partner—some guy Ray knows—have done those articles and TV shows that publicize poaching."

"I know who she is. I've seen some of her documentaries and photographs. And the man's name is Josh Gregory. I also remember you advised the tribe and the NPS to refuse them permission to enter our lands. You said her filming would disturb the hatchlings—and maybe interfere with the investigation of your father's death."

"Yeah, well, that was a year ago, and I thought I'd have caught Dad's killers by now."

"You've changed your mind?"

"Yes. She's exposed poachers all over the world. She gets publicity for animals at risk and creates public awareness of the problem." He paused. "Her work even led to the capture of some poachers—in Australia, I think.''

"But you said you were going to catch the poachers yourself."

"I intend to. However, I need a distraction—a tactical diversion—while I'm doing it. Today's was a bust."

"We wanted to come."

"I shouldn't have agreed. I endangered my family and nearly got killed in the process. I'm the ranger here. This is *my* job, not yours."

"Carson, don't."

"I've been going about this all wrong," he mused. "This woman just might be our ticket to success. Alisha Jamison's business is documenting damage done by poachers. She's a very public figure. If we bring her onto Seminole land, the poachers will have to lie low or, more likely, retreat to park land—where I've got NPS assistance and trained firepower—more than we have here. While everyone's watching her, we'll be waiting for the poachers to come out."

"If they come. They could cut and run."

"They don't run. *They kill.*" He shook his head. "Time to put an end to it," he said again. "So, I need you to go back to the council."

Deborah frowned. "It won't be easy to convince them to change their minds, especially since you were against Alisha's earlier request."

"They'll listen to you." He felt himself getting sleepy, but forced his eyelids to stay open. "Don't bother with a letter—have Ray fax Ms. Jamison from the casino. I want her here by the time I'm back on my feet.''

Deborah continued to stroke her nephew's head. ''Only if you promise to stay away from any more bullets.''

Carson grimaced. ''That's certainly my intention. Oh, something else…''

''Rest.''

''No. One more thing.''

He felt his aunt's touch, felt the sedative effects of the tea, and heard his voice grow fainter. But he refused to sleep until he'd finished.

''For her own safety, I don't want Alisha Jamison involved in my fight. I don't want her knowing any of the specifics—about these poachers…or my father's death.''

''If I were in her position, I'd want to know.''

''Absolutely not. She'll be our gundog who either flushes our prey or drives them into hiding. Nothing more. Do you understand me, Aunt? *Nothing more.*''

CHAPTER TWO

Amazon jungle, Brazil

ALISHA JAMISON RUMMAGED through the rusting refrigerator for the clear plastic container. She gently shook it, causing the small tree viper trapped within to flex its coils.

"For heaven's sake! Aren't you asleep *yet?*"

Ordinarily the cold would send the reptile into a lethargic state, making it easy to handle. Alisha could then safely position her chilled subject, its lowered body temperature keeping it immobile long enough to let her shoot a decent roll of film.

But the ancient refrigerator wouldn't even freeze water, the light outside her bungalow was fading, and if the snake didn't cooperate soon, she could kiss those shots goodbye.

"No slides for me means no freedom for you," she warned the snake, her blue eyes narrowed in frustration. "Shape up or else!"

The snake angrily flexed its coils again as she replaced him in the refrigerator and shut its door.

"Hey, Al?"

"Josh!"

Alisha spun around at the sound of her partner's voice, her straight brunette hair swinging below her shoulders. At fifty-five, Josh Gregory was twenty years older than Alisha. He'd quit his studio job to team up with a then-unknown filmmaker-photographer. His faith in her had paid off. He'd become an award-winning writer-producer whose magazine and media documentaries were illustrated with her award-winning photography, both stills and film, and her meticulous research.

Both their names were now internationally recognized, thanks to Alisha's instincts. Early in their partnership, Alisha zeroed in on one passionate cause: documenting the animals poachers preyed on. Her stories ranged from kidnapped family pets used for medical research to slaughtered rhinos whose tusks were turned into so-called aphrodisiacs, and her investigative work saved animals and often jailed poachers while providing TV specials the networks fought to air. Alisha, who'd never been interested in fame, still couldn't believe how successful she'd become.

Fortunately, Josh had never doubted it. The older man had seen something in Alisha that others hadn't. Their relationship—always platonic—had quickly evolved into a dynamic business partnership that had earned them a respected name, healthy bank accounts and world travel. The team of Jamison and Gregory was willing to tackle any subject, any location, from cloudy mountaintops to tropical caverns, for everyone from *National Parks* and *National Geographic* to the Disney Channel and Discovery Channel. They often traveled together, Alisha out in the field doing her research and videotaping or photographing, Josh writing the scripts and packaging her work. All in all, they were perfect business partners.

Except when it came to snakes. Indiana Jones had nothing on Josh's fear of snakes. Any snake photos Alisha took were on the sly. Because of an almost fatal childhood experience with a striking Florida cottonmouth, Josh became hysterical just *thinking* about snakes. Fortunately for him, this assignment concentrated on the nocturnal Brazilian tapirs.

And here he was now—waving a piece of paper in her face. If he caught her with a live, poisonous reptile in their refrigerator, next to the fresh groceries he'd bartered for last night, there'd be havoc.

"What are you doing back so soon?" she asked guiltily. Both the container and its snake were in danger of forcible ejection from the bungalow, a situation Alisha was determined to prevent. It had taken her hours to find and capture the viper, whose beautiful coloring made it a favorite with poachers and belt-makers. Alisha edged slowly away from the rusting refrigerator.

"I thought you were interviewing the locals one last time," Josh said.

"I was, but...uh, I decided to tally up my statistics." That wasn't *exactly* a lie. She could count one possible statistic right now—in the fridge. Alisha checked her watch. "I didn't expect you for another hour."

"I came back early. We need to talk. Plus I need a drink."

Alisha refused to give ground. "Let me get it."

"I'll get it."

"Oh, all right, dammit, you caught me. But I swear, Josh, I was just going to submit the slides and captions and maybe a little sidebar, nothing else." She shrugged lightly. "You know I won't be able to work for a while on account of my health. I'm just trying to prepare financially…" She tried to disguise her fear that "a while" might become "forever."

"Alisha, I—"

"Yes, yes, I know how you feel about snakes." Alisha talked fast, hoping to stave off Josh's usual phobic outburst. "But we haven't firmed up our next assignment, and this little critter really needs publicity. Let me cool him down, and I'll turn him loose just as soon as I—"

"Al, forget about the snake."

"Forget about the snake?" she echoed incredulously. "What's wrong?"

"Look!" He waved the paper again. "We're going home!"

"Home?" she echoed.

"Let me grab a couple of beers, and we'll celebrate."

Alisha was astounded. She followed Josh into the tiny bungalow's main room and sank onto the rickety bamboo lounge. "Our home? As in the good old U.S. of A.? Chicago?"

"No, Al. Florida!" Josh opened the first bottle and warmish foam spilled out. "Which *used* to be my home."

"But...you're from Los Angeles."

He lifted his beer and took a sip. "I'm originally from Florida, remember? Born there, bred there."

"So what's this all about?"

"A trip to the Everglades, courtesy of a friend of mine."

He shoved the wrinkled sheet of paper her way. A fax. Alisha carefully scanned the letter from the Seminole Tribal Council.

After careful consideration, we have reconsidered our earlier refusal of your request to enter our lands. We hereby grant you permission to photograph, videotape and publicize any indigenous life on our reservation. We extend this invitation only for the next month and apologize for the time you may have lost. The following contact will assist with your goal and can be reached at—

Alisha stopped reading. "Wow. Last year when you wrote the Seminole Tribal Council, they refused because... What *was* their reason? A tribal member was shot and killed by poachers last summer, and his family didn't want us involved. They didn't want to talk about it—right?''

''They do now.''

''Those poor people. Why the change of heart?''

''Who cares? Isn't it great?''

''Josh!''

''I meant it's probably our last job together for some time and we're going home to do it!'' Josh opened the second beer and held it out to her. ''Come on, let's toast to fast planes, first class and Miami in June.''

Alisha took the beer, clinked bottles with Josh and took a sip. Grimacing at the warmth, she set the bottle down.

''Why'd the council members change their minds? And who's the friend you mentioned?''

''A man named Ray Weaver. His mother's on the tribal council. His father used to be an old poker buddy from my Florida days. Oh, and Ray's first cousin is the ranger we're supposed to contact.''

Alisha stared. *Something's wrong here.* Long ago she'd learned not to distrust her instincts. *Like now.*

''Tell me about this fax.''

''What's to tell? It came, I read, I made reservations. We leave. End of story.''

''But it's so strange. Before, we couldn't buy that assignment in the Everglades. Now the Seminoles are *inviting* us to make a documentary on their land— and they're willing to go before the cameras to talk about a painful death? After a whole year? What changed their minds?''

''Wise people, Native Americans. Always admired them.''

''Would you listen to me? According to this fax, I'm supposed to contact some park ranger—your friend's cousin. But the number they gave me is for your friend—Ray—at work.'' She waved the paper at Josh. ''Why him? Why not the ranger himself? Why only one month and no longer? Why a deadline? We should check this out before we commit ourselves to anything. I don't want to push the grieving family into our documentary unless they're willing. If they keep changing their minds…I have to question it. We could always use newspaper archives to research the death and do our filming on public land.''

''You'd better commit yourself to packing or we're going to miss the bush plane to our commercial flight. You'll miss those snake shots, as well.''

''I… Are you *sure* nothing's wrong?''

''No—but so what if there is? It won't be our problem. This is our last assignment together, thanks to your lousy health. *I'm* the one who should be complaining.''

''You win,'' she said lightly, seeing that Josh was in no mood to cooperate right now. *I'll find out what's going on, but it'll have to be later.* ''I'm off to take a couple rolls of the snake.''

''That's my Al.''

She retrieved her camera case, grabbed her chilled snake and headed for the door. "What's this ranger's name, anyway?"

"Ward. Carson Ward."

ON THE LONG FLIGHT NORTH, they were served boring food and shown a boring in-flight movie whose plot made no sense, despite the English subtitles.

Too bad, Alisha thought. *I could have used the distraction.* Josh napped, leaving her with uneasy thoughts and unanswered questions about the job. *My last job.* Poachers had attacked her in Africa three years ago, and her health never did bounce back. *Now it's rocking chair time…and me only thirty-five years old. Should've stuck to endangered ferns or threatened insects,* she thought wryly. But no, they'd targeted poachers. *So I'm going home—one step closer to doctors and hospitals and boredom and retirement. Life's so unfair!*

Alisha was glad when Josh awoke. The two engaged in their usual routine of briefing each other on the upcoming assignment.

"All right, we get one month on the reservation." Josh dumped peanuts into his mouth directly from the package. "That's plenty of time for you to get critter shots and tape the Everglades for the Seminole angle. As for accommodations, we have rooms at the Lucky Lady Hotel and Casino."

"A casino?"

Josh shrugged. "It's owned by the Seminoles…

has a four-star rating and a five-star chef. And great wine.''

''Any other entertainment besides the casino?''

''Cable TV. A pool. Not much else, but the rooms are gratis. Although I guess you'll be spending some time in the swamp.''

''I thought you'd be coming out in the field with me—this being our last assignment.''

''I can write in a bungalow. I can't write in a canoe. Nor can I plug in my computer if I'm living in some hut in the Everglades.''

''Chickee. It's called a chickee,'' Alisha said, shuffling through her papers and spotting a picture of the raised platform with open sides. The structure kept Seminoles dry when it was raining and cool in the worst heat. ''The roofs are made out of palm fronds. In fact, you can see them on the beaches, as well—for tourists.''

''I'm from Florida, and I know what a chickee is,'' Josh reminded her. ''Full of mosquitoes, *Ms. Chicago.*'' He shuffled through his own papers. ''All right, we've got multiple endangereds here right at our fingertips. Doesn't Florida have the most endangered or threatened species of the fifty states?''

''Nope, Hawaii does...*Mr. Native,*'' Alisha tossed back with easy camaraderie. ''Florida is second.''

''Whatever. Since the gator farm opened in St. Augustine, both *National Geographic* and the university in Gainesville have worked on saving the critters.

Gators are big news again. Apparently, numbers are down, but not seriously.''

"They're the keystone animal of the wetlands. They go, and everything goes. Still, there's no reason to limit ourselves to gators.''

Josh looked up so sharply, his reading glasses slipped down his nose. He shoved them up again. "Oh?''

"Everyone's doing alligators, and they're not endangered. If we finish in enough time, why don't we get some footage of the American crocodile, as well? They *are* in trouble.''

"Crocs prefer brackish, coastal areas. It's easier for official patrols to keep tabs on them, and harder for poachers to get 'em,'' Josh observed. "We'll be inland where the freshwater alligators—and poachers—are.''

"I know, but if we wrap this up early, we can do both.''

"Nah. With all the competition on gator and croc stories, you know everybody wants us because of our poaching angle. Plus, we'll get even more markup value if we add the Seminole angle. And they don't have any large coastal reservations.''

"Oh.'' *I didn't know that.* "Well, as long as we're there, we could broaden our horizons. What about endangered sea turtles and the Eastern indigo snake?''

"We're talking saltwater Everglades again, not inland fresh,'' Josh said, rubbing his chin. "Let's skip the coastal stuff. Just give me inland. How about mammals?''

''Florida panther?''

''That's more northern Big Cypress than Everglades. The cats need trees. Vegetation in the southern wetlands can't support their weight or hunting habits.''

''Well, yes, but—'' usually *she* was the one with all the information and Josh was the one shuffling through notes ''—the Seminoles own land in Big Cypress.''

''We haven't been given permission to stay *there*. It's a different tribe, different reservation. What's the big deal, anyway?''

''I'm in no hurry to—''

''—check into the hospital for more surgery?'' Josh shrewdly asked. ''You're the one who's been insisting that you're well enough to work. If you're feeling worse, we can always cancel.''

''I don't want to cancel. Look, right now let's just worry about this assignment. Did you tell your contact I won't have any problem roughing it in the field?''

''Yep. By the way, you've got the reservation permit. I won't be needing one. When I'm not in the hotel, I intend to stay with family. It's been a while.''

''You didn't tell me that.''

''I'm telling you now. That's why we have these little meetings.'' He dumped the rest of the peanuts into his mouth and crumpled the wrapper.

Alisha, who didn't like nuts, slid him her un-opened pack. "It won't be the same without you."

"I've *been* to the Everglades. I'll pass. You don't need me there, anyway. You'll have local guides. Like this ranger."

"Yes, but still…"

Josh studied her carefully. "What are you worried about? We often don't do fieldwork together. I think you're just nervous about going into the hospital when this is over."

Alisha shot him a sideways glance. "I am not." *Yes, I am.* Which was why she'd taken this assignment, despite her health. She needed to keep busy as long as she could.

"Surgery makes everyone nervous," he said. "Now look at this, and get your mind back on business." He tapped a notebook with his pen. Alisha leaned over the armrest. "You want to document the big cats, which would mean doing a night video. We've just done an all-night safari. Are you seriously in the mood for another?"

"I'd like some more sun." *Need* some sun was more like it. Her resistance to illness—and to cooler temperatures—was slowly but surely failing.

"All right, then."

"Let's put the Florida panther on the 'maybe' list." Alisha scribbled in her notes. "Supposedly there's only thirty of them left in the state. The other mammal would be the West Indian manatee. They're freshwater and saltwater, but mostly fresh. Could we fit them in?''

''As a Florida resident, I can tell you they've been done to death. Literally and figuratively. The beasts are still dying in droves, thanks to the almighty powerboat. Lucky for them, they get lots of coverage. Almost as much as the whooping cranes. They're not good money. Too much media exposure.'' Josh stared at her. ''Besides, poached animals are our specialty, and no one's poaching them.''

''Yes, but still... They're endangered. Beautiful animals, the manatees. So graceful.'' The memory of a colleague's documentary film played in her head.

''Beautiful?'' Josh snorted. ''Graceful? They're fat hippos, U.S.A.-style.''

''But we could chance it, if we had time to go up north.''

Josh frowned. ''It'd be dicey getting decent shots unless you were lucky enough to find them in the shallows. Anything deeper and you'd probably need to scuba, for stills or video. You can't dive anymore, remember?''

''I thought maybe I could get away with just snorkeling.''

''You'd come up empty. And anything else would be too risky for you. I can dive, but I sure can't operate those fancy cameras of yours. Sorry, kid.'' He patted her on the shoulder like a kindly old uncle. ''Ya gotta watch that bum lung of yours.''

Yeah. The same lung that's ending my career, unless the doctors can fix me up.

She didn't like remembering the time three years earlier, when ivory poachers had almost carved her into a carcass like the African elephants they'd slaughtered. The poachers had unexpectedly returned to a killing field she'd discovered and was photographing. Josh had stayed behind to set up their camp and when Alisha didn't return as scheduled, he'd gone looking. He'd found her, close to death, and taken her to the hospital in Nairobi.

The hospital stay was hell. The doctors feared the worst, and Josh had left a message for her mother. Alisha couldn't speak to her family until she was out of danger, recovering from emergency surgery. That phone conversation went downhill after a scant five minutes.

"Maybe they can take your life story and make it into a movie when I bury you," Fran Jamison had sobbed over the phone, "Like Dian Fossey and *Gorillas in the Mist*. My God, Ali, I can see your tombstone now. 'She died so fake furs could flourish.'"

"Mom, it was African elephants and they don't have fur."

Her attempt at levity had fallen flat.

"Your father left me plenty of money when he died. Your brothers are lawyers, living like normal people. Yet you let this Hollywood writer talk you into getting killed! What does he do, produce assignments from hell? Is this what you want?"

Her mother's phone calls to the Nairobi hospital, although upsetting, were the least of her worries. She'd been scarred deeply—physically, and emotionally. She'd never sleep soundly again. Nights were the worst, and the damage to her right lung continued to plague her. Bronchitis was common, as were more serious bouts of pneumonia.

"Find a less physically stressful type of work," the doctors said. "Either way, you're going to need surgery again soon."

Easier said than done. The hospital costs had already been horrendous, and last year, her medical insurer had cancelled her coverage.

That knife in the dark had cost her health, a diminished capacity to do her job, and her peace of mind.

I need a big story and some big money for my retirement—fast. I have to do this while my health holds up. I might have to quit, but I intend to remain independent. I want a nest egg. I refuse to live off Mom and my brothers' charity.

Sadly, this Everglades story didn't seem to promise Alisha her goal. The strange fax still bothered her; so did fears that her health might prevent her from doing this job—possibly her last—as well as she wanted to.

"There must *something* we can use besides the gators. There's always bird shots," Alisha said.

"You hate doing birds," Josh groaned. At Alisha's stare, he gave in. "Oh, all right. Whaddaya have for rare or endangered feathered?"

"Well..." She looked through more notes as Josh tore into the second bag of peanuts. "Five. There's the snail kite."

"Let me guess—it eats snails."

"The wood stork, the Cape Sable—"

"Whatever the hell that is."

She gave Josh an impatient glance. "The Cape Sable *sparrow*. Plus the Arctic peregrine falcon."

"What's it doing in Florida?"

"Migrating, I guess. Hey, there's the southern bald eagle."

"They aren't easy to find. We'll come across lots of other bird shutterbugs, though. They're *not* a rare species." Josh washed down his peanuts with a swallow of rum and cola. "Like I said in the beginning, let's stick with what we do. Poachers. Poached animals. Gators are it for now. Ace producer that I am, kid, stop questioning my smarts."

The old Alisha would have grinned. She hadn't been a naive "kid" for years. "I think I can come up with a two-for-one, Josh. Maybe write up some of the endangered birds that gators prey on? I could tie them into the story—no," she corrected herself, knowing what Josh would say, "I could mention them in the alligator piece, and do a second special highlighting them on their own. Twice the pay."

"Obi-Wan has taught you well, Young Skywalker.'' Josh grinned. ''I can die in peace. Hey, flight attendant...'' he yelled out.

''Can't you use the call button like everyone else?'' Alisha hissed, glad she'd at least trained him not to use the term *stewardess*. ''This isn't a Cubs game.''

''Hey, it's not my fault. We're in first class. She's not supposed to disappear for so long. Can I get a beer now, sweetheart?''

The approaching flight attendant put on a phony smile. Alisha wasn't surprised. Josh was fit and trim for a man his age, but his personality would always have rough edges. He was a hard man to know, a man who rarely showed a vulnerable or tender side.

Alisha knew it was there. She'd found that out after her attack. Josh hadn't left her side from the moment he'd discovered her bleeding in the dirt. All during that wild jeep drive to safety, those long weeks in the hospital, his hand had held hers until she no longer needed his strength. She'd never forget it.

Too bad he's never had children to bring out the best in him. But if he was with family, I'd have died alone in the midst of freshly killed elephants. The memory sent chills down her spine. *Well, maybe he'll settle down, meet a woman, fall in love, while I'm recuperating. It's only a matter of time before we finish this last assignment and I have to quit for the lung surgery.*

''You want anything, Al? I'm buying.''

"Very funny. I know perfectly well that drinks are free in first class. But I could go for a ginger ale. I'd like it over there." She gestured to an empty seat. "I'm going to move, Josh. I need some quiet time," she explained with a smile to both partner and flight attendant.

"Come on," he protested. "Let's check out the casino layout. I have the brochures. Plus I bought some electronic games at the airport so you can practice."

"Thanks, but I'll pass. You know how I feel about gambling." *I do plenty of gambling on the job. My life is high-stakes enough.* "Give them to your nieces or nephews."

"Come on, be a sport. You need some fun. You don't laugh anymore, Al."

"I'll play later. Right now, I can't wait to get into my research," she said slyly, stepping over Josh's legs. "Did you know the crocodile still looks like its Triassic ancestors? They haven't changed much since then because their method of survival's so perfect. In fact, they've even shrunk in size, they're so efficient. Guess how much."

"Umm…"

"Saltwater crocs are twenty-eight feet long, down from the ancient Phobosuchus, which was seventy feet long with—"

"You know, viewers hate statistics. So do I. Besides, I thought we were doing gators."

"Gotta complete my research if we want to document anything else. Do you know how to tell them apart? I read that…''

A glazed look appeared in Josh's eyes, just as Alisha knew it would.

"Umm, maybe you'd better sit where I won't disturb you." Josh buried his nose in the casino pamphlets. "I have reading of my own."

Alisha stifled a smile and started down the open aisle to the empty seat. "Okay, Josh."

"A relative?" the flight attendant asked sympathetically as she brought Alisha her drink.

"Friend and business partner," she said vaguely, not mentioning Josh's or her own well-recognized names in front of the other passengers. *Thank goodness I stay behind the cameras. Even if I didn't, I'm usually so grubby, I can't possibly look "presentable."* She was presentable now, clad in warm slacks and a wool pullover for the chilly flight, complete with light makeup and her brown hair down and loose instead of neatly braided. Ever since the poacher attack, she was almost paranoid about using her real name. In public, she was Alisha Jamison only to Customs, government officials and her bank.

It'll stay that way until the poachers who tried to kill me are caught, or I'm six feet under.

No trace of her poachers had ever been found. They'd been organized and shockingly bold. They'd had the nerve to masquerade as environmentalists, closing the gas pump at an African field station— citing fictitious leaks in order to do that. Then they'd used the deserted station as their base of operations, complete with free fuel for their vehicles.

"Would you like anything else?" the flight attendant asked.

"Could I please get a pillow, if you don't mind?"

Soon after, Alisha relaxed with Vivaldi's *Four Seasons* playing in her headphones. Her empty glass taken away, she burrowed comfortably into her blanket.

Ah, first-class service. I don't get much of this. Better enjoy it while I can.

She could easily have drifted off, except for her niggling thoughts.

Why did the tribal council change its mind? Why let me in a whole year after refusing me? Why is Josh pushing this? I didn't really need Seminole land to do a story on gators or panthers. I can get local color elsewhere, no matter what Josh says. Something's not right. And my future depends on this job.

Every instinct told her one thing.

There's trouble ahead.

CHAPTER THREE

Miami, Florida

THE HEAT SIZZLED off the pavement, causing rippling silver mirages on Miami's runways. Carson and Adoette were waiting in the arrivals lounge. Carson glanced at his wristwatch, then out the window.

"That should be their plane now."

Adoette shivered. She tugged the edges of her sleeves even lower. Seminoles, whether in modern or traditional dress, tended to cover as much of their skin as possible against the ferocious mosquitoes. Dressed in her traditional long, layered skirt and light blouse with three-quarter sleeves, Adoette was no exception. Only now her clothes protected her from air-conditioning instead of bugs.

"Here, take this." Carson removed his brown NPS uniform jacket and held it out for her to slip over her chilled arms. He himself usually wore the long brown pants, long-sleeved shirt and boots of the National Park Service. Today, as a concession to being away from the Everglades and around hot tarmac, he wore a short-sleeved shirt and the jacket above a pair of uniform shorts. On most men they would have looked ridiculous. Carson wasn't most men.

"How do these people stand it?" Adoette asked, her teeth still chattering.

"They get used to it, I suppose. Like we get used to heat and bug spray."

Adoette looked miserable. Carson slung his good arm around her shoulder—his other was still a bit stiff—and pulled his friend close.

"Better?"

Adoette smiled, her face framed by long black hair, the smile a thing of beauty beneath the dark brown eyes so many of his people shared. Adoette had inherited her family's small frame; Carson had taken after his father, a tall man with a strong, lean build and a stubbornness in his jaw.

Watching Adoette, Carson thought, *Ray's a damn fool. And Adoette's an even bigger one for waiting. She needs a man who's like her—not a guy more interested in bright lights and excitement than finding a wife. Well, maybe she'll change her mind. Ray never will. Not after Susannah...*

Adoette interrupted his thoughts. "What do you think Alisha Jamison looks like? I've never seen pictures of her. Have you?"

"No. Does it matter?"

Adoette kept her gaze on the plane as it taxied toward their gate location, and switched to Seminole for privacy. "I hoped to spot her early...see if she looks friendly. I want to be her assistant while she's here," Adoette announced.

Her reply caught Carson off guard. "Assistant? She has a partner. He does the writing and producing."

"I know, but I understand Alisha does most of the fieldwork. She'll need a local guide, and he's not it. *Someone* needs to lead her in one direction while you men go after those poachers in the other. I want it to be me."

"What are you talking about?"

"Come on, Carson! Your plan to let the famous Ms. Jamison scare the poachers off Seminole land is so obvious."

"Is it, now? How did you arrive at this conclusion?"

"Easy. You've made sure she does her research on reservation instead of public land. And you're meeting with her tonight. Everyone will know about it because you had Ray call the media. You're setting her up as a bird dog to flush out our poachers, aren't you?"

"There's more to it than that."

"Then fill me in."

Carson swore in Seminole, but didn't bother denying it. He never lied, and even if he did, he doubted he could fool Adoette. "First, tell me how you found out."

"Easy. I'm invisible, you know." Her words were

bitter, contrasting with her youthful beauty. "Especially to Ray."

"You're *not* invisible."

"I don't want to discuss it. I don't want poachers on our land, either, and I know these waters as well as you do. Alisha Jamison needs a trustworthy guide. Let me help. Deborah doesn't really need me, and God knows I have nothing better to do."

"Adoette—" Carson marshaled his thoughts before speaking. Adoette had tried college but she'd grown depressed away from the land she loved. Whereas, he was comfortable in both worlds, even if he preferred the wetlands.

Adoette, on the other hand, was like those earlier Native Americans who, taken away from their land, died of heartbreak. She wasn't invisible, at all; she simply fit into her beloved home so well she was a timeless part of it. Ray was the odd one out, the proverbial sore thumb. He'd left to find his own place to belong, something Adoette already had.

"Ordinarily I'd ask for your help." Carson chose his words cautiously. "But my plan's already settled. Ray's going to show Alisha around reservation land while I continue to hunt for the poachers."

"Ray's in on this?" Adoette said, shocked. "He hates the Everglades!"

"He loved his uncle. My father was Ray's father after Deborah's husband died. So Ray's taken some time off from his job. He insisted on coming along to help."

"Well, I'm insisting, too!"

"It's not a good idea. Your…problems with Ray could make trouble on this expedition. Three people is all I need. I'm guessing the poachers won't stay on the reservation while an antipoaching celebrity like Alisha Jamison is there. That could be the break I need to find them. Besides, Ray and I are family. You aren't."

"That's no reason for me to stay behind," Adoette argued. "What if the poachers don't do what you want? What then?"

"They won't have any choice. As long as I keep Alisha on our land—tribal land—the poachers have to lie low or move onto park service land. The NPS will close off the area to tourists and patrol the borders. I've already been given the green light by my boss. Our poachers are greedy bastards. They won't want to wait a whole month for her to leave. Sooner or later—and probably sooner—they'll strike."

"It's a good plan, Carson. *If* it works."

He shrugged. "Well, if it doesn't, I'll have to come up with something else. But I figure chances are good that it will. We know they're operating here now—and we know it's the same group. So…"

"You're forgetting one thing."

"What?" Despite her feelings about Ray, Adoette had wisdom about others he rarely disregarded.

"It might not fool Ms. Jamison. What if she figures it out?"

"Since she'll be safe, I don't intend to tell her. Do you?"

Adoette pulled his jacket closer. "No. But since *you* won't be guiding her, she'll get suspicious. How will you explain your absence?"

"I'll say my duties take priority."

Judging by her expression, Adoette didn't seem convinced.

"The main thing is, she'll be safe," Carson reiterated. "No poacher would risk hurting her again—not with the massive publicity and official manhunt we saw after her first attack. That's why Ray announced her arrival to the media."

"Since you claim this is such a safe operation," Adoette continued, "I want in. Ray won't distract me."

"Ray's your life. He affects every move you make." His voice was tinged with big-brother overtones—the wrong tack to take.

"Finding your father's killers is *your* whole life. It affects every move *you* make," she shot back.

"My situation is different."

She switched back to English. "No, it isn't. You're just as obsessed with revenge as I'm obsessed with Ray, but at least I know what I'm up against. You can't even *prove* that the poachers who killed Ferris are the ones who shot you. You're just guessing! You can't identify your enemy."

Carson frowned but didn't dispute her words.

"Don't even think of shutting me out," Adoette

continued angrily. "Because if you won't let me act as Alisha's guide, I'll follow you on NPS land and I'll shadow you. Don't forget, I own my airboat. I'll be there the next time a bullet knocks you out of a canoe—and that's something you should be *grateful* for!"

"Dammit." His jaw tightened. "I won't risk your safety again."

"You won't if I'm with Alisha. You owe me, Carson. I want in."

Carson counted slowly to ten. "How does Ray figure into this?" he finally asked.

"Ray?"

"Yes. What's in this for you?"

"Nothing."

He'd heard *that* answer before, and it meant *something*. "Come on, Adoette. Spill."

"I hate poachers on my land."

"That's a given. What else, younger sister?" he asked in Seminole.

It seemed that the kindness in his tone, more than the words themselves, had the desired effect.

"Oh, all right." She slipped back into English. "It's no big deal. I've decided to change from an invisible woman to a visible one."

"Huh?" Her answer caught him totally by surprise.

"You heard me. I'm tired of Ray treating me like some dreary little wallflower. How can I compete against the casino hostesses dressed like this?" She flipped one hand disdainfully at the bright colors of the Seminole skirt, then at the beads around her neck, the strands added one by one since birth. They represented every special event in a female's life until, by middle age, a woman wore so many, she could barely turn her head.

"You look beautiful to me."

"Only because I'm your friend. To Ray, I look like something out of a history book. I sit at an ancient loom in my antiquated clothes and weave all day. Even on the airboats I dress like this, and I feel like an idiot when tourists snap my picture. It's time for me to…to change my life. I want a more active role. Alisha Jamison is my chance to see how it's done."

"Adoette, you couldn't even finish a year in college. You were too shy."

"I was very young. I was away from home—and I didn't have the proper motivation." Adoette's eyes narrowed. "I do now."

Carson was suddenly conscious of Adoette's curves; he remembered how her yearning gaze followed his cousin with a hunger that seemed to grow more and more every day.

"I'm not a kid, Carson. I know what I need to do."

"Changing yourself because you *want* to change is one thing. Changing yourself for a man who isn't interested in you is another." Ordinarily such rare bluntness from him would have caused Adoette to burst into tears. Not now.

"I'm doing this for both of us," she said urgently. "Ray'll notice me by the time I'm finished—he won't have a choice. I'll get what I want, you'll get what you want. Alisha Jamison and I flush the poachers onto NPS lands. I get Ray. And you get your father's killers."

Carson started to argue, then stopped and lightened his tone. "Whatever. But this isn't TV, Adoette. Don't be surprised if Ray doesn't fall into your arms when you put on a pair of tight jeans and mascara. Besides," he added, "Alisha Jamison's high profile comes from risking her life on the job. She's a crusader—not the type of woman you'll want to emulate."

Adoette's patience was obviously at an end. "How do you know? Maybe she *is*." She moved closer to the terminal gate, away from him. The first passengers were trickling through.

Carson was shaken by Adoette's words and the pain that had prompted them. Denying who and what she was could only make matters worse. Still, letting Adoette go with Alisha Jamison might not be a bad thing. Carson had already accepted Ray's help and originally planned to have him guide Alisha. This way, though, Ray would have an extra pair of eyes. Not only that, Adoette would be driving the airboat.... He felt responsible for her, but she'd be safe with Alisha and Ray, who, like Carson, carried a handgun. He could look after himself and the women, despite his distaste for the wetlands.

I have nothing to worry about.

Adoette noticed the couple first. Carson immediately recognized Alisha's partner from Ray's description. Josh Gregory was large-framed with graying hair and a handsome physique—although that positive first impression was marred by his loud voice. *That's got to be the producer.* Carson deliberately hung back, letting Adoette greet the couple—giving him more time to study the woman at the man's side.

Alisha Jamison wasn't what he'd expected. She certainly wasn't a thick-muscled glasses-wearing stereotype of the female bush observer. On the other hand, she was nothing like Adoette. There were no delicate curves, no fragile beauty. At first glance, Alisha Jamison seemed run-of-the-mill ordinary—not tall or short, heavy or thin, striking or homely, just an average woman who would never grace a magazine cover but could easily be the girl next door.

Until he looked closer...

The eyes were an ordinary blue, but they were alive with interest, their gaze moving everywhere, missing nothing. The smile was more than polite—there was a hint of generosity in the subdued yet welcoming curve of her lips. The woman's bearing was graceful, almost proud, with a certain dignity that reminded him of stone cuttings of Mayan royalty. *No,* he corrected himself. *It reminds me of my own people.*

She conducted herself in a manner that made those around judge her as definitely not average.

Men—including himself—found her attractive. Women, he noticed, including Adoette, found her a definite threat. He saw either awe or envy in the eyes of any woman looking at Alisha Jamison. She wore simple clothing, little makeup and no jewelry except a plain silver cross, but Alisha was the most desirable woman there. Carson had to fight down a surge of pure male excitement as Adoette led the travelers his way. He was surprised to find himself jealous as hell that Adoette reached Alisha's side before he did.

This woman's trouble. Big trouble.

Alisha Jamison's gaze targeted him in the crowd. He saw her take in his appearance, the brown NPS uniform, and make the connection. She detached herself from the small group and approached him alone, her carryall slung over one shoulder, her hand outstretched.

"Mr. Ward? Alisha Jamison."

Carson took her hand. There was self-assurance in the grip of those feminine fingers. "Welcome to Florida, Ms. Jamison."

"Thank you, and please, it's Alisha. Or Ali, if you prefer."

"Then call me Carson."

She released his hand. "Carson. If you could lead us to the baggage carousels…"

He nodded, and the four of them went through the tedious practice common to all airports. Alisha walked beside Carson. Behind them, Josh was complaining to Adoette about Customs, muttering that he hated how long the routine took in Florida. Adoette, still wearing his brown jacket, talked politely to Josh. Carson enjoyed having Alisha to himself.

"I hope you had a pleasant flight," he said as they walked along.

"A long one, anyway."

"You must be tired."

"Just a little. I slept on the plane," she said with a smile.

"You'll feel better once you get to the hotel. It's not a long drive."

A surge of people from the same flight arrived at the luggage carousel from the Customs area, which precluded further talking. That didn't stop him from trying.

"What do your bags look like? I'll grab them if you point them out."

"Thanks. They're black, with silver name tags."

They waited in front of the empty carousel.

"I hope you haven't arranged for a guide," Adoette said, finally managing to make her way to Alisha's side. "I'm available. I'm familiar with the area, and I'm also a fully qualified airboat operator." She spoke quickly, frowning a little in her seriousness.

"I'd love your help—if it's okay with the ranger here." Alisha glanced at Carson, who merely shrugged.

"I guess that means yes." Alisha laughed, a deep, delighted laugh that spoke of hidden passion—bedroom passion, if his hormones could be trusted. "Well, good. My résumé leaves much to be desired in that department."

She found her first piece of checked luggage and pulled it off the carousel instead of pointing it out. Before Carson could react, Alisha started to reach for a second bag, one that obviously held camera equipment.

"No one carries Al's cameras but her," Josh informed him.

"That's not true, Josh. No one carries my *film* but me. Or my tape. The cameras I check."

As Alisha passed Carson a second camera bag, she said, "I have a question for you."

His senses were immediately on alert.

"Why did you and your tribal council change your position regarding my earlier request?" she asked. A direct hit. Carson hadn't expected this so soon—if at all.

He saw the intelligence in her eyes—and it made him uneasy. *Adoette's right. This woman might discover my plan, after all. What if she won't play along? What if she wants to join the hunt, instead? I refuse to be known as the man who put Alisha Jamison at the mercy of poachers…again.* Suddenly he changed his demeanor from friendly to strictly business.

"No time for questions right now," he said.

"Adoette will take you to the pickup area. Please wait there with her." His voice left no room for refusal. "I'll get the car."

ALISHA FLOPPED BACKWARD onto her bed, hair wet from the shower. She wore the fluffy terry-cloth robe provided by the Lucky Lady Hotel and Casino.

"Oh, Lord, that feels so-o-o-o good," she groaned.

She heard a knock on the connecting door. "Are you decent, Al?"

"Yes, come on in."

Josh appeared. "Comfy?"

Alisha reached for a pillow and shaped it more comfortably under her head. "I'm getting there. Nothing like a good ol' American mattress."

"Yeah, well, before you nod off…" Josh shook a bottle of pills. "I just got your prescription refilled."

"I still have some left."

"I know, but there aren't any pharmacies in the middle of the Everglades, you know. I didn't want you to run out. Did you take today's dose? You didn't—I can tell by your face. Take them *now*. Here." He held out the pill bottle and an open can of soda.

Alisha groaned again as she sat up and took the pills and the drink. She'd been on a low dose of antibiotics ever since the poachers' attack; it was the only way to keep in check the numerous bouts of bronchitis and pneumonia that had plagued her since.

"You're almost as bossy as our host was at the airport," Alisha said.

Carson Ward. An interesting man. On the drive here, she'd observed him with the same intensity she brought to her work. *He doesn't give much away. He certainly clammed up when I asked him about the fax. And then he played nonstop tour guide during the drive—so I didn't have a chance to bring it up again.*

"The ranger wasn't wearing a wedding ring. Did you notice?"

I noticed. She didn't guard her expression carefully enough.

Josh pounced. "Yep, you did."

"Bastard." It came out too affectionately to sting.

Josh laughed and pulled the covers over Alisha and gently tucked her in. He smoothed her wet hair back from her face. "You should've dried your hair. It can't be good for your lungs. Cold in here, too." Josh kicked the air conditioner regulator up a few notches. "There."

"If you're done fussing, tell me what's on for tonight."

Josh was all business again. "I've ordered lunch from room service—it's on the way up. And, hey, there's a copy of the local rag, today's, with a story about you. Don't bother reading it—nothing there but standard P.R. stuff. Just eat your lunch. Then get some beauty sleep. You look like tapir dung."

"Gee, thanks, Mom."

Josh didn't even blink. "After that, a wake-up call at 6:00 p.m. Plenty of time to dress and meet Carson Ward, his delightful friend Adoette, and Ward's cousin, Ray, for dinner."

"Ray's your old poker buddy's son?"

"Yes. By the way, Ray Weaver manages a shift here at the casino and got us the rooms. So be nice to him."

"Of course."

"I've ordered a dress from the gift shop. It's being pressed now."

"My size?"

"No, mine. Of course your size! Long-sleeved, high back."

Josh didn't add what they both knew—that she wore dresses like this to hide her scars.

"Oh, and some new underwear, as well. Last time I did the laundry, your bras all looked like linguini. I got you some tans and whites, plus one black strapless, no underwires in the bunch."

Alisha hated underwires. "Josh, I have to say, you're a partner among partners."

"Yeah, well, not for long. Dammit, Al, what'll I do without you if you can't work after the operation? No, don't answer that," Josh said impatiently. "Anyway, it's drinks at seven and dinner at seven-thirty. Watch your p's and q's. This guy Ward isn't just some park ranger."

"I remember, you told me his aunt—"

"Yeah, Ray's mother. She's a big muckety-muck

on the tribal council. Don't step on any toes. I won't be there, by the way."

"Where *will* you be?"

"At my brother's, but first I'll be getting your supplies for the trip."

"Don't forget toothpaste!"

He made a rude gesture, and she laughed. "I'd tell you to skip the supplies shopping, but I know you wouldn't listen. Besides, I don't think dinner in a nice hotel with a good-looking man is going to be any hardship." Josh raised one eyebrow at the "good-looking" part. Alisha pointedly ignored him. "Even if it *was,* you always say suffering builds character. Look at me."

Josh's smile faded. "Yeah. Look at you." His expression became thoughtful. "Eat your lunch, take your nap, have a great time. Fill me in tomorrow."

ALISHA STARED INTO the bathroom mirror. A stranger stared back at her. With her hair up, carefully applied makeup and the classic dress, she hardly recognized herself. As usual, the clothes, from the long black skirt and jacket top to the new underwear beneath it, were a perfect fit.

"Thanks, Josh," she murmured, but she wasn't really thinking about her partner. Their relationship wasn't only business; they shared the affection and companionship of good friends. But not lovers.

In fact, there hadn't been much romance for either of them. Their work left little opportunity to meet potential lovers—or spouses. Josh had been married briefly, in his thirties; Alisha had experienced a few short-term affairs. That was it. Not much success on the romantic front, she thought, resigned as always. She did have regrets about it, though, especially now, with her career about to end.

Alisha patted her hair one last time. She intended to enjoy tonight. She'd be eating dinner with new people at an actual table instead of over a campfire. Carson was a handsome man. With luck, he and his cousin would provide interesting dinner conversation. And she'd have a chance to get better acquainted with Adoette, a good idea if they were going to be spending the next few weeks together.

She left her room and, on impulse, skipped the elevator for the grand staircase. The hotel-casino complex took up more horizontal than vertical space. She knew that was because skyscrapers were rare along the coast with its porous limestone bedrock. The building was carefully designed to bring the vivid greens and blues of the outside in, creating an attractive sense of openness.

Alisha went past the casino entrance to the slot machines, crowded with people dressed in swimsuits, jeans shorts and T-shirts. Beyond, she noticed the more high-stakes gambling areas, where quiet men and women dressed in formal clothes sat at games tables presided over by tuxedoed dealers.

She smiled as she continued walking, not breaking stride. The background cacophony of whistles, gongs and excited chatter was no temptation for her. Gambling in general paled in comparison to the safaris she'd been on. As for high-stakes games...

I've played the real thing.

The hotel had several bars, and Josh's instructions led her to a lovely indoor oasis set far from the casinos and overlooking a spectacular view. Florida bloomed with the fullness of summer. The oranges and yellows of late sunset could still be seen in the west. She paused, unable to pass such beauty. Seconds later, she was rewarded as a flock of snowy egrets lifted off the wetlands. Wings open, they rose from the Everglades to roost in trees, secure from the night's predators. The sun glinted off the water and the birds' wings, turning them into a surrealistic fantasy of gold.

The sight was spectacular. She continued to bask in the pleasure of it as she approached the maitre d'.

"Ah, yes, Ms. Jamison. Your party is waiting. Please, follow me."

Time for pleasure—and for business. Time to find out exactly what Carson Ward's hiding.

CHAPTER FOUR

"OOH, LA LA, IS THAT *HER?*" Ray asked as a woman in a black gown and fitted jacket approached their table. "She—" His comments were cut short by Adoette's elbow jab to his side.

"Ray, don't embarrass me," Adoette warned. "Hush and stand up."

Carson was already on his feet. He pulled out Alisha's chair, then took her arm when she approached.

"Good evening, Alisha."

"Carson. Adoette, you look lovely."

"This is Ray Weaver, my cousin," Carson said. "He works here at the casino."

Ray took Alisha's hand and gallantly kissed it before Carson seated her.

"Welcome to Florida." Ray added a string of compliments that caused Adoette to droop and Carson to seethe. Carson noticed that Alisha didn't seem impressed by Ray's flattery—which, he had to admit, pleased him.

"I'm not as gorgeous as Adoette," Alisha said lightly. "What a beautiful gown! Only someone as young and stylish as you could carry that off. I envy you."

Adoette brightened. "Why, thank you! I—it's new," she stammered. "Do you really like it?"

"That color suits you perfectly," Alisha complimented.

Adoette wore a lime-green slip dress, a tight sheath slit up the side. It left nothing to the imagination, and Carson felt uncomfortable seeing so much of his friend in it. A pair of panty hose seemed to be all she had on underneath, while every line of her body was visible through the thin, clingy material. It wasn't the kind of outfit he'd choose for his woman—if he had one.

Strangely, or perhaps not so strangely, Carson found Alisha's outfit much more exciting. He wanted to peel off those layers to discover what lay beneath, a reaction Adoette couldn't possibly evoke in her dress.

Conversation switched to casual comments about the fine quality of the house wine—which Alisha regretfully passed up due to her medication, although she blamed jet lag—the local landscape and the casino business until their food was served. Then Alisha introduced a more personal topic.

"I'm still bothered about your fax," she said to Carson. "Care to explain the tribal council's change of heart?"

"Certainly. But first you tell me why you chose this place," Carson said. He knew he'd have to confront the issue; it might as well be now.

Alisha's fork hovered over the fresh grilled marlin.

"I specialize in documenting dangers to human life and wildlife...especially from poaching. Josh suggested the Everglades after hearing about your father's tragedy last summer. He was murdered by alligator poachers, I understand. My condolences to you and your family, by the way."

"How did you learn about it?" Carson asked.

"Josh has family in this area." She leaned closer to Carson. "The Seminole population here numbers about twelve hundred. Violent incidents like murder can hardly be hidden in a community that small. There were articles in the local papers, as well. His brother forwarded some to him. Josh originally thought we could cover gator poaching and its consequences—including murder."

"I'll help you as much as I can," Carson said before taking another bite of fish.

"But why? We understood your reluctance to cooperate last summer. Such a topic would be painful in a very personal way. Plus, with the ongoing investigation..."

"It's been a year. I've rethought my position."

"Have you captured the poachers since we last talked?"

"Well, let's just say if there *is* a problem, it's nothing for you to worry about," Ray cut in.

Dammit, Ray, now you've given her a reason to worry—and that patronizing tone won't sit well with any woman. Especially this one.

He was right. It didn't.

"So you haven't caught the poachers." Alisha turned toward Adoette. "I need to know what's going on. Adoette, what can you tell me?"

"Nothing…nothing! I mean, I—" She switched to Seminole. "Shouldn't we tell her about the poachers?"

Ray suddenly pulled Adoette away from the table. "Let's dance." Alisha and Carson were left alone.

"It seems you'll have to tell me what Adoette knows about poachers."

"You speak Seminole?" he asked, amazed.

"No, but Josh and I do our research. You'd be surprised what I pick up. I can say *poacher* in twenty-three languages."

She's furious! He saw it in her eyes, her mouth, the tight neck muscles.

"Are you going to fill me in, or am I leaving?"

Carson's smile was equally tight. "Okay, I'll fill you in." So much for keeping any secrets from her. He told her about the poachers, his own shooting, his plan. Everything.

When he finished—silence. The waiter approached with the dessert menu. Alisha waved him away. Carson's patience ran out.

"Well? Will you help us or not?"

"Help a man who deceived me? Who intended to go on deceiving me, despite the presence of armed criminals? Men who shoot to kill?"

"That," he said, "is not an answer."

She swiveled toward the massive picture windows,

her profile expressionless. When she faced him again, the anger under control, her gaze distant, whatever hope he'd had vanished.

"You're not going to help. Are you?"

"You've got that right."

"Mind telling me why?"

"Because my job is to document and publicize the *effects* of poaching.... I'm not a game warden, not a law-enforcement officer—I'm a filmmaker and photographer! I've learned the hard way to stay within the bounds of my expertise. Trapping poachers isn't part of that."

"Trapping poachers *is* my area of expertise," he insisted. "I'd keep you safe."

She rose. "Judging by the bullet hole in your shoulder, I seriously doubt it."

Carson flinched, but not from the violence with which she threw her napkin on the table.

"Find yourself another sucker, Mr. Ward. This expedition is off."

BACK IN HER HOTEL ROOM, Alisha removed her evening jacket. The black silk slithered down and onto the bathroom tile.

He lied to me! That handsome, winning bastard fed me dinner and a smooth line! She yanked open the skirt zipper and kicked it off as it slid to her ankles. *Just what I need in my life! More poachers!*

She glanced at her scarred chest and shoulders in the mirror, then reached for the hotel's white terry robe. As she turned to leave, she nearly tripped over the balled black material. Ashamed, she bent down and picked up the outfit. *No sense kicking these. Carson Ward—now that's a different matter.*

She neatly placed her clothes and shoes in the closet, removed her panty hose and reentered the bathroom. She was about to brush her teeth when she heard a knock.

"You can go straight to hell," she yelled at the door. "Because you aren't coming in here!"

"It's Josh."

Alisha belted her robe more securely and crossed to the door. She opened it, the chain still on. "What? I thought you weren't coming back tonight."

"Nice manners, Al. Let me in."

"Sorry." She slid off the chain and opened the door. "You wouldn't *believe* the evening I've had."

"Let me guess. Your dinner was a big bust?"

"That's putting it mildly." She closed the door behind him and sat down at the table. "What are you doing back so soon?"

Josh removed two ginger ales and a pack of peanuts from the minibar, then joined her. "My evening was no picnic, either. My brother and his kids all had the stomach flu. One or other of 'em was always locked in the bathroom. Plus my mom and sister-in-law were busy with the patients. I left, did our shopping, and decided to come back here. I was only in the way at home."

"Oh, Josh, I'm so sorry! I know you were really looking forward to your visit."

"Yeah, well, that can wait. A couple days and they'll be fine." He popped open the soda and took a swallow. "Now, what about *your* evening?"

By the time Alisha had finished relating her tale, she was shaking. "Josh, how could you set me up with a story like this? With active poachers? He was going to *use* me..." Her voice was anguished.

"It's been a year since Ferris Ward was killed. I didn't know about Ward's injury—and it's to his credit that he told you. Still, I'm pushing for this story."

"My God, Josh! I thought we were friends!"

"We are. That's why I did it."

Alisha bit her lip, confused, angry, hurt. "Why?"

"You have the guts to listen?"

"What kind of question is that?"

"You tell me. Ever since those poachers did their carving job on you, you haven't had the stomach for much. You need this assignment for three reasons. One—" He held up a forefinger. "You've got to make some money. The documentary and article are presold. We have an obligation to honor."

She nodded reluctantly.

"Two, your health is getting worse. You've got to quit this business, at least for now. The doctors know it, I know it, and so do you."

Alisha lifted her chin. She refused to feel sorry for herself.

"Back to point one," Josh said. "I've managed to get you a book deal. I wasn't going to tell you, but... I think you need to hear it. I was on the phone this afternoon with the agent I hired. Here's what happens. You write the story of your life, it gets published for big bucks. There might even be a movie deal attached to the whole thing. We could remain business partners regardless of your health."

I'd like to write a book about my work. Not about me but my work...

"Look, Al, you and Carson Ward break this Everglades poaching ring, you've got yourself a happy ending. You'll go out in a blaze of glory. You'll draw attention to the poacher problem—and you'll be telling a good story. A *positive* story, which is what people want. You'll be a winner—not a victim."

Alisha shivered. "When you put it like that—how can I refuse?"

"Skip the sarcasm, Al. I'm your friend, but I'm not a miracle worker. I can't fix your bum lung. You're living on pills and inhalers, and it'll get worse before it gets better. Surgery's waiting."

"Don't remind me."

"Pull this off, and you can retire a wealthy woman."

"If I don't die from a bullet in the swamps first!"

"Carson says you'll be safe. He's the one risking the bullets. Let him chase after the bastards! Just do your thing, snap a few shots, take some videotape, get your documentation for me to write up—and we're home free. You sign on the dotted line for enough money to retire in style.''

"I might not have to retire."

"But if you do, this one last gamble is all you've got."

Her eyes remained dry.

"Say something, Al."

Alisha struggled to find her voice. "You said there were three reasons. I've only heard two."

Josh ran his fingers through his hair, a nervous gesture that was unusual for him. "You won't wanna hear this."

"The evening's already ruined. Go for it."

Josh toyed with his soda can, tracing the rim. "Those poachers did something to you. Not just physically, but…mentally. Emotionally. You're not the same Al I used to know and love. She's gone."

What do you mean?

"In her place is a frightened little *victim*—a woman afraid to take chances, afraid to sleep without a light on, afraid to live life as it's meant to be."

"I'm more cautious, yes," she said angrily. "What did you expect?"

"More than I'm seeing." Josh crumpled the empty can in his fist. "I want you take this assignment."

"You don't know what you're talking about!"

"Yeah, I do. Listen to me, Al. You can't spend the rest of your life hiding under the bedcovers or looking over your shoulder! I want the real you back again. No matter how the surgery goes. I don't mean to be cruel, Al, but you might not survive the operation, and if you don't, I want you to die a hero. A winner.'' He swallowed hard.

Shocked, this time she felt the tears start.

''It's one last chance to find yourself. I've pulled in all my favors, done all I can. The rest is up to you.''

Josh tossed his empty soda can across the room to the waste basket and missed. He got up from the table to correct his error.

''So, what's it to be? You gonna let your life go down the dumper?''

I'm afraid. I've been afraid of everything for so long....

''Think about it. Like I said, you can finish up in style—one big bang. I'm going to need your answer in the morning, Al.''

Better give it now, before I lose my nerve. ''I don't know about the big bang part, but the big bucks part sounds sweet.''

Josh's grin chased some chill from the room. ''Atta girl. I knew you were no wimp. I'll go call Carson. You'll meet with him tomorrow, okay?''

''Okay.''

''Good night, Alisha. Sleep well.''

''Yeah.'' *I'll try...my last night in this lovely bed. Next stop, the Everglades.*

CHAPTER FIVE

Day one—late morning in the Everglades
NPS land

CARSON WARD WAITED outside in the humid air of
an Everglades morning, his eyes on the only road in,
the old Seminole Tamiami Trail. U.S. 41, the cross-
state highway from Miami in the east or Naples in
the west, led into the heart of the Everglades.

There were clusters of Miccosukee homes here
and there along the road; some were built on stilts
with palm fronds, others of sturdier cinder blocks and
asphalt roofs. His own parents had had a cinder-
block house for the winter rains, with an open
chickee for the rest of the year. Since his father's
death and his mother's move, Carson had shut down
the house. He preferred the chickee, although overnight stays at isolated ranger bases were common for
him.

Directly south of the trail lay Everglades National
Park land, while the Miccosukee Cultural Center, the
Tamiami ranger station and the Shark Valley infor-
mation center were on the road itself.

The early-morning message from the ranger station surprised Carson. The expedition was back on. Alisha would meet him around lunchtime. According to the information he'd received, Josh had managed to reach Ray, who'd drive her in.

There were few tourists, but Carson stayed where he was to answer their questions—about directions, airboat tours, Seminole culture. All the while, he thought about the phone message. *She's coming after all—but why?* There was a mystery about this woman that had nothing to do with poachers. *Now I have two mysteries on my hands. I'll solve them both,* he vowed, continuing with his morning duties. Somehow Alisha's presence had provided a respite from the thoughts of death and violation that had pursued him since his father's murder.

Noon passed, then one o'clock. Carson grew restless on the job. He'd been scheduled to work on the information center's tram tour, which carried visitors out to a popular observation point and back. Carson switched tram duties with one of the other rangers so he could stay near the station in full view of the road.

A shame she's so late. I'd like her to see the observation point. Carson's pride in the land was something he suspected Alisha could share...would enjoy. *If she ever gets here.*

Deborah and Adoette arrived in Adoette's truck, Adoette's gear in the bed. Adoette would drive farther west to pick up her airboat, but they stopped to talk to Carson first.

"Where's Alisha?" Adoette asked. Both women were in traditional dress, their layers of skirt material protection against the mosquitoes.

"On her way, I guess."

Deborah frowned. "When's she due to arrive?"

"Any time now. Ray's driving her in."

The casino knew about Carson and Ray's hunt for the killers. A replacement was quickly found whenever Ray requested time off, even at short notice. The tribe was family, and they understood.

"I wouldn't worry, then. Tourist traffic's always heavy on the weekends," Adoette said. "Or maybe Ray had a last-minute problem crop up before leaving work. I'll go inside and get us some sodas. Usual orders, everyone?"

Deborah elected to remain outside with Carson. He continued to peer down the road, sunglasses over his eyes. Deborah wore none. Instead, her hair—like Adoette's—served that purpose in traditional Seminole fashion. It was coiffed and stiffened into a large, flat, slanted disk that provided abundant shade for her face and neck.

Deborah spotted the car first. "That looks like Ray's car. I think that must be Alisha next to him, but I'm not sure."

Carson squinted. "It is." Already hurrying toward the parking lot and Ray's car, he missed his aunt's speculative gaze. "Hello, Alisha, Ray."

"Sorry we're late," Alisha apologized.

"Problems?"

"You should know—you're the one who arranged the media blitz. Alisha and I were waylaid by reporters." Ray's gaze swept the area. "Where's Adoette?"

"Inside getting drinks. Let's go. We've got a lot to do."

Soon after, Carson and Alisha climbed inside Carson's truck. A canoe was secured in the back. Ray left his car at the ranger station, and Deborah drove Adoette and Ray down to the airboat dock. Deborah would drive Adoette's truck home, but for now the two vehicles caravanned. Carson and Alisha had reached the canoe-launching area and stopped.

"We'll catch up with you at the hammock!" Adoette yelled out the truck window as they traveled on.

Carson beeped his horn in acknowledgement, then parked at the edge of the paved road. The vast expanse of wetlands was before them—nothing else was visible between the road and the horizon. He and Alisha would take a canoe to the hammock or small island where his family had their chickees.

"I hope you packed light," Carson said.

Alisha lifted her backpack. "This is it. A few changes of clothes and my camera gear. Plus a light-weight sleeping bag."

"We won't have room for the sleeping bag. Leave that in the truck. You can pick it up later at the ranger station." He watched her unfasten the bag from the pack's frame. "Leave the frame, too. It's less weight, and you won't be hiking much."

"Is someone coming for your truck?"

"Yep. Your gear will be okay. Come on, let's unload the canoe." At her questioning look, he explained, "Four people is too much weight for an airboat in these shallow waters. So we're using Adoette's airboat and this canoe."

Within seconds they'd lifted the canoe out of the truck bed, letting half rest on the paved road, the other half in the water. Carson slipped the keys under the driver's seat, then locked the door. He'd made sure that the ranger coming later had a spare set. When he straightened, he saw Alisha had already loaded their supplies into the craft. The weight was nicely distributed—the gear strapped down securely and away from the oars and first-aid kit.

"That was quick."

"I'm eager to get started." Alisha ignored a swarm of insects buzzing near her face.

He noticed that none of them landed. "You wearing bug repellent?"

"And the proper clothing, and carrying a canteen," she said calmly. She was dressed like him, in long sleeves and long pants, plus a brimmed hat.

"You might want to change into comfortable shoes," he warned, glancing at her feet. "The canoes aren't that large."

"I prefer boots around poisonous snakes. I understand you have water moccasins, coral snakes and two kinds of rattlers. Eastern diamondback and pygmy, isn't it?"

"Yes, but I'd still suggest you change the boots."

She shook her head. "I heard five feet is the average length for the Eastern rattlers. Josh told me they're the largest snakes in Florida. So the boots stay."

"He's a snake buff?"

"No—far from it—he's originally from Florida." She tossed him the end of the tie-line and moved to the front of the canoe. "Let's head out."

He grinned. She was a no-nonsense woman, this one—unlike many of the tourists he'd guided. "Ray and Adoette will meet us at Deborah's with the airboat. They'll probably get there first."

"Okay."

She and Carson shoved off. She didn't scrape the canoe bottom, but carefully lifted the keel above the pavement before advancing it down into the water. When she hopped in, boots and all, the craft barely rocked. Even he couldn't have done better. She had her life jacket on and paddle in hand, flat end in the water, as he took his seat at the stern.

It wasn't until they were under way that she turned halfway to face him. "What's our schedule for today?"

Carson settled himself more comfortably. "About an hour's paddle due north. There's a natural open-water trail through the slough—the saw grass expanse. We travel north. You'll spend the night at Deborah's place.''

''The current seems to be against us.''

''If you want to call it that. You won't need that life jacket yet. The southern Everglades has an average depth of only about six inches, and the riverbed slopes a mere two inches to the mile. It's the drainage pattern of a fifty-mile-wide river.''

Alisha immediately removed the life jacket, since less bulk would keep her cooler in the heat. ''Okeechobee's the source, isn't it? The lake north of Big Cypress?''

''Right. We'll paddle north through the saw grass to my family's hammock, pack more supplies and load up the airboat.''

''Hammocks—those are the small Everglades islands, right? Full of trees. I'm looking forward to seeing one.'' Alisha's research had told her the vegetation was mostly tropical hardwoods, plus palms and mahogany. The trees grew on the few elevated areas. ''I read that most of the Everglades' land mammals live on the hammocks.''

Carson murmured agreement, then made a minor course correction with his oar. ''Tomorrow, the four of us will take the airboat north to Big Cypress. Once there, you and Adoette will stay with the airboat on reservation land, while Ray and I take the canoe and quietly patrol the park's boundaries.''

''Tell me about your job,'' Alisha said, reaching

for her Nikon, one of the two cameras she carried. "Won't I be interfering with your normal duties?"

"Right now, catching poachers *is* my normal duty."

"I mean like reporting to your boss, or doing paperwork, or checking into the office. It's hard to float a desk in the middle of the wild."

Carson grinned. "I check in by radio. There's not a lot of paperwork—just routine stuff—unless something's seriously wrong."

She attached her wide-angle lens to take a photo of the wetlands. On sudden impulse, she framed the shot to include Carson. "Where do you live?" she asked.

"The park service has scattered shelters throughout the Everglades for ranger use. My father and I also set up our own shelters on Seminole land. And there's always my family hammock. I have a chickee there, and I have lots of friends I can stay with when I'm off the hammock."

"So you're saying…you won't be within shouting distance after tomorrow?"

"Don't worry. Adoette knows her way around. You'll be safe."

"With poachers, there's no such thing as safe—which you know as well as I do. Since I'm supposed to flush 'em out, I prefer being prepared for the worst. I mean, what if they don't fall right into your lap like they're supposed to?"

There was silence in the canoe. A huge flock of

egrets took to the sky at their noiseless approach. When the birds had settled again, directly behind them, Carson spoke.

"You don't like my plan."

"It stinks. You're assuming far too much."

"Then why did you change your mind?"

Alisha pivoted completely around to face him. "It's my job. Could be my last one." She placed the oar inside the canoe at her feet and rubbed her arms.

He continued to paddle alone, his strength easily transporting the two of them across the water. "Your partner getting ready to retire?"

"Heavens, no. Why would you think that?"

"He's a good deal older than you. And he's come home after all these years. I just figured—"

"Josh isn't quitting." Her lips compressed into a tight line. "I'm the one who might be doing that. I'm thinking of cutting my losses." Alisha swiveled forward again, leaving the oar untouched.

"I know you were injured by poachers that time in Africa. Why risk it again if you're retiring?" he asked bluntly.

"You said it wouldn't happen!"

"I believe that, but you obviously don't. So why not quit now? Why this one last gator story?"

"You're not responsible for my decisions. I take my own risks, Carson. I made the choice back in Africa. I'm making the choice now."

Carson thought of his father, dead in his arms that rainy day. He remembered the bullet slamming into his own shoulder just weeks earlier. "I won't knowingly put you in danger. I promise."

"The only one who does that is me."

Carson didn't know how to respond to that somber, cryptic remark. "It's going to take us twice as long to get there if I'm the only one paddling," he said, hoping to change her mood. He lifted her paddle and offered it to her. "Be careful of splinters," he said.

"Splinters are the least of my worries."

"You know, it's not too late to change your mind."

Her eyes narrowed. "Oh, I might change my mind, all right. Just not the way you think." She smiled, but there was no joy in her expression. "I don't retreat. I've got too much at stake. Remember that."

She dipped the oar into the water, her gaze locked with his. Carson felt more than a moment's ease—he felt an ominous premonition. She turned her back to him and began paddling again.

"Is there something I should know?" he asked.

"Well..." She hesitated. "I've been offered a sweet deal to write my autobiography. I just wanted you to know I wouldn't refer to your father's death without your permission."

He had the distinct feeling there was more. "And?"

She continued paddling and didn't respond. After a moment, his oar joined hers.

An hour later they stopped at his suggestion.

"Let's take a breather. I need a drink." He passed Alisha her canteen. "You?"

"Thanks." She set down her oar, uncapped her canteen and took a long pull.

"Hey, not so fast," he warned. "You'll get sick in this heat. It's close to a hundred, maybe more."

"Don't worry. It's ginger water."

"It's what?"

"Warm water flavored with ginger. You can drink as much as you want and it won't make you sick." She held out her canteen. "Want to try it?"

"Sure—thanks." He took a swallow and made a face as he handed the canteen back. "Tastes funny," he said.

"I know. There's sugar and vinegar in it, too. It takes some getting used to, but it won't cramp your stomach."

"You'll have to give me the ingredients ratio. Where'd you pick up that tip?"

Alisha capped her canteen as he continued to drink from his. "It's an Old West trick. Laura Ingalls Wilder even wrote about it in one of the books in her *Little House* series. I'm not sure whether to describe them as fiction or autobiography. Anyway, the book's called *The Long Winter.*"

"Hmm. I read mostly nonfiction. Biology, local history, that kind of thing and so on."

"I like all kinds of books. Reading's generally the

only form of entertainment around—where I work, anyway.''

He nodded, then slapped at a mosquito buzzing around his canteen. ''Where'd you pick up your bug repellent? It doesn't smell like any commercial mixture. From a book, too?''

''No. It's a Masai concoction.''

''What's in it?''

''I have no idea. I asked, but the tribeswoman who gave it to me said it was better if I didn't know.'' She grinned. ''I think she was afraid to upset my delicate sensibilities—as if I have any left with this job.''

''Too bad—about the recipe, that is.''

''Yeah. It works great. When it's gone, I won't be able to replace it.''

''I'll give you some of our stuff—Seminole, not store-bought.''

''I'd appreciate it. It'll beat chewing garlic.''

''Sweating garlic may work for some insects, but it isn't enough for Everglades mosquitoes. We get isolated cases of sleeping sickness, malaria and spinal meningitis every year. Our mosquitoes can kill. When you run out of repellent, tell me immediately,'' he ordered.

''I will.''

''Lucky for us humans, the birds get fat on all our insects here. You ready to get started again?'' he asked reluctantly. Carson wasn't in any hurry. He'd genuinely enjoyed these few minutes of face-to-face conversation.

"In a minute. I need a snack." She reached into her pack and withdrew some beef jerky. She held out a piece to him.

She's generous. Is it just good manners or does it mean she accepts me as her partner? "No, thanks. You're hungry already?"

"Not already. Right on schedule. I'm still on Amazon time. Brazil's two hours ahead of us."

He rolled up his long sleeves as he watched her eat. He noticed how she first took several pills from a small waterproof pouch attached to the wristband that held her watch. She swallowed them dry.

"Must be hard living in all those time zones," he remarked.

She shrugged. "This is the last time I'll be out of sync for a while."

"The active Alisha Jamison, stuck at a desk, scribbling away? Seems...wrong, somehow."

"That's why we have to catch these poachers. So I can go out in style." She tore off a chunk of the jerky with her teeth and chewed. "One last bang, as Josh says."

Carson froze as the memory of the bullet's report, of his father's death, washed over him. "I wouldn't joke about it. My father was killed by poachers— almost certainly the same men operating in these waters now." His words were cold, terse. "It's not proven yet, but I believe they're the same ones who took a shot at me. Ballistics is working on it—they've got both slugs.''

She blinked, the blue of her eyes darkening. ''I'm sorry—I didn't mean to offend. Nor have I ever considered this a joke.''

''Then listen carefully. You document, I'll hunt. Once we reach the park border tomorrow, Adoette's your partner and Ray's mine. We split up, I'll go after the poachers, you photograph them afterward. You'll get your story…and stay in one piece.''

''I think it's time to reconsider the strategy. You and I will catch the poachers. Ray can take my place with Adoette.''

''What are you talking about?'' He didn't know which was more frustrating, her calmness or her ignorance. ''Look, you're not a trained ranger—you said so yourself. The camera's your weapon against poachers. We have a plan—''

''Well, now we have a different one,'' she replied.

''Have you ever actually *caught* a poacher?''

''You know I haven't.''

''Do you know how to shoot? Do you even own a weapon?'' he pressed.

''I have a more valuable weapon than a gun. I know how poachers think. I know how they act. They attack with absolutely no regard for life or limb, whether it's animal or human.''

''You think I don't know what these bastards are like? I've been trying to catch them since last summer!''

"Without success," she said bluntly.

"I've caught poachers before."

"Yes, but these aren't just poachers. They're your father's killers. You need fresh ideas—a new perspective—from someone like me. I've seen poachers in action all over the world. I've seen the ravages they leave behind."

He, too, was brutally blunt. "Your perspective won't cut it. You said yourself this is just one last story before you pack in your cameras. But to me, it's personal."

She smiled then, and something about her expression disturbed him. "You don't think it's personal for me?" she asked quietly.

Carson watched Alisha drop the rest of the jerky stick inside her breast pocket, then unbutton her shirt. When she slid it off altogether, he couldn't help himself.

He gasped—not at the lovely lift of her bustline beneath the brightly colored bikini top—but at the mass of scars from old slice and stab wounds. They, along with surgical scars, were everywhere. Her torso, her arms, her shoulders, her belly—all were covered with puckered ridges.

My God… How did she even survive such an attack? There certainly wasn't anything in the papers about *this!*

"It's personal," she repeated. "And believe me, I know the risks." She swiveled around in her seat. He was treated to the same brutal scars on her back.

He watched, shocked, as she reached for her discarded shirt and plucked the jerky out of the pocket. She picked up her oar again, glancing at him over her scarred shoulder.

"Let me explain something. Last night I turned you down because of this—" she gestured at her body "—because of what they did to me. I was afraid to take that kind of risk again. Today, I'm here—for the same reason. Because of what they did to me. I *have* to try to help you catch these poachers. Do you understand that?"

He heard the determination in her voice. He compared her face, the only scar-free area on her entire exposed body, to the rest of her. Now he knew what she'd been hiding—and he wished he didn't.

"Good," she said, without waiting for his answer. She popped the jerky stick back into her mouth and started paddling again. "Come on, Ranger Ward. We're wasting daylight."

CHAPTER SIX

Day one—Late afternoon
Ward family hammock

ALISHA PAUSED, TAKING a moment to stretch. Her shoulder muscles were only a little sore from the canoe trip. It felt good to be standing on solid ground again, her shirt and hat once more protecting her skin, the shade of the hammock's hardwood trees a welcome change from the glare off the water.

"You okay?" Carson asked. She passed him supplies, which he tied down in the docked airboat. Adoette and Ray had obviously arrived sometime before, but she hadn't seen them yet. "I can finish up if you're tired."

"I'm fine. Besides, we're almost done here." She lifted a tightly wrapped box of dried food, then placed it in the cooler for protection against scavengers. "Only a few more boxes to go."

"I wonder where Ray and Adoette are? They were supposed to help load supplies."

"I'm sure they'll turn up. This stuff's not heavy, anyhow."

They quickly finished loading the airboat. Alisha came aboard with the last of the gear.

"You ever driven one of these?" Carson asked.

"No. I've never even been aboard one."

"They can cover ground faster than a conventional canoe, or even a Seminole canoe."

Alisha studied the controls. "What's the difference between canoes?"

"The Seminole canoes are carved out of wood, and one end is higher and wider to form a platform. The canoe can either be paddled in the traditional way or poled through the water by someone standing on the platform."

"I imagine it's healthier to be able to change from sitting to standing once in a while," Alisha observed.

"It also means fish-spearing and other hunting is easier. It requires fantastic balance, though."

"Mine's not bad. Maybe I'll try poling sometime," Alisha said. Airboats were a big improvement over motorboats, but they still disturbed the environment. Alisha knew noise pollution could be just as disruptive to feeding and nesting animals as propellers were to vegetation. She finished studying the airboat controls and hopped back onto the hammock shoreline. "Another thing—poachers can't hear canoes as easily."

"True." Carson finished tying down the last crate, doubled-checked the lines and joined Alisha on shore.

"Now what?" she asked.

"We'll hook up with Ray and Adoette at Deborah's later on. Right now, let's get something to eat."

"Where?"

"At my place. I have my own chickee, and my parents' cinder-block house is there if you prefer more shelter."

"How many people live here on the hammock?"

"Six families—around twenty people in total. We're all related. This way." He took her hand, startling her. "The trail's rough," he explained as she hesitated. "And we have poison ivy."

"I don't need to be led around like a child. I know what poison ivy is." To his disappointment, she withdrew her hand.

"Yes, but do you know what poisonwood looks like? Or manchineel?"

"Not...really, no."

"Poisonwood is just as toxic as poison ivy, but looks very different. As for manchineel, it's one of the most poisonous trees in the world. They're protected, so we can't clear them out."

He continued to extend his hand. He felt her awkwardness as she let his large fingers curl around hers. Then he led her through the vegetation, explaining the dangers of his world.

Alisha allowed him to guide her safely around the hazards, the poisonwood with its orange fruits and shiny compound leaves, the larger manchineel. "I guess I should start watching for them instead of staring at the orchids. Beautiful, aren't they?"

He stopped. Her face was vibrant, transformed by her rapt interest in the orchids. *She has as many moods as these flowers do colors,* he thought.

"Yes...beautiful." *When was the last time I stopped to admire the orchids? And held a woman's hand while doing so?* "Actually, the Everglades' orchids have needed a conservation write-up for some time."

The beauty of her expression faded, the spell broken. He immediately regretted his businesslike words, but she urged him to continue.

"Go on."

"Everyone's concerned with saving the manatees and crocodiles—and rightly so—but our orchids are neglected."

"I imagine they suffered from hardwood harvesting on the hammocks over the years."

"That, and poaching."

"Orchid *poachers?*"

"Yes. There are hundreds of ground-dwelling species to steal. The air plant orchids—only a dozen—are even more spectacular, and easy targets. In fact, all our orchids are subject to theft. The cowhorn orchid is a perfect example. It weighs up to seventy-five pounds. Its size has almost eliminated it from the park. The vanilla orchid is quite fragrant, another favorite target. Easy to find, too."

He gestured overhead, and her eyes tracked his finger. "The air orchids grow on rough-barked trees—not much of a challenge for a serious collector.''

Alisha recognized the pink and white of the clamshell orchid, the pale blues of the spread-eagle orchid, the yellows of the butterfly orchid. ''And I thought the Amazon had fantastic specimens,'' she said in awe. The indigo of the sky and the emerald canopy of the trees framed the orchids' riot of colors. ''They're even more beautiful here.''

''And disappearing rapidly. I don't suppose you and your partner would be interested in doing a special—or even an article—on orchid poaching?''

''Let me worry about this job first.'' She stopped staring overhead to meet his gaze, her hand still in his. ''My plans for the future are…undecided. But, like I told you, this assignment takes precedence over everything else right now.''

''You're motivated, I'll say that for you. What you told me in the canoe, about why you're doing this—I hope revenge isn't your motive.''

''Revenge isn't it.'' *Salvaging what's left of my lung is my first priority. Salvaging what's left of my backbone is a close second. I can't live the rest of my life afraid.*

She shrugged. ''I guess it has to do with dedication. And, of course, money. My health says it's time for some medical treatment…and that's got to be paid for. I don't know how long it'll take to recuperate, so I'll need money for that, too.'' *Or to pay for my funeral if I don't make it through surgery.*

"Oh." His voice sounded strange. "Well, I hear plastic surgeons are doing great things these days."

"A plastic surgeon? Who said anything about a—" She bit her lip. *Damn, but that hit a raw nerve. Drop it, Alisha.*

There was a moment of profound embarrassment between them. Alisha uncurled her fingers, but his tightened even more.

"Sorry. I've been told I assume too much. Your plans are none of my business."

His discomfort and apology were sincere. She felt terrible—because she'd caused the misunderstanding. *This is my own fault. I should never have taken off my shirt in the canoe. What else could the poor guy think?*

"I'm not offended," she said in as light a voice as she could manage. "But maybe we should stick to botany lectures."

She gently pulled her hand from his, and this time he released her fingers.

"Now, about that meal?"

DARKNESS SETTLED GRADUALLY over the Everglades. The night feeders emerged from their shelters, as did the larger predators.

From inside the women's chickee where Deborah and Adoette lived, Carson listened to the familiar sounds of the wetlands. It was late now, close to midnight, but Ray, Adoette and Deborah still hadn't returned to the hammock. They'd left a radio message with a friend on the same hammock, saying they'd be late, although they hadn't explained why. Dinner somewhere, he supposed. The message said not to wait up.

He waited, anyway. Alisha had already retired for the night. She slept on a loom-woven hammock, suspended over the floor, covered by mosquito netting and a light sheet. He could see her motionless form from where he sat next to Deborah's loom. The chickee had no walls, just a few overhead rails where blankets could be suspended for privacy. None were hung now. Blankets kept out the cool evening breezes, which defeated the purpose of a wall-less house.

He found himself watching Alisha. *I sure screwed up,* he thought. *The best-laid plans…* It was all supposed to be so easy. He'd catch his poachers, she'd get her story….

Instead, he had a woman here who was more intent on seeing poachers brought to justice than in grabbing any personal glory for herself. That he admired. But he couldn't understand her eagerness to put herself at risk again. Why subject herself to the same dangers? Why not let someone else, someone qualified, someone like him, take the chances? That'd been *his* plan for her…and she'd rejected it. Obviously she was a woman of courage—or a stubborn fool.

Either way, she hadn't needed his tactless comment earlier. Carson winced. *Plastic surgeon. Way to go, Ward. I wonder what she needs the doctor for? She seems healthy enough.* Very *healthy*... Despite those scars, he found rare beauty in Alisha Jamison, both inside and out. She reminded him of those exotic air plant orchids, found in places you didn't expect them, just out of reach and straining toward the light.

She'd be an interesting woman to get to know. Intellectually, emotionally...physically, too.

That idea surprised him. He hadn't thought about wanting a woman for a long time. His job as a ranger, plus his year-long quest for his father's killers, had kept him too busy and too obsessed to even consider a romantic relationship. Yet Alisha tempted him, the way he imagined a butterfly orchid tempted a would-be possessor.

That's one tree I'm not going to climb, he vowed. But he couldn't help glancing at her now and then. *Just to keep an eye on her,* he told himself. *Nothing more.*

An uncharacteristic blush spread across his bronze cheeks as he watched her sit up. *Great, caught like some kid sneaking a peek.*

''You okay?'' he asked.

She wrapped the sheet around the bikini that she used as both underwear and sleepwear, and lifted the mosquito netting.

''Someone's coming,'' she said.

''I don't hear...'' He strained to listen. His ears picked up Ray's voice. ''You've got good hearing.''

"I'm a light sleeper," she told him. Her sheet trailed past the loom frame as she joined him at the edge of the chickee. "Who is it?"

Only then did he notice the tense muscles, the wariness of a stance poised for fight or flight. He remembered her scarred body and understood.

"Family." He stood and found his arm encircling her waist. She didn't pull away. "You have nothing to fear on my hammock, Ali."

He felt her relax beneath his arm. "Thank you," she whispered. She gathered her sheet closer around her.

He hoped it was because of the night air and not to hide her scars. "You're a very beautiful woman," he said in a low voice.

She smiled, then surprised him with a quick kiss on the cheek. Before he could react, she moved a step or two away.

He studied her carefully. "Is retiring going to create a serious financial problem for you?"

She was unmistakably startled by his question. "That's an awfully personal thing to ask."

"I apologize. However, if you're concerned about money, you could consider retiring here."

"In the Everglades?"

"Yes. On Seminole land. You don't need money to live here. We have a bounty of food available to us. You contribute to the tribe, and you share in its wealth."

To his satisfaction, she seemed to think about his

suggestion. "It sounds good," she said after a moment, "but I'm not Seminole. I wouldn't fit in."

"What do you know about the history of the Seminoles?"

"The usual stuff from history classes and my own research, I guess." The original tribes living in Florida were completely wiped out by the Spanish conquistadors. After that, northern tribes migrated south to the now-vacant Florida lands. These peoples, especially the Creeks, met with some early settlement success—but they, too, suffered the fate of their predecessors at the hands of the Spanish. Then later, the English, Colonial Americans and the United States Army almost finished the job. "All the killing—very sad."

"By the early 1700s, only scattered survivors remained. They all banded together, forming one new tribe, and named themselves Seminoles. It means free, untamed. Our new tribe retreated to the Florida Everglades for safety. It was a harsh land even the whites didn't want. But our presence was still considered a threat. We were given a choice. We could relocate to a reservation in Oklahoma or be hunted to extinction. Some of us relocated rather than face siege and starvation. The rest chose to stay and fight."

"I know about the three Seminole Wars."

"In those years, the Seminole population dropped from five thousand to a few hundred. The last of our great chiefs, Billy Bowlegs, was taken captive, yet we still fought. We still hung on. You see, in the Everglades, we learned to survive where no white man ever had. Do you know why?''

"You were left with no choice."

"Partly, but mostly because we were extremely flexible. We adapted to new situations by changing to fit the circumstances. We discarded whatever culture and customs hampered us. We accepted into the tribe anyone—*anyone, Alisha*—who swore allegiance. Whites, runaway slaves, other tribes' members…you see? Being Seminole is more than birthrights and traditions, important as they are. Being Seminole means staying free. I think of it as a state of mind, of heart. A state of *being,* Alisha. It's here, if you want it.''

"If I have something to contribute, you mean." She smiled, but her eyes were cheerless. "The only thing I have—my work—I'm going to lose. If I don't pay the dues, I can't join the club, right?''

"That's not what I said.''

"Carson, your story—your people's story—ends happily, and I'm pleased for you. My story has…an unfinished ending. Maybe it'll be happy, maybe not. But I know one thing. I'm out of this business— permanently. I've done my good deeds for the planet. It's time for a change…and for me to take better care of myself. I can't do that here.''

His chest tightened with disappointment, and something else. "I hope you find what you're looking for.''

Alisha merely shrugged.

Adoette, Ray and Deborah were now in view. They ascended the chickee steps with weariness and an air that immediately alarmed him.

"What's wrong?" Carson asked.

"Poachers," Deborah spat out. "Oh, hello, Alisha. We found three gator carcasses."

Ray brought up the rear. "What was left of them."

"How bad was it?" Carson asked.

"You don't want to know," Deborah answered. She and Adoette hung their privacy blankets. "I'm going to bed."

"What happened? Tell me, Ray," Carson ordered.

Ray stole a look at Alisha, who took in every word. "Nothing to worry about, Alisha." Carson wasn't fooled. He grabbed another flashlight as Ray said, "Let's take a walk."

Carson followed Ray down the chickee steps, his boots scraping against the hard, honeycombed limestone that was the base of the Everglades.

"Wait, I want to go," Alisha called after them.

"There's no need for that. You might as well go back to bed. We didn't mean to disturb you." Carson heard Ray's practiced, patronizing casino voice, and knew immediately it wouldn't work on Alisha.

"I'm coming with you. Don't even *try* to stop me." Alisha didn't think she'd ever dressed so fast in her life, pulling on loose jeans and a long T-shirt. She shoved her feet into her boots, grabbed a flashlight from Adoette and hurried after them, boot laces trailing.

The walk to the airboat was quick, despite the darkness. Carson kept an eye on Alisha. With a keen memory for geography, she avoided the poisonous plants and trees he'd pointed out earlier. *Darkness or not, this lady knows her way around.*

They stopped only once, at Carson's request. "Hold on, Ray. Alisha, tie your boot laces."

He held the light for her as she knelt to tie one set of laces and then the other. They made faster time after that. Ray's path led them straight to the dock. His canoe was tied next to the airboat.

Carson's flashlight played over the scene. "Dammit to hell!"

The carefully loaded supplies had been pulled off the boat and dumped in the water. The boat seat was slashed, and wet clothing lay scattered across the dock. Over everything was splashed the gory viscera of skinned gators, staining surfaces with dull red and tainting the air with the smell of decay. Already smaller scavengers, rodents and insects, covered the airboat and feasted on the remains.

"How could this happen?" Carson shone his light around. The darkness and the destruction made any salvage efforts virtually pointless.

Ray shook his head. "Adoette's airboat broke down at the docks. Turns out someone slashed her fuel line. Deborah and I went with her by canoe to pick up a new line from one of the other hammocks.

On the way, we saw a few skinned gators and stopped to check out the area. Didn't see any poachers, though. Guess we know why—they were all over at the dock, dumping gator guts.''

Carson frowned heavily. ''You should've called me.''

''We didn't have fresh batteries in the radio, or I would've. By the time we made it back to the dock an hour ago…'' He gestured. ''This is what we saw. Right in our own backyard.''

''Looks like someone's flung down the gauntlet,'' Carson said.

''Despite the fact that you let them know I'm here. They've got nerve, this bunch.'' Alisha approached the dock, flashlight up, carefully picking her way through the gator waste. ''Where do you want me to start?''

''Start what?'' Ray asked.

''Cleanup. Oh, and let me get my camera to document this.''

''We'll wait for morning to do both,'' Carson said. ''It'll be safer then.''

''Fine with me.'' Ray headed back toward the trail. ''I'm in no hurry to get my hands in that muck,'' he grumbled. ''I'm a casino *manager,* not a janitor.''

''But—look what they did! You're just going to leave it here?'' Alisha asked.

''The scavengers will take care of some of it. Either way, our early start tomorrow is canceled.''

"Are you sure? I've done this kind of work before. I'll do my fair share."

"I know that," Carson said.

Alisha stared one last time at the destruction before them. "In Africa, we had to leave the dead rhinos and elephants where they fell. We moved camp because we couldn't move the carcasses," she remembered.

Carson saw her shiver, and felt she was remembering more than dead animals. "Tomorrow," he repeated firmly as he placed a comforting arm around her.

This time she didn't argue. They hiked back to the women's chickee in silence. The other two were already lying on the chickee floor on mats, covered with the requisite mosquito netting. They weren't asleep. Across at Carson's chickee, Ray hadn't even bothered changing for the night. He stood gazing into the darkness. The two women sat up when Alisha entered.

"Did you see it?" Adoette asked.

"Yes." Alisha climbed back under the mosquito netting covering the hammock, and balanced there cross-legged.

"I'm so sorry this happened," Deborah said. "Will you all be able to leave tomorrow as planned?"

"It depends on whether they did further sabotage to the boat." Carson spoke across the short distance separating the structures. "If not, we'll settle for a delayed departure time. Thank heavens Alisha left her cameras here and not on the boat.''

"You did? Well, that's a blessing,'' Deborah said.

"I tend to be a little paranoid about them. I even pack my clothes around them for added protection.''

"Speaking of clothes…Adoette, how do you feel about Alisha borrowing yours?'' Carson asked.

"What for?''

"Because of the media coverage, the poachers know Alisha's here—and the damaged boats prove it. Her high profile was the first part of my plan, an attempt to draw them into the open. Now, though, it's time for all of us to fade into the background. So if Alisha dresses in Seminole clothes and I stop wearing my uniform…we'll be a lot less identifiable. The four of us will split up. I'll take Alisha with me by canoe. We'll go through the more heavily vegetated waterways to track the poachers, while you two take the airboat through open water. So…with your permission, Adoette?''

"And if it doesn't violate any tribal customs,'' Alisha broke in, "Your traditional garb will help me blend in better.''

"Like a disguise?'' Adoette asked.

"Yes.''

"Well…sure, I guess,'' Adoette said. "But I'd like to borrow your clothes in return. Maybe a pair of jeans or two?''

It was Alisha's turn to be surprised. "Why?''

"Until dinner the other night, I've never worn

non-Seminole clothing. Not even at college... I thought I could give it a try now. We're about the same size.... So, can I?''

"If you want," Alisha said. Deborah started to object. "Adoette will be perfectly safe in my pants and heavy-duty long-sleeved shirts," Alisha reassured her. "My clothes are pretty nondescript."

"Okay," Adoette said. "You borrow my things and I'll borrow yours."

"What about your hair?" Carson asked Alisha.

"I can dye it black. You're a weaver, Deborah. I'm sure you have something I can use."

"This is ridiculous," Ray scoffed. "What do you think this is, the movies? You're acting like spies with disguised identities—"

"Don't forget murder," Adoette said fiercely. "Your uncle's death. We have to do whatever it takes to find his killers. And that's *not* ridiculous."

"I never said that!" Ray had the grace to look embarrassed. "But we can't even be sure that these poachers murdered him—although I know Carson believes they did. I guess we have to try to prove it," he murmured.

"Then it's settled," Adoette said. "Right, Carson?"

"It's settled, unless anyone wants to take my earlier suggestion and back out. Now's the chance." He glanced at everyone in turn. "The NPS is patrolling the main waterways. I'm checking out the more deserted areas myself. Remember, this is my job, not yours.''

''We already had this discussion,'' Adoette muttered.

''That's right,'' Ray seconded.

''You already know what I think, Carson.'' Alisha lay back on the hammock. ''Please make sure you wake me up. I'm still jet-lagged. Good night, ladies…Ray. And Carson, would you do me a favor?''

''Yeah?''

''Leave your lantern on.''

CHAPTER SEVEN

Day two—Seminole Everglades

THE MORNING SUN ROSE bright and orange. The night feeders retired, even as the day feeders awoke, for the Everglades teemed with life. The sights, sounds and smells of the wetlands filled Alisha's senses every waking moment.

This is a gorgeous place, she thought, finishing her breakfast of fish and fruit with Adoette and Deborah. The men had already eaten and were down at the dock cleaning, repacking and repairing the airboat. *I wish I could enjoy it, instead of worrying about poachers and hospitals and death and money...*

Last night's grisly scene had sickened her. It wasn't because of the carnage, though that was bad enough. In her career, she'd seen enough to develop the proverbial cast-iron stomach. It was what the poachers represented—the danger to their lives—that made her sick. Only Carson's arm around her waist had kept her nerves in check.

She'd expected the usual nightmares, too, but her sleep in the swinging net bed was surprisingly dream-free. Somehow, the memory of Carson's saying, "You'll be safe on my hammock," remained with her.

Just words. Words can't protect anyone, no matter how sincerely they're spoken. Still, her sleep was uneventful. Alisha awoke rested and ready to start the trip.

Deborah carefully cleaned and stacked the last of the dishes. "Ready for your transformation, ladies?"

"I'm game," Adoette said.

"I'd like to freshen up first," Alisha said.

There was a camping toilet with biodegradable chemicals and paper in its own little chickee, with blankets hung for privacy, but other than that and the fresh tank of bottled drinking water, Alisha could see no modern amenities—like a shower.

"You can bathe in the water—but then you have to watch for snakes," Adoette said. "Or you can do a camping bath with a washcloth and bucket of water."

"When it's raining, we just hang some blankets, drop our clothes, soap up and rinse in the rain," Deborah said. She rummaged around in the box of dyes next to the loom. "The men and women are separate, of course."

Alisha frowned. "It's not raining now, and I'd really like more than a bucket." *But without the local critters.*

Deborah's eyes twinkled. "Then that leaves our alternative shower. Oh, yes, we have one," she said at Alisha's eagerness. "It's a rainwater catch with a sieve system—simple and effective. We'll need to wet your hair to dye it, anyway. Alisha, please grab a change of clothes for Adoette. Adoette, you'd better do the same for Alisha.''

A few minutes later the three women were inside the privacy of the blankets. Without embarrassment, the other two women started to strip. Alisha, her sheet wrapped around her, paused.

"There's only one shower," Deborah explained. "If we don't want to wait for the next rainfall or lug water from the glades, we have to share."

"Oh." *Great.*

"You aren't...shy?" Adoette asked in amazement. "A famous woman like you?"

If your skin looked like a jigsaw puzzle, you'd be hesitant about baring yourself, too.

"We could turn our backs," Adoette suggested.

"Or Adoette and I could go down to the water if you want," Deborah said. "Snakes are easy to spot in the daytime."

"No, no... It's not a problem." Alisha reached for a piece of their soap—a "harmless to the environment" brand she recognized as one she often used herself—and sighed. *So much for privacy. Here goes.* She dropped the sheet, and her bikini pieces.

It wasn't as bad as she'd expected. Adoette gasped only once, and Alisha couldn't even register Deborah's reaction. In true Seminole tradition, Adoette and Deborah made no comment and averted their eyes. Alisha saw no need to maintain the silence on her end. She gave them a one-word explanation. "Poachers."

The showers and Alisha's dye job proceeded quickly and without any personal comment, although it seemed that Deborah's hands on her wet hair were kind, even motherly. Adoette deftly guided the conversation away from Alisha and toward herself.

"I'm glad you decided to go with Carson. I'd much rather be with Ray," Adoette said easily. "I've got a thing for him, you know. So don't get any ideas, Alisha."

"Adoette, such talk!" Deborah scolded.

"Deborah doesn't approve of women throwing themselves at men, but Ray is so obtuse— That's one of the reasons I want to wear your jeans and blouses. I want a change of image. I need him to notice me the way a man notices a woman—the way Carson notices you."

Alisha didn't know how to reply, whether to deny Adoette's words or ignore them.

"Adoette…" Deborah scolded again.

"Carson watches every move you make," Adoette repeated. "I want that with Ray. I'm getting desperate. Deborah doesn't approve of *that,* either. But I thought I'd tell you, anyway. Since we're sharing clothes…"

And since I shared the reason behind my scars?

"We might as well share confidences," Adoette finished, just as Deborah finished with the dye. Adoette handed Alisha a body towel.

"There!" Deborah said, shutting off the water. "All done."

Towel clad, Alisha lifted a strand of her hair and peered at it. *My face was pale enough with brown hair. I probably look like a corpse now.* "How does it look?"

"Very, very black," Adoette said.

"It's not really you, but it looks fine," Deborah said tactfully. "Let's dress before the men show up."

"Ray will hate it. I wonder what Carson will say."

I wonder what Carson will say, myself.... "Why do the Seminoles wear so many colors?" Alisha asked as the three women rummaged through the stack of clothing.

"There's a pattern to the colors," Deborah said. "Have you heard about our snails?"

"I read about them." Alisha remembered mostly that the Everglades snails were very large, and could grow up to two and a half inches in diameter on account of the plentiful tree lichens. "I know they're big."

"And colorful. The snails are banded. Their shells have many stripes, and were the original inspiration for our dyes. Look closely, Alisha," Deborah said. "You'll notice a definite pattern."

Adoette dressed first. Alisha was a little taller, but Adoette simply rolled up the sleeves of the beige safari shirt, did the same to the cuffs of the beige pants and cinched the belt tighter. She wore her own boots and braided her long hair instead of wearing the traditional style.

The other women deliberately kept their backs to Alisha as she dressed. First came a fresh bikini, then the full, billowing Seminole skirt with its horizontal, multicolored stripes. Alisha studied the colors with new interest. Thanks to Deborah's explanation, this time she saw a definite pattern instead of a mishmash of colors. The loose, long-sleeved blouse with its overcape and stripes was next.

Not a bad fit, she thought, reminding herself to look for snails on the trip. It was comfortable and cool, although a little bulky. *I'll have to be careful getting in and out of a canoe in this outfit.*

She finished dressing at the same time Deborah finished with Adoette's hair. Alisha and Adoette faced each other.

"You both look…different," Deborah said. "Not like yourselves at all."

"That's exactly what we want. Wait—one more thing!" Adoette reached one hand to her neck and the thick, heavy strands of beads that completely filled the expanse from chin to chest. "Help me, please."

Deborah blinked. "Adoette, are you sure? All your life-strands…"

"The outfit isn't a disguise if it's not complete. Alisha wants to blend in. And I want these off—all of them! I want Ray to see *me,* not a bunch of outdated customs!"

"Well, you wouldn't be the first young woman to discard the old ways for new. Though I hate to be part of this."

Alisha stepped forward. "Adoette, you don't have to go this far."

"No, I want to. Really, I do. Take them. I insist."

"All right...but this is just a loan. I promise to take good care of them. And I think you should keep your birth-strand. Just leave that one on."

"You know about that?" Deborah asked.

"I came across it in my research." Alisha remembered that Seminole necklaces traditionally showed a woman's wealth and personal favor with family and friends. They also commemorated birthdays, pregnancies and births, weddings, and a young girl's physical maturation. Some women had as many as two hundred strings of beads, weighing up to fifteen pounds, around their necks.

"Fine, the birth-strand stays," Adoette conceded.

Deborah was relieved. "One strand less won't be noticed on Alisha. And Adoette, I wouldn't feel right seeing you without it."

Alisha instinctively felt she'd said the correct thing. Finally, the transformation, jewelry included, was complete. How do the women walk around with all these necklaces? she wondered. The weight was annoying, and the thickness of the beads made her neck feel sticky.

"You don't like them, do you?" Deborah said on

the walk back to the family chickee. She fondly touched her own beads.

"I imagine if I'd put them on one at a time while I was growing up, they'd feel comfortable." Alisha flipped her fingers through the massive strands. "It's hard getting used to them all at once."

"When you reach middle age, you get to take them off, one by one," Deborah explained. "Until only our birth-strand is left before death."

"I'm not middle aged, or six feet under," Adoette said tartly. "So I'm stuck with the whole lot of them. Or rather, Alisha is. For now, anyway. I'm not even married and I've never had children, yet I still ended up with tons of beads."

"You must be well-loved." Alisha lowered her head to stare at the mass of beads. "They *are* kind of pretty. At least I can take them off later—not like some women. In Africa there's a tribe who solders rings of metal around their women's necks every few years to elongate it."

"I've heard about those," Deborah said.

"If they're removed—and sometimes they are as punishment—the woman suffocates. The neck muscles atrophy from years of imprisonment in metal, and the weight of the head collapses the breathing tube."

"Antiquated traditions. In some things, modern is better. Like airboats instead of canoes. Or these clothes." Adoette smoothed the collar of Alisha's shirt for emphasis. But Alisha saw that Adoette's hand crept often to her almost-naked neck, feeling for the missing beads and finding only the birth-strand. She was still doing it as they reached the chickee. Even Deborah noticed.

"This is only for a short time," Alisha said quietly to Deborah. "I'm not trying to drag Adoette away from her heritage."

"I know you aren't. She'll do that on her own. Adoette's restless, and has been for some time. I've seen this coming. But she's an adult and must be allowed to choose her own path. Since Ray has discarded many of the old ways and Adoette wants to be his wife, perhaps it's just as well."

It was time to prepare for departure. The younger women hung their towels, retrieved clothes and camera gear, and said goodbye to Deborah, who preferred not to accompany them to the boat dock.

"I already said my goodbyes to the men," she said. "I'll say my goodbyes here." She kissed Adoette's cheek, then Alisha's, too.

"Be careful. Both of you. Safe voyage."

THE TWO WOMEN QUICKLY HIKED to the boat dock, Adoette leading the way. Though not squeamish, Alisha was relieved to see that the men had cleaned everything up. Nothing remained of the previous night's carnage.

Carson noticed them first, and nudged Ray.

"Talk about a switch!" Ray said.

Adoette strolled casually down the dock and just as casually asked, "What do you think?"

Ray grinned. "Wow, Adoette! You've got curves!"

That obviously wasn't the answer Adoette wanted. She frowned, climbed aboard and stowed her gear. "I always had those. Well, Carson, how do you like what we did with Alisha? She'll fit right into the scenery."

"What do *you* think?" Alisha asked.

"I don't like it." He gestured toward her hair. "The color makes your face look washed out. And the skirts... It isn't you," Carson concluded.

"That's the point. You're the one who let the media know I'm here. You're also the one who wants me to keep a low profile—remember? I just don't want poachers to be able to spot me right off as an outsider. *I* know it isn't me."

He looked at her skeptically but didn't continue the argument.

She stowed her camera case and clothes next to Adoette's pack and tied it down. "At least I'm wearing a braid instead of that lacquered pancake style."

"Even I passed on that," Adoette said. "I hate all the lacquer in my hair. Give me a pair of sunglasses any day."

"I hope I don't trip and fall out of the canoe in these skirts," Alisha murmured.

"Better get used to it quickly," Carson suggested.

He took his place before the airboat controls. "Everyone ready?"

As ready as I'll ever be. Alisha held on to a bracing bar. "Let's go."

FULLY LOADED WITH passengers and supplies, the airboat maintained a slow speed as they made their journey through the deeper northern waters. Just as slowly, Alisha watched the Everglades' topography change.

They were headed toward Adoette's family hammock on Big Cypress. The four of them planned to spend the night there, then borrow a Seminole canoe, which Carson and Alisha would use in the morning. Carson's new strategy was to start their search at the extreme edges of the park.

More limestone outcroppings appeared as they traveled along with the usual hardwood hammocks. However, unlike what she'd seen in the southern wetlands, Alisha noted pond apple, willow and pop ash trees in the depressions between hammocks. Denser populations of bald cypress trees were visible, too, mostly in thick clumps.

Alisha edged closer to Carson. "Why aren't there more cypress trees down south?" She raised her voice, so as to be heard above the airboat's fan propeller.

Carson shook his head in confusion and idled the engine. She repeated her question.

"The ground is different. Here in Big Cypress the

soil has more quartz in the limestone. Cypress strands thrive on it.''

"Strands? Not stands?''

"A strand is the name for the big clumps of cypress.''

"Of course, these trees aren't really that big. You should've seen this place years ago,'' Adoette put in. "My grandmother said the average diameter of the cypress was three to six feet. Some were actually twenty-five feet wide, and over a hundred feet tall.''

"Are any left?'' Alisha asked.

"Most were heavily lumbered before we were born,'' Carson said. "The non-Seminole locals made coffins and pickle barrels out of them. The government used them for PT boat hulls during the Second World War. It'll take a century or more for these empty areas to grow back.''

"What a shame.''

"There're a few giants left, mostly on the Norris Tract,'' Carson said. "It's protected by the National Audubon society. The trees' disappearance is what led to our wildlife being endangered.''

"The wild turkey, bobcat, deer, bald eagle, black bear and Florida panther—their numbers have dwindled since the trees were cut down,'' Adoette said.

"So have the Seminoles','' Ray added quietly.

Alisha gazed over the clumps of cypress, trying to imagine the Everglades with trees all over a hundred feet high.

Carson gestured upward. "My grandfather said

when he was a child, the bird life was so plentiful, there'd be total darkness underneath when the flocks took to the air. He said you couldn't see a patch of sky between wings. You could only tell how big the flock was by how many seconds it took for daylight to become visible again. Those days are gone.''

''Maybe they'll return,'' Alisha said hopefully.

''I doubt it,'' Ray said. ''There used to be millions of wading birds. Now there are a few hundred thousand.''

''You'll find disregard for life in all generations, past and present,'' Carson said.

Alisha didn't argue with that statement. Carson started the airboat again, and they continued on their journey.

The trees grew thicker now. Carson had to use water trails; earlier, he'd been able to navigate in the more open southern wetlands. They stopped once for lunch and a drink. From the silent craft, Alisha noticed the freshwater otters, amazed at their large size. Like river otters, they were delightful to watch. Plentiful fish meant extra energy. They played and cavorted in the water as if they knew they had an audience.

Even when the airboat was underway again, wildlife was everywhere.

''I hope I brought enough film.'' Alisha exchanged another exposed roll for a fresh one. ''This is a photographer's paradise.''

Common mammals, such as the white-tailed deer

and the opossum, contrasted with the rarer species—marsh rabbits with their tiny ears and the Everglades swamp snake, with its black-dotted yellow belly. Black and white frigates and kites fed near the anhingas—the water turkeys—and the rare pink flamingos. Their similarly colored cousins, the roseate spoonbills, guarded their younger, paler offspring.

If I had my health, I could work on all kinds of different pieces, Alisha thought. They don't *all* have to be dramatic life-and-death stuff. Carson had started her thinking last night. She didn't consider his invitation to join his tribe as viable. Her personal identity was firmly established; she wasn't searching for a new one. But his invitation to stay, *that* was something else. Her whole life she'd concentrated on large mammals. But the orchids and birds and some of those endangered banded snails—they were just as exquisite. Surely the public would be interested in stories on them.

If only things had been different. If only her health wasn't failing because of her entanglement with those poachers...

She shivered, an involuntary movement that caught Carson's attention.

"How's it going?" he yelled above the noise of the airboat.

"Fine," she yelled back.

"We're almost there. A few more minutes and we'll be docking."

Soon after, they pulled up to a much larger hammock than Carson's, this one settled by Adoette's family. Relatives were waiting at the dock. Adoette excitedly called out to them as Ray tied up the airboat and Carson shut off the engine.

"Carson, if I'm not being nosy, what are they saying?" Alisha asked.

"I don't know. They're Cow Creeks."

"Pardon?"

"Muskogee Seminoles. Traditionally soil tillers and cow herders, hence the name. They comprise about a third of Florida's Seminoles. Ray and I are Miccosukee Seminoles—descended from Creek hunters and fishers."

"You Seminoles don't speak the same language?"

"No."

"According to my research, your traits and cultures are similar. You share the same reservations."

"But our ethnic backgrounds are very diverse, remember? Adoette's parents were Muskogee and Miccosukee. She speaks both. Her Miccosukee father was a friend of my father's—my family kept in touch with Adoette's when he moved north to his bride's hammock. That's how Ray learned Cow Creek, enough to get by, anyhow. And most of us speak English, so we communicate that way, as well."

The next hour was a busy one. Adoette chatted with relatives and translated, helping Carson secure the Seminole-type canoe set aside for his and Alisha's use. The four new arrivals quickly split up and repacked their gear. Ray's and Adoette's things were left on the airboat; Carson's and Alisha's supplies were placed aboard the canoe.

By then, it was getting late. Dinner was served, and Adoette and her family retired to their cinder-block house. Alisha was offered a room there, and Ray and Carson were offered use of the family's spare chickee. However, Alisha preferred the peace of the outdoors to Adoette's noisy family reunion, while Ray preferred his creature comforts and, unlike Alisha and Carson, spoke the language. He fit in more easily with Adoette's family. In the end, it was Alisha and Carson who bedded down on the raised platform floor beneath the palm fronds.

Clean woven mats with hand-loomed blankets and the ever-present mosquito netting were invitingly present. Alisha stretched out on top, completely dressed, and moaned with contentment. "Lord, that feels good."

"You'll feel better riding in the canoe." Carson remained standing, his gaze focused on the night. "Less vibration than airboats. Better visibility. Quieter, too."

"Good. My ears are still ringing from the fan. I'm surprised Adoette doesn't get a headache from it." Alisha kicked off her boots and pulled the mosquito netting over herself. Her thick skirt rustled, and Adoette's beads clicked and slithered around her neck, adjusting to her change in position. She pulled off the skirt, and lay in her bikini bottoms and blouse, enjoying the cool night air.

"So, were you comfortable today...dressed as a Seminole?" Carson asked.

That's a curious question. "A skirt's a skirt. Though I'm not sure I can get used to the beads. I hope I can sleep in them. There's too many to untie and then redo in the morning." She paused. "As long as I'm not easily recognizable to any poachers, I guess it doesn't matter. Why?"

"Because tomorrow we do this in earnest. This is your last chance to change your mind and back out."

"You don't give up, do you. This is the last chance for you to change *your* mind," Alisha reminded him. "Why not bring others in on this chase besides just us four? According to my maps, the park-Seminole border areas are very isolated. Surely some of the local men could help."

"They could, if I asked them. Which I won't. They're civilians. I don't know how effectively they work or whether I could trust them to watch their backs...and mine. Besides, I don't have enough radios to coordinate a large group of searchers. What if they *did* happen to find the poachers? There's simply too much potential for a dangerous confrontation. I don't want to be responsible for innocent people being injured or worse." He frowned. "As it is, I have reservations about allowing the three of you along on this mission. I'd prefer to handle it myself, but I do need the extra eyes..."

She sat up, the mosquito netting safely tenting her. "Why must you be so *alone?* I've learned a little about you, Carson. You've made patrolling the border your life's work, ever since you were a child. Your father's been murdered by poachers, and you almost were, yourself. Maybe *you* should think about retiring. Trying something different. Something where you're around more people."

"Easier said than done." He pivoted her way. "Until I find my father's killers, it's not a possibility I'd ever consider."

"What if you don't find them? My attackers were never caught, and I've accepted that."

"Yes, but you survived. My father didn't. I blame myself for his death. He was retired and I wasn't, yet I allowed him to continue our routine. Did you know that?"

"I—just know what I read in the papers."

"It's no secret. I'll tell you."

Alisha listened as his story softly floated to her on the moist, tropical air.

"My father loved the Everglades. He spent his life patrolling the borders of our land and public land. In his day, there were very few rangers who were Seminole. There weren't any ranger chickees along the miles of waterways. They had no cell phones or miniature radios, just walkie-talkies that were full of static—when the batteries lasted. Dad didn't care. He helped map the trails I use today. I grew up in his canoe, learning all he learned. When I turned eighteen, I joined the rangers, just like my father."

Carson smiled, the happiness of those memories

softening his usually serious features in the moonlit night.

"Dad was so proud when I followed in his footsteps. The first day I wore a ranger uniform in the Everglades, he made me a surprise for my birthday—the traditional Seminole canoe. He'd carved it for weeks in secret. Even the push-pole was hand-etched with his personal designs." His voice warmed with affection. "My father was a master woodworker. He said anyone would be able to stand in this craft because the balance was perfect. And it was."

Carson adjusted his mosquito netting. "Dad and I used that canoe for years. Then it was time for him to retire. He worried about me patrolling the borders alone, just like I'd worried about him when I was young. I told him my job was easier because of all the groundwork he'd done. That Mom needed him. Dad finally did retire, but occasionally he'd come along with me to check things out—for old times' sake. His health was good, and he was a retired ranger. It wasn't exactly legal, of course. Officials aren't supposed to have civilians with them, but everyone looked the other way. No one had any problem with us continuing our work together until—"

Alisha braced herself. She knew what was coming next.

"Poachers were working one of the borders. They figured it would take some time for the NPS to find someone to replace Dad's and my two-man team.

They didn't figure I'd continue the patrol without a partner. Plus, it was raining heavily that day. Visibility was reduced. The poachers didn't expect to airboat right past our canoe with a stack of fresh gator skins piled on their deck. They almost ran us over before they saw us—and then it was too late. Dad was standing and poling, I was sitting. He took a bullet right in the chest.''

"Oh, Carson, no."

"I grabbed him as the canoe flipped us both into the water. The poachers fled, and I swam to shore with him. By the time I made it—'' He swallowed. "He never had a chance. You know, I never should've let him come along…should have done my job alone like I've done for the past year—without him.''

"You can't blame yourself. Those poachers killed your father. It wasn't *your* fault.''

"True, but I feel I played a part in his death. Until I find his killers, I'll never rest. Never be able to draw a peaceful night's sleep. Never in good conscience be able to marry, have children.''

"That's a terrible way to live your life. Driven by—''

"Vengeance? Guilt? Is that what you were going to say?''

"No! A…a search for justice, perhaps.''

"Call it what you will. You're right about one thing. The last year hasn't been much of a life—

alone in a canoe, always looking over my shoulder. Which makes me even more determined to end this.''

''What if you never find them?''

''Then I guess I die looking.''

''But to put your life on hold... No family, no personal involvement—it's such a waste.''

''That's been my family's argument. But my decision stands.'' He was silent for a moment. ''I thought you, of all people, would understand. Is your story any different?''

''In some ways, I guess it isn't,'' she admitted. ''I ended up doing this work because I loved the land and the wildlife it supported. I was raised in the city—Chicago—and felt starved for nature. I became a silent·crusader, with Josh's support, and I think we may even have accomplished something in alerting the police to the damage done by poachers.''

She sighed deeply. ''Now I sometimes think I've seen too much killing, too much slaughter of animals. Seals in the Arctic, dolphins in the Orient, elephants and rhinos in Africa, tigers in India... You name it, I've witnessed it.''

''That has to affect you.''

She nodded wordlessly. ''But...I *have* learned that even something as ugly as poaching can be more complex than it seems. In Third World countries, tribal customs and social structures are disappearing. Economies are collapsing. Immigrants to the city often lack the specific skills and education to thrive, and people who stay in rural areas are subject to droughts and floods and their farms fail. So they're forced into desperate ways of life.''

"Like poaching."

"Especially poaching."

"Granted, it's a vicious cycle," Carson said. "But surely you knew that when you took this on. And these people are a much smaller percentage than the professional poachers."

"I know. I firmly believe that saving the animals and educating the public will protect our ecosystem and the health of our planet. However, a machete in the dark did to me what all the poaching couldn't."

"It scared you away from your work."

"Yes." She took a long, shaky breath. "I lost my nerve."

She watched shock register on his face.

"I won't lie to you. I hate poachers, and vengeance *is* part of it. Still, I know I'll never find *my* poachers, Carson. But here in the Everglades, facing my fears, my own cowardice—*that's* what this last trip is about."

"Alisha, this is no place for that kind of bravado! This terrain is just as dangerous as any Third World country's. If I'd known your reasons for coming here, I'd never have agreed."

"You don't have to live with my conscience. I do. If I can handle this, I can handle anything."

Even surgery. She couldn't tell him about it. She needed a new lung. She couldn't say, "You know how they replace a bad lung? They'll cut out *both* lungs, *and* my heart, and transplant three replace-ments. Apparently that lessens the chance of rejec-tion—if I survive the surgery. I don't want my heart cut out, Carson! I'm scared! I have to learn to face the unknown again...." No, she couldn't tell him these things. It was her burden, not his. He had bur-dens of his own....

Carson shook his head. "Go home, Alisha. After tomorrow, there's no turning back."

"Then I'd better get some sleep, hadn't I?" she said calmly. She lay back down. On a sudden im-pulse, she pushed the mosquito netting away from her face.

It's just my imagination, she told herself. *Don't be silly.* But try as she might, she couldn't force herself to use it again.

It reminded her of a shroud.

CHAPTER EIGHT

Day three—morning
Carson's canoe

STANDING, CARSON POLED the canoe through the cypress strands, his motions smooth and rhythmic. Alisha sat in front with her camera. Paddling and poling didn't go together, Carson told her. For now, she was free to enjoy the ride and take all the still shots she wanted.

They'd made an early start, before the sun and the day's insects had made their appearance. Even though it was barely midmorning now, the heat had grown intense, and with it swarms of mosquitoes had arrived. Alisha didn't mind; she felt prepared for all eventualities. The bugs weren't biting, thanks to her insect repellent. The bright Seminole scarf she wore over her newly black braided hair kept her head cool. Canteens were filled and easily accessible.

"Ready to stretch your legs?" Carson asked.

"That would be lovely," she agreed. Sitting in a canoe for hours, then balancing her cameras whenever she wanted to use them, didn't make for the most comfortable ride. She wished Josh was there to help.

"There's a large hammock to our right. We can take a break there."

A few minutes later, Carson poled the canoe to shore. Alisha climbed out first and pulled it higher onto land as he poled forward.

"Better?" he asked, stowing the pole and joining her.

"Oh, yes. Thank you." She slung her canteen over her shoulder. "Lead the way. I'm dying to walk out the kinks."

"Grab your camera," he said. "There should be some gator nests here."

"Great!"

"Not so loud—we might be able to get close enough to take a few snaps."

"Just as long as they don't take a snap at me," Alisha whispered. She took her video camera, as well.

He grinned. "Let me worry about that. The mounds are on the other side of the hammock, if I remember right. That's why I docked over here."

Alisha scanned her memory as they hiked. Alligators built their nests above the ground out of leaves, branches and mud. Females laid twenty to seventy eggs in the center and covered the hole. As the vegetation rotted, it generated incubating heat for the eggs.

"Hope I get a few good ones," she murmured, checking her film. Good—most of a roll left.

"You might not get that many if we're running for safety," Carson warned.

Alisha knew alligators were rarely a danger to grown adults. Everglades alligators were fairly harmless—unless they were protecting their nest. "I'll be careful," she promised. "Though I wish I could get up close with my video camera. They're pretty maternal for primitive creatures. I'd like the public to see female alligators guarding their nests—help change those stereotypes."

"Unfortunately, we can't camp out at the nests with poachers in the area. You'll have to take what you can get quickly."

"Okay." Alisha carefully picked her way through the vegetation. She began to hear a strange noise that became louder and louder the closer they hiked to the nest area. She tapped Carson's shoulder.

"What in the world is that?" she whispered.

"I don't like what I'm thinking. We may have poachers around. Stay close." He reached for the holster at his side and flipped off the leather holster guard. He drew his weapon as they advanced.

Alisha continued to follow, hating the way her nervousness grew with every step. Wild animals rarely frightened her; poachers did.

They cleared a copse of mahogany and suddenly stood where tree line met water. Alisha looked straight up and gasped in horror. They'd found the source of that strange sound. A trapped female alligator roared and squirmed, trying to free herself. She was strong, but the nylon mesh net suspending her just above the mound of eggs she must have been guarding was stronger. For a second, the two of them stared.

Anger flooded her veins. "How could anyone *do* this?"

Carson put away his gun. Alisha started taking pictures as he surveyed the situation, then switched to her video camera, capturing the frantic struggles of the alligator.

"Tell me what I can do to help. I'll dump the cameras whenever you need me."

"Just stand clear. Better yet, climb a tree. I'm going up this one to cut her free."

Alisha studied the distance from net to ground. "The fall might injure her," she said, worried.

"The sand's moist, and gators have tough hides. Besides, there's no other way. I'm not going to carry her down. Go up that tree, and watch for snakes and intruders."

"Great." *It's like something from* The Wizard of Oz. *"Gators and poachers and snakes—oh, my!"* Alisha left her canteen behind. Carefully she inspected the limbs of a cypress, then slowly climbed it, her two cameras swinging at her neck. Carson climbed his tree much more quickly.

"You focused?" he asked. "Should be one hell of a shot."

"I'm doing video." She balanced on a sturdy tree limb, holding the camera in front of her face. With growing excitement, she flicked on the record button. "Ready when you are."

Carson unsheathed his buck knife. His blade sliced through the nylon. In seconds the roaring female fell to the ground, her struggles and cries ceasing as she hit the sand.

"Oh, no! She's not moving...." Alisha continued to record as she spoke.

"She's probably winded. Maybe in shock. No telling how long she was up there. Give her a few minutes."

It didn't take long. The female started moving, jerkily at first, then more smoothly. She reached her egg mound and examined it frantically. She opened her mouth, the white of the teeth stark against the pink of her mouth as she hissed her displeasure at the humans in the trees. After a final check of the mound, she raced to the water. For a few seconds she was visible, then she ducked her head. With a massive whip of her powerful tail, she was gone.

"Well. That's gratitude for you." Carson grinned nonetheless.

"I appreciate your finesse, even if she doesn't. You do good work, Carson."

"Thanks, partner."

Partner. She liked the sound of that. "All I did was take some video. I should get some stills of the nest, too."

He shimmied down his tree, approached hers and held out his hand. She passed him her two cameras, which he carefully set on the ground, then she hopped lightly down. He placed his hands on her waist to steady her. They remained that way as she turned from the tree trunk to face him.

"Quite an adventure," she murmured.

She felt the exhilaration of the moment change into something intense, a mood she recognized as attraction. An excitement that had to do with being a man and a woman together. His face, his lips, drew closer to hers. She didn't resist—

Until she saw something out of the corner of her eye. She shoved him away and pointed.

"Carson, look! Poachers!"

He swore and reached for his gun; she grabbed up her video camera. She managed to focus on the single intruder for a good five seconds before he ran into a tangled mess of vegetation. Carson didn't have time to fire his gun. Almost immediately, they heard the sound of a fan engine—an airboat blasting free of its hiding place.

"Get him!" Alisha screamed. She dropped her video camera onto the ground and ran toward the shore with her Nikon, telephoto lens already attached, to get a better picture. She flipped on the auto-shutter. The camera whirred as she yelled, "Shoot at the engine!"

Carson grabbed her arm and spun her behind him.

"Hey!" She shoved at him, trying to get around him. "I want pictures!"

"Dammit, he probably has a gun!" He shoved her back again, she tripped over the video camera, then she was up, up, up in the air, a second nylon trapping her as easily as it had trapped the female alligator.

She gasped, squirmed, swore. The intruder or intruders, whoever they were, had gone. "Carson!"

He tipped his head back and blinked in surprise. "Alisha? Are you okay?"

"Get me out of here!"

"I'll cut you down. Don't move."

"Do I look like I'm going anyplace?" Fury raced through her. "You're not laughing...are you?"

"No. It's just—if you could see yourself..."

"If you hadn't got in my way, I wouldn't be up here in the first place!"

"I didn't want you hurt." He began to climb the tree from which she was suspended.

"Do I look like a helpless female?"

"Right at this moment? Yes."

"Dammit, you *are* laughing at me."

"I'm not laughing. I'm merely smiling. Sure you're okay?"

"I'm fine. Let's hope my video camera is, too. I tripped over it." She placed the strap of the other camera around her neck as best she could.

"Did you get any pictures of the guy?" he asked, climbing the tree.

"I don't know. Maybe a couple—and they're

probably a big blur, because of this net. Didn't you notice it?''

''No. All my attention was on the boat.''

''So was mine.'' Alisha pulled a chafing portion of net away from her nose. ''Why didn't we hear it before?''

''They probably poled in so as not to disturb any gators, then motored out when they saw us.''

''Damn!''

He climbed higher up the tree until he was at her face level. ''If you're done griping, take my hand.''

''What for?''

''So you don't fall on your head when I cut you free.''

She pushed one of her hands through the mesh. He grasped her wrist, she grabbed his, and he sliced through the net.

Her body was suddenly freed as the net fell to the sand below. She dangled in the air, her feet a few yards from the ground.

''Ready to jump?''

Alisha grabbed the Nikon with her free hand so it wouldn't hit her in the face. ''Okay, let go.'' She landed feet first in the sand, then overbalanced. Her knees hit the ground, but she was uninjured. Still on her knees, she crawled over to her Camcorder and retrieved it.

''Everything okay?'' Carson asked, scurrying down the tree. He reached for her elbow just as she stood on her feet again and fiddled with the buttons.

"I'm *fine*." She shrugged away, then brushed the sand from the front of her skirt with a violence that was far from necessary. "But my video camera's power switch isn't working! The plastic around the switch is broken."

Carson studied her. "Calm down. Better the camera than your head."

The gaze she threw him could have melted metal.

"I'm just relieved you're okay—physically and emotionally."

"Emotionally?"

"Seems your nerves aren't as bad as you thought. We've had some unexpected surprises in the last few minutes. You haven't cried, frozen, become hysterical or passed out. As I said, I'm relieved...and impressed."

"Skip the compliments and listen carefully. I respect your skill as a guide. I need it. But in the future, please don't play baby-sitter or bodyguard except for natural hazards. When it comes to poachers, I decide what risks I take."

"My job as ranger is to protect you." His voice was as cold and hard as hers.

"Yes—on NPS land. We're on Seminole land. Your idea, remember? As far as the legalities are concerned, your park service duties ended when we crossed the reservation border."

"I refuse to let you walk into the nearest bullet, no matter where we are." Carson bent over and retrieved the second net, bundling it up.

"Look, Mr. Ward. I don't have the energy to argue. Only a bottle of pills is keeping me going right now. That won't last long, either—so I have to save my strength for the job. I really do know what risks I can—"

"You're that sick?" Carson interrupted, frowning.

She paused, watching him, feeling unexpectedly warmed by the concern on his face, in his voice. "You were honest with me back at the casino," she finally said. "It's time I returned the favor and told you the truth."

She told him everything. When she was finally finished, there was a long silence before he spoke again.

"You're…on the transplant list? And you're out here? Shouldn't you be—"

"What? Wrapped in a blanket at my mother's house, waiting for the phone to ring? As long as I can walk and talk, I can still work. Like I said before, this really is my last big effort—and it has to be a good one. I respect your uniform and your dedication. But here's the bottom line, Mr. Ward. Stop trying to save a corpse."

RAY CAREFULLY HID his airboat behind another hammock before shutting off the engine. Adoette was as white, as shaken, as he.

"Did you know those nets would be there?" he asked in Seminole.

"No. But this is my home. All the locals know that hammock is a favorite nesting ground. That's why I thought we should pole in—so we wouldn't disturb the females. I had no idea we'd find nets...or Carson and Alisha!''

Ray swallowed hard. ''Adoette, do you think it's possible?''

''Don't say it.''

''I've got to. If only the locals know that hammock is a good nesting site, then our poachers might be—''

Adoette bit her lip. She reached for her canteen with a shaking hand. ''We should have stopped. Why didn't we tell Carson we were there? Why run?''

Ray gave her a sharp look. ''Think, Adoette. Think! If a local—one of *us*—is killing alligators, then he could've killed Carson's father!''

''You don't believe that, do you?''

''I don't know. Maybe. No outsider would know about that nesting ground. Do you want to be the one to tell Carson?''

''No!''

''Me, neither—so I gunned the airboat. I wanted to talk to you first.''

''My God, Ray, what are we going to do?''

''I don't know. It isn't poaching if Seminoles are taking gators on reservation land.''

''But Carson's father—your uncle... Ray, it's still murder.''

''I know, I know! Shut up and let me think!''

Adoette took a swallow of water and passed him the canteen.

''Thanks.'' He drank deeply, then wiped his

mouth with the back of his hand. "I shouldn't have told you to shut up."

"It's okay. I—I have an idea."

"We sure could use one," Ray said.

"Let's keep a quiet eye on Alisha and Carson, too—without letting them know. As long as we're both in poaching territory…we'll try to beat Carson to the poachers."

"You sure you want to go hunting for possible killers?" Ray asked, returning the canteen.

"Alisha is."

"This is Alisha's work. And Carson and I are family. What's *your* reason?"

"Ray, if Carson finds the man…or men…who killed his father, he'll kill them," Adoette said slowly. "What if he ends up in jail?"

"He…wouldn't go that far."

"He might. I can't see Carson reading his father's killer his rights and handcuffing him, can you?"

A muscle twitched in Ray's temple. "You've got a point there."

"If the killer is one of our people, we'll find him ourselves. My family will help. Then the tribal council can take care of him—without Carson's interference."

"But what about Alisha? If she finds the poachers before we do, no telling how she'll handle it. It'll be a media frenzy. I can hear it now—Indians slaying gators…and each other."

"What do you suggest?"

Ray studied Adoette carefully. "What do *you* suggest, wise sister?"

She flushed with pleasure. "Well, I know this might sound silly—"

"No. Tell me."

"If we don't want Alisha doing a story on Seminole poachers, it seems to me the first thing we do is take her cameras."

"Makes sense." Ray slung an arm around Adoette, his admiration clearly visible. "So," he said in English, "you ready for our first mission?"

"Yes. If you think we're doing the right thing…"

"Keeping Carson out of jail and Alisha from spreading us all over the news? Believe me, Adoette. We're doing the right thing."

CHAPTER NINE

Day three—afternoon on the nesting hammock

CARSON MARSHALED his thoughts, taking in Alisha's shocking confession. "You're—dying."

"Yep. There's a very good chance of that."

"You can't be serious!"

"We haven't known each other long, but do I seem like someone with a warped sense of humor?" Alisha straightened her skirt layers.

"No, but you're so…" He gestured toward her.

"Hearty? Hale? Roses in my cheeks?"

"Something like that. I find it hard to believe that you're—"

"One foot in the grave? My left lung is pretty much shot. It was scarred badly by the attack, and then by subsequent infections." She cautiously approached the alligator nest. "Think I could take a few photos here? I doubt Mom's in the mood to return."

"Go ahead, I'll watch out for her. But why are you worrying about work at a time like this?"

"I don't have a choice. It's what I do. Carson, my bad lung's getting worse. I've got pills and inhalers, but it's only a matter of time before the whole thing quits on me. It's infecting the good one now, too.''

"Can't they do *anything* for you? Besides that transplant? I mean, if your heart's okay..."

She knelt down on the soil for a close-up. ''They *have* to do a heart-lung transplant.'' Alisha clicked and refocused, missing his horrified expression. ''The doctors tell me no one's ever survived with just one lung. And the risk of rejection is terribly high for any lung transplant. For some reason, a double lung-heart transplant reduces the chance of rejection. They aren't sure why, but it's standard procedure.''

"You're *positive* there are no alternatives?"

"Yes—or I wouldn't be on the waiting list.'' She frowned. ''What a boring shot.'' She lay on her back, catching the top of the mound and the lower end of the gator net trap in the frame. ''Still lousy. Spread that extra poacher's net around the nest, would you, please?''

He did, and she reframed the shot.

"That'll work. Thanks.'' She clicked a few shots of the overhead trap as she lay on her back, then moved to her knees. ''Anyway, about the surgery— you need three things to qualify.''

"A donor, of course.''

"That's actually the last. First, you need as healthy a body as possible under the circumstances. The cure can kill you otherwise. Lucky for me, I haven't developed any secondary infections other than in my other lung. My vitals are pretty good, and my age is a plus."

"Then comes the donor?"

"If I get a match. I'm lucky here, too. I'm not a rare blood type. I'm A positive, the most common after O positive. So with my health and blood type, I have a shot at a transplant. Two out of three isn't bad. But there's no guarantee I'll survive the surgery, or my body won't reject the donated organs later. If it *doesn't* reject them, I still don't know how healthy I'll be after it's all over. I might be able to work— at something—or I might be an invalid the rest of my life. That's why I have to take the risks now. I'm working on a tight schedule. Very tight." Alisha finished with her shots.

"I'm…sorry."

She held up her hand. "Carson, I'm way past pity. It's a waste of time. We have enough to worry about with these poachers, okay?"

"But there's a good chance the doctors can help you?" Carson asked.

Alisha shrugged. "If I'm a good match, maybe." *Except that the actual donors are a mere fraction of the multitudes waiting on the list. There's so many other variables. And, in addition to everything else, I have to survive the surgery. Still, it's better than nothing.*

"It's the only chance I have. So forgive me if I'm a little overzealous going after my retirement fund. Or if my temper gets the best of me—like when my

Camcorder's broken! Right now, patience isn't my strong point.''

Carson reached for her hand, squeezed it, and after a silent moment, released it. Finally he said, ''I'll go get the canoe. Will you be all right waiting here?''

She nodded, and as he left, she busied herself checking her camera gauge. *Half a roll of film left.* She began to put the camera back in its case, then paused. *I don't know if I caught the face of our intruder, but if I did, I don't want anything happening to this film.*

She pushed the button triggering multiple-shutter shots, knowing the film would automatically rewind when it reached the end. As soon as it did, she removed the roll. But she didn't plan to stash it in her backpack. Alisha slipped it into one of the voluminous pockets of her skirt, instead. She'd pin the pocket closed with a safety pin from her gear as soon as she was back in the canoe.

And as soon as I get my backpack, the rest of my film goes in here, too. I'll take my spare camera out and sleep with the thing on my neck, if I have to. I can't afford to have anything else happen to my equipment—or this film. I'm already out one Camcorder.

She patted her skirt pocket one last time. Alisha was about to start hiking toward the other end of the hammock to take additional pictures when she saw Carson poling the canoe around the bend. ''Your chariot awaits.'' She made a wide track around the gator nest for the beach. Carefully she climbed into the canoe.

"Where to now?" she asked in her most businesslike voice.

"If you're up to it—"

"I am."

"I thought we'd check out a few more hammocks for nets. Then find a safe place for the night."

Safe. Now, that might be easier said than done. "What did you have in mind?"

"There're some smaller hammocks with only a few trees, a couple miles east of here. One of them has a chickee my father built—kind of a way station I sometimes use. It won't have much in the way of gator nests. Any poachers working the area won't bother with it."

"Sounds good to me."

After visiting three more hammocks—all mercifully free of nets or gator carcasses—Carson took her to the chickee where they'd spend the night.

"I think I see a gator nest. They seem to be everywhere," Alisha said as they secured the canoe.

"It's that time of year," he said. "As long as we stay on this side of the hammock, we'll be fine."

"Okay. If you don't mind, I'm going to wash up a bit."

Carson scouted out a safe area for her with a fairly clear freshwater pool. Alisha sponged off, applied more bug repellent, rinsed out her bikini and put on a fresh one, then changed into a fresh blouse. She kept the same skirt with its carefully pinned pocket.

That's not much of a safeguard, considering this is poacher county. I need to do more.

When she and Carson had traded places in the pool, she spent a few minutes dividing her camera gear in half. She placed equal numbers of fresh film rolls with each camera, and secured her Nikon in her pack, along with the broken Camcorder. She decided to leave the videotape in the Camcorder until she had it repaired. If only she could operate the playback and see who was out there... The smaller spare, the Canon, she hid in her bedroll.

It's not exactly Fort Knox, she thought, *but anyone wanting my film will have to rip this skirt right off me.*

After a short fishing session with poles Carson had stored in the canoe, they had the usual meal of grilled fish and fresh fruit, both plentiful.

"Good thing you're not allergic to fish," he said, carefully banking the embers to avoid giving off light to any passers-by.

She nodded as she finished up the last of her meal. "What we need now is dessert."

Carson reached into his pack and withdrew a candy bar.

"Chocolate? I don't believe it!"

He tossed it her way.

"Bless you. What about yours? Do you have more?"

"No. But eat it, anyway."

"I think I'm in love. Thank you, Carson." She peeled the wrapper, then broke the bar in half. "Want some?"

"Sure."

They munched contentedly, and Alisha savored each melting mouthful. "I was afraid to bring empty calories because of the animal life," she said. "I could just imagine raccoons or rats rummaging through my pack."

"Raccoons live in the dryer areas of the park. I'd worry about the bears and ants getting your chocolate."

"Not if I eat it first." The sun flooded the trees and water with a brilliant gold, and she smiled happily. "I could get used to this."

"Really? I thought after the type of life you've led, you'd want all the creature comforts...especially with your health problems and all."

"I love the outdoors. Even as a kid, I always felt happier outdoors than in. Though I'd enjoy it more if I wasn't hustling for a story and watching my back."

"I know what you mean." He grinned, then suddenly looked serious again. "Alisha—Ali—where will you go...after? When this is over?"

"Home to Chicago. My family's there, and I need to be near a major hospital. I'll write my book, enjoy the sunshine..." *And wait for the telephone to ring.*

"What about you? What will you do if—when—you find your father's killer?"

"Take it easy, I guess. Something we should both be doing." Carson cleared the rest of the dishes. "I've got the hammocks up for sleep, and the mosquito netting."

She groaned. "Great. Just what I need. More nets."

"I guarantee these won't yank you up to the top of a tree. But if it makes you feel better, then sleep with your knife. It's not really necessary, though. I have my gun. And my radio."

"You sleep with your radio?"

"I won't leave either radio in the canoe. They're too accessible to any midnight intruders. I'll give you the other one, if you'd like."

"Please."

Carson immediately retrieved one of the radios and gave it to her. "You weren't nervous before, but you are now. Try not to be. I'll keep you safe."

She thought of all the scars on her body, the price she'd paid—was still paying—for her work. "Better to be overcautious than overconfident." *I won't make that mistake again.*

Maybe it was the gator net that had trapped her earlier, or all the talk of poachers and weapons. Whatever the reason, Alisha had nightmares. She was back in Africa, dead elephants all around her, tusks missing. In her dream, she was being stabbed over and over by poachers using the tusks to pierce her body. She cried out for help, but no one was there except her attackers. They were laughing, she was dying....

Alisha moaned. "No, no...please," the same words she'd cried back then. Raising her arms, she reached for safety from those stabbing tusks, and felt another pair of arms. Someone was saving her, lifting her away from the horror.

"Alisha, wake up."

She tossed her head, still in the throes of the nightmare.

"Come on, Alisha. Open your eyes."

She did. Carson's arms were around her, holding her upright. Her fingers grasped his shoulders, and there were tears on her face.

"You were dreaming," he said.

Alisha shivered uncontrollably. He tightened his arms around her until the shaking stopped.

She wiped at her eyes, embarrassed. "Sorry. Damn nightmares."

"They're a pain."

"You, too, huh?" She dried her cheeks.

"Usually it's my father dying."

Her lips curved in a trembling smile. "Mom insists I find myself a good therapist. In my *spare* time."

"*My* family thinks a woman would fix me up fine."

"Sex instead of a shrink... Sounds good to me."

He paused, his fingers lightly roaming her arms. "Was that an invitation?"

Alisha suddenly realized what she'd said. "I didn't mean it to be but...I'm flexible." He'd been so kind, and she'd been so lonely. She'd never slept with strangers—but he didn't seem like a stranger. *And I have so little time left....*

He released her. "I'm not here to take advantage of you—just make sure you're okay."

"I'm *not* okay! I'm tired of being alone. Tired of sleeping alone. Tired of waking alone. I want a home with two kids, a dog and a white picket fence. I want a man to love, a man who loves me...." She took a deep, shuddering breath and steadied her voice. "With my health, I have to be realistic. So, here it is. Let's dispense with courtship rituals, feminine wiles and mating games. I'm feeling particularly needy right now. And if you're feeling anything along those lines...why not?"

Even in the dark, she could see his physical interest in the tenseness of his stance.

"With your health problems?"

Alisha smiled. "The only health issue I have to worry about here is safe sex." *Although you don't need to be concerned about catching anything from me. I've been out of circulation since the attack.* "Pregnant women don't get transplants," she said matter-of-factly. "Despite my inactivity, my doctor insists I travel prepared."

Carson remained standing. She remained carefully balanced, sitting cross-legged in the hammock, the skirt covering all but her feet.

"I don't take advantage of women. Especially women who've just awakened from a nightmare."

"I can't believe you're going to play the gentleman." Alisha wasn't sure whether to laugh or cry, whether to feel grateful or insulted.

"No hard feelings?"

"Bruised ones, but I won't take it personally." She kept the disappointment from her voice, then lay back in the woven folds of the hammock and covered herself with the sheet and mosquito netting. She watched him do the same. After a few minutes, she said, "Thanks for listening."

"Anytime."

"If you ever get out of these swamps, you'll make someone a lucky woman." *Too bad it won't be me. Just my luck—I've got one foot in the grave when I finally meet a decent guy.*

"Good night, Alisha."

"Good night."

She tried to sleep. She really did. The heavy skirt, the netting of the hammock beneath her, the mosquito netting above her, the memory of the gator netting around her... *Trapped.* She couldn't stand it anymore.

She pulled off the skirt. She took the sheet and placed it on the ground, then lay down on it. Carson's deep voice came to her in the dark.

"That's not a good idea."

"Sorry. Did I wake you?" she asked.

"No, but you shouldn't sleep on the ground. What's wrong?"

"It's too much like that damn gator net. I don't like feeling—" *Confined. Helpless.* She started again. "It's not comfortable."

Carson rose, took her hand and led her to his hammock. He lay down and, his hand still in hers, gently tugged her toward him. Alisha hesitated. "But you said no."

"I said no to sex. I didn't say anything about sleep. I won't get any with you on the ground—and neither will you."

"I'll be fine," she insisted.

"Humor me."

Alisha let him pull her down beside him, bringing the sheet and netting over their heads. *Five minutes,* she thought. *I'll just lie here five minutes.*

Slowly she relaxed against his warm body.

"Better?" he asked after a while. Five minutes? She wasn't sure.

She nodded, and Carson gathered her closer.

"What do you do when you have nightmares?" she asked, her head on his shoulder.

"Me?"

"Yeah."

"Promise myself I won't have them anymore."

"Does that work?"

"No. But I think they'll stop when I catch Dad's killer."

"I pray you do."

He stroked her head softly and kissed her hair.

"What was that for?"

"I just felt like it."

Alisha yawned once, then again. "Like I said, you'll make some lucky girl a wonderful husband."

"If we find our poachers."

"When..."

"When," he agreed.

Minutes later, she was asleep in his arms.

"I'LL SNATCH THE CAMERAS," Adoette whispered in the dark. "You stay here with the airboat."

"Let *me* go," Ray suggested.

"No. I'm smaller and quieter. What if you fall over some tree root?"

Ray grimaced. "I hate the great outdoors. Watch out for gators."

"I will. If any poachers come, move the boat and pick me up later."

"Just hurry." Ray slapped a flashlight into her hand. "I had to pole us in here to stay quiet. I'll have to pole us out, too. Go in, grab her cameras and get out. Be fast, be careful."

"I will." Adoette hopped off the airboat, her feet making no noise as she cleared the water. "If I run into trouble, I'll whistle. Crank the engines and get ready to roll. Just in case."

"Please—be careful," he repeated.

The night air felt good. Adoette inhaled happily, glad to be home, glad Ray was with her. Not that he'd ever want to *live* here. Big noisy man that he was, he'd always want to be around big, noisy buildings.

Adoette liked the quiet. It was something she'd grown up with, something that was second nature to her. She moved lightly, quickly through the brush, barely needing her torch to see the way. The moon was almost full. *Poacher-bright,* she thought.

Her happiness drained away. Adoette concentrated on finding the camp. Suddenly, two hammocks were visible. Only there were *two* people in *one* hammock. Adoette couldn't help her gasp.

Alisha stirred against Carson's arms. Adoette froze, motionless as a cypress on a windless day. Alisha settled down again, Carson's arms still around her. Adoette continued to stare.

They didn't…did they? They're both still dressed, but—together in a hammock? That was quick work! How did Alisha do it? Why can't I get Ray to notice me like that?

She picked her way to the empty hammock. Alisha's beige backpack hung from one of the anchoring trees. Adoette hesitated. *This isn't stealing,* she told herself. *It's not.*

For safety's sake, she shut off her torch. Reaching for one strap of the backpack, Adoette lifted it away from the tree. An ungodly noise broke the stillness of the night—aluminum cup, plate and silverware rattling against one another. Adoette yanked at the string holding the pack and camping dishes to the tree, snapped it and freed the pack, then ran.

She heard Alisha's sleep-rough voice cry out. Worse, she heard Carson coming after her. *Carson carries a gun.* Adoette ran even faster, raising two fingers to her mouth for a piecing blast. The airboat engine roared to life. Ray pulled away from the shore, aligning the boat for a speedy retreat. Adoette continued to run full-tilt, jumping from the shore to the boat.

"Go, Ray, go! Alisha booby-trapped her pack!"

Ray needed no urging. With the throttle wide, they made their escape.

RIGHT BEHIND THEM, shoeless and skirtless Alisha made it to the water—but not before the boat disappeared behind another hammock. The sound of the engine retreated in the distance. It didn't matter. She knew what she'd seen.

"Alisha, get over here!" Carson emerged from the brush, her boots in one hand, his gun in the other. "Are you trying to get yourself killed?"

"Put your gun away. Those people are no danger."

"You don't know that! Are out of your mind, chasing after them half-dressed? You ran right past me!" He dropped her boots in front of her. She removed the socks, shook them out, then gratefully wriggled her feet into them. "Thanks."

"Did you get a look?"

"Yep, and you're not going to like it. Our intruder was Adoette."

"*Adoette?*"

"The one and only."

Carson shook his head. "No."

"Yes! Come on, Carson, don't you think I'd recognize her?"

"Not in the dark."

"She's wearing my clothes. I know those clothes, and I know her. I booby-trapped my pack. When it rattled, I was awake in seconds. I had time to see. It was Adoette."

"Are you sure you weren't still half-asleep? What with your nightmares…"

She fought down her anger. "No, no, no! Believe me, it was her! Which meant Ray was driving the boat." Alisha pivoted to head back up the trail. "I'm getting dressed."

Unfortunately, that wasn't as easy as she thought. All she had left was the single Seminole skirt—lying soiled on the ground, the shirt she'd worn to bed, and the socks inside her boots, plus the bikini she'd rinsed out earlier.

"She took my video camera and tape. And my main camera… Oh, no! My spare!" She hurried back up the trail faster than was wise, considering her lack of familiarity with it. She'd left her spare camera— the Canon—lying in the net hammock when she'd gone to sleep with Carson.

No telling how long that little sneak was rummag-

ing around in my things! If I hadn't rigged my pack, I'd never have heard her....

Alisha reached the camp, immediately rushing to her hammock. *Yes!* The skirt with the film pinned into its pocket and the spare camera were still there. *Now all I have to do is convince this stubborn man his friend and his cousin are up to no good.*

Carson arrived and lit the camping lantern. Alisha slipped the skirt back on—grimacing at the dirt.

"I hope you have extra clothes I can wear, because your little friend just stole everything I own. Even my toothbrush and comb!"

"I wish I'd seen the culprit."

"Adoette," Alisha emphasized. "And Ray. He had to be driving the airboat."

Carson surveyed the campsite. "Anything else missing?"

"My Camcorder and videotape, my Nikon and the fresh film stowed inside the pack with my clothes."

"Sorry about that."

"I've got my spare camera, but they have everything else—including my video of the captured gator!" She gasped at a sudden thought. "What if it was *them* we saw earlier? With the trapped gator and the other net? Don't just sit there shaking your head—it's possible!"

"You have no proof."

"Maybe I do. I kept all my exposed film *out* of my pack. Where's the nearest civilized outpost? We need to get it developed."

"You...actually...think...Ray and Adoette are involved in *poaching?*"

"Why else would they sneak around? Oh, Carson, they could be covering for someone. You've got a radio. So does Ray. Use it—then you tell *me* what's going on!"

Carson didn't argue. He grabbed his radio, clicked it on and keyed the mike. "Carson to Ray. Carson to Ray. Come in, please."

Nothing.

He did it again...and again...and again.

By now, Carson's face was fierce with anger. "This isn't funny."

"Who's laughing? First light, we head for civilization to develop my film and replace my clothes and dishes."

"That can be arranged—after I talk to Adoette and Ray."

"They aren't answering. We could wait until doomsday."

"I'll talk to them *before* I make any decisions. That's final."

Alisha nodded curtly. She returned to the hammocks. This time, she climbed into hers, and he climbed into his. Alisha couldn't sleep.

This isn't working. It's time to take matters into my own hands.

When Carson woke up, he was alone. Alisha and the canoe were gone.

CHAPTER TEN

Day four—Adoette's airboat

"CARSON TO RAY. Carson to Ray. You'd better answer me, Ray, or I swear this is your last week on earth."

Adoette stared at the radio, then at Ray. They were both on the airboat, which was docked at a small hammock, Adoette at the controls. "Aren't you going to answer it?"

"I don't know what to say! Why do you think I turned it off last night?" Ray ran his fingers through his hair.

"Well, you've turned it on now. You can't ignore it. Maybe there's trouble," she suggested nervously.

"Yeah, and guess who's in it. Us."

"We can't let him keep calling us forever! Sooner or later he'll call my family and they'll get up a search party, which'll scare off every poacher in the area." Defiantly Adoette picked up the radio. "Adoette here, Carson. Over."

She winced at the loudness of Carson's transmitted voice. "Where the hell have you been? Over."

"I—uh—"

"Never mind, tell me later. Get over here *now* and pick me up."

Ray took the radio. "Something's wrong, Carson?"

"Yeah. My canoe's gone. Alisha Jamison took it. She's gone. Who knows where she is now? If you'd answered my call—"

"We're on our way, Carson. Over and out." Ray shoved the radio back into Adoette's hand, and she quickly stowed it.

They stared at each other with mournful expressions, then Adoette fired up the airboat. "Alisha missing..." Adoette maneuvered them away from the hammock. "Where could she be?"

"Maybe taking pictures. Or maybe she's afraid of Carson's temper."

"I doubt it. Carson and Alisha slept in the same hammock."

"What?"

She nodded, carefully navigating the boat.

"Don't tell me she—he—?"

"I don't know! I certainly wasn't about to stop and ask, was I? Either way, she's still missing."

"Carson's gonna kill us," Ray said darkly.

"Don't be ridiculous. But I wonder... It'd be nice for Carson if they do have something going. No fun being alone," Adoette said wistfully.

Ray's glance was sharp. "Don't tell me you're jealous of Alisha?"

Adoette shook her head, her eyes on the waterway.

"Carson's like a brother to me. But that doesn't mean I wouldn't like someone special in *my* life. You know, when this is over, I think I'm going to find him. And if I really, *really* like him, maybe I'll let him sleep in my bed, too."

Ray swore in Seminole. "What is wrong with you? I thought you were a traditional girl! Put on a pair of jeans, take off your beads, and suddenly you're ready to jump into bed with a stranger."

The soft expression left Adoette's eyes, replaced with something harsher. "Alisha Jamison went after what *she* wanted. Why shouldn't I? Besides, what do you care? I've wasted too much time waiting for you. It's obvious you aren't interested. Maybe I *should* move on instead of growing old at the looms."

"What—you're too good to be a weaver all of a sudden?"

"You haven't got a clue, have you. I'm lonely! I don't have a casino full of flashy bed partners like you do."

"I don't believe in using my job to seduce women. Even if I did, I wouldn't have a job for long." Ray studied her closely. "What's gotten into you, Adoette? Stop trying to be someone you're not."

"You're wrong. I'm trying to become the woman I want to be. Need to be. With or without you."

Try as he might, Ray couldn't get her to say another word.

CARSON PACED UP AND DOWN the shore, searching the horizon for any sign of his ride.

Alisha cut out on me? I can't believe it—she left me high and dry! How does she expect to maneuver without a guide? I don't even know what her course is.

He paced again, almost upsetting his pack and the personal supplies at his feet. Alisha had left him half the canoe's bottled water and food.

"When I catch up with her…" *She's going to hear a thing or two. Right after I finish with Ray and Adoette.*

He heard the sound of the airboat and saw Adoette at the wheel. In seconds he'd slipped his pack onto his shoulders, then lifted the boxed supplies in his arms. Ray came out to help, a welcoming smile on his face.

"Drop the friendly act." Carson boarded the boat without assistance. "What the hell's going on?"

Both spoke at once, Ray loud and fast, Adoette soft and slow, he in English, she in Seminole.

"Stop! Just stop."

They did.

He dropped his gear with little regard for the contents. "I'll ask the questions. Number one, was that your airboat speeding away from the netted gator?"

"Yes, but " Ray began.

Carson held up his hand, then faced Adoette. "Number two, was that you who stole Alisha's things last night?"

"Yes, but if I'd have known you were sharing the same hammock—"

Carson interrupted again. "Question number three. Are you poaching?"

His answer was violent negatives from both of them.

"I didn't think so. Last question. *Why did you act as if you were?*"

Ray and Adoette were suddenly quiet.

"What, no one wants to talk now? Do you know what you did? You sent Alisha Jamison off with photos of the two of you to be developed! I can see it now—on the news at eleven."

"But I stole her camera and film!" Adoette insisted. "And her Camcorder!"

"There's a very simple answer, Sherlocks. She hid the exposed film—and a spare camera."

Ray groaned. Adoette flushed and dropped her eyes as Carson continued.

"Which brings me back to this. Why did you two run when we spotted you?"

Ray stared at Adoette. Adoette stared at the ground. Finally Adoette spoke. "You're not going to like this, Carson."

"Try me."

"Tell him, Ray."

Ray looked his cousin straight in the eye and told the truth. "We think our poachers are Seminole."

"On what evidence?"

"Blazed trails—new trails—to the nesting grounds. We didn't want you and Alisha to find out that our own people are involved in this."

"You're wrong. Our people would use existing trails."

"Then how do you explain them knowing where to look for nesting sites?"

"Ray, think! There isn't that much land in the Everglades. Nesting sites are easy enough to find. It's the waterway trails that aren't easy for anyone who isn't local. Neither my father nor I ever found evidence of local poachers in all these years." He paused, shook his head. "Too bad that'll be hard to prove, since Alisha has film of you two speeding away from the scene of the crime."

"Surely Alisha can't suspect *us*," Adoette whispered.

"Of course she does! She recognized you, for heaven's sake. When she gets those photos back—well, I've seen her work, people. She's a whiz with that camera. I wouldn't be surprised if both your faces come out clear."

"We have to stop her," Ray announced.

Carson finally stored his gear. "We have to find her first."

ALISHA CAREFULLY POLED the canoe through the shady water trails beneath the cypress trees. After sitting all morning paddling, she'd decided to test her luck and balance poling. It wasn't hard, she discovered. The canoe must have been carefully designed and perfectly balanced when it was carved. That was half the battle right there.

Sometimes the old ways were best.

She enjoyed the silence of her ride and the security of knowing where she was headed. Her park guidebook of mapped waterways seemed easy to follow, and quite a few Seminole waterways were included. Once she left reservation land, the park trails would be simple to follow. The natural water trails sported such names as Alligator Alley, while man-made canals were also labeled, often with bright red signs carefully attached to trees. These northern waterways were dotted with enough hammocks to make navigation easier than in the south with its vast expanse of grasses.

Alisha checked her book again. According to what it said, eight public campgrounds existed in the park preserve. She was headed for the largest one of these. It didn't say one way or the other, but she figured they had to have some kind of film service...or mail pickup. She could either send out the film or mail it directly to Josh for developing. Too bad he wasn't here. She felt on edge without a partner.

Alisha followed her route along the Seminole waterway canals. In some areas, the water was much shallower than that described in her guidebook. It was easy to gauge depth with the canoe pole. Luckily she hadn't run aground anywhere.

Still, the water itself fascinated her. The colors reflected the myriad plant growth within the shallow depths and the reflection of the larger trees above. Patches of green were made a brilliant emerald in some areas by certain species of algae; in other areas, they darkened to rich cocoa for the same reason. Occasionally a gator broke the surface of the water, and as it did, birds lifted suddenly into the air. The birds' legs made tiny trails in the water until they, too, were high above.

She felt relaxed for the first time since she'd fallen asleep in Carson's arms. There was something about him that felt comfortable, as if they'd known each other all their lives. Her damaged lung notwithstanding, Alisha would never have offered herself to him otherwise. It was an invitation that had surprised her—as much, no doubt, as it had surprised him. It had been a one-of-a-kind instance where her emotions led the way.

Was it one-sided, all on my part? I hate to think that. Still, I have to admire the guy's morals. Most men would have jumped at a no-strings opportunity.

She continued to pole along the water. When the sun came out from behind the clouds, rainbows tracked from the water to the humid air above, only to disappear when the sun ducked behind the clouds again, or a large flock of egrets flew overhead, disturbed by her sudden presence.

Alisha inhaled blissfully. The superheated, humid air felt good in her lungs; it was easy to breathe, easy to exhale. The quiet of the surrounding preserve tempted her into an effortless contentment. It was a temptation she would have readily succumbed to except for thoughts of poachers...and Carson.

After what had been a lovely—albeit passion-less—night, his actions after their rude awakening puzzled her. Attackers burst into their camp, stole her camera and pack, and when she identified the cul-prits—

Carson didn't believe me. I thought rangers were supposed to be men of action, ready to leap into any fray. But not on my say-so, it seems. Instead, he'd insisted she wait until he could confirm the intruders' identity.

Okay, so they're his cousin and his close friend. But what if they're poachers? Then what?

Would he prosecute? Ignore their crimes? Deny her assertions? What if the film didn't show Adoette clearly? *I need to know if I have proof!*

Patience might be Carson's strength, but it wasn't Alisha's. How could she trust him? Right now, she didn't know which side three-fourths of the people on this expedition were on and until she reached the park, this was Seminole land. The others belonged here; she didn't.

What else could she do but set out on her own?

And what exactly was going on with Ray and Adoette? Why would they steal her camera unless they were afraid she'd captured something incrimi-nating on film? But if they *were* involved in trapping gators, would they be helping the son of a man mur-dered by poachers? She was sure Carson wouldn't have asked them along if he suspected their involve-ment.

Which brought her back to Carson again. What-ever the other pair was doing, Carson could sort it out. Her goal was to finish this job. That meant lo-cating the poachers, photographing them—whoever they might turn out to be—and developing this film.

As the day wore on and Alisha continued canoeing toward park land, her uneasiness increased. She missed Carson's easy commentary on the beauty around her. She was reduced to frequently checking her guidebooks, both to identify the flora and fauna around her and to track her progress.

Poling these canoes wasn't as easy as it looked, either. Her balance was good, but her shoulders were sore from poling, and from occasional stints of pad-dling when the overhead trees dipped too close to the water to allow her to stand. As for the canoe itself, wet wood wasn't nearly as light as the Fiberglas ca-noes she was used to. Alisha was hot, sweaty, tired, and not nearly as close to the campground as she'd expected. In fact—

She sat down and studied her maps once, twice, again.

Give me a break. I'm lost.

Not exactly lost. Just not where she was *supposed* to be. She was still on reservation land instead of park land. She'd taken a wrong turn.... *Probably when I was rubbernecking at the scenery or mooning about Carson.*

She confirmed her present coordinates one last time, annoyed at how much backtracking she'd have to do. It was already late afternoon. Time to set up camp, she decided. She had plenty of supplies; she'd start fresh tomorrow. For now, she'd find a likely hammock, have something to eat, try to sleep. And she'd paddle while she looked. No more poling.

There seemed to be quite a few hammocks to choose from. The area was thick with them, trees from one hammock touching the cypress limbs on others. The waterways were shaded into actual tunnels in some areas. Alisha glanced overhead for panthers. She hoped she was big-enough prey to disturb the Florida cats, but her presence could startle them. The canoe paddles sounded awfully loud to her, and the wildlife seemed unnaturally quiet now.

Then she heard the voices—and saw the men standing beneath nets that hung heavy with gators.

Poachers!

Ever so slowly, ever so carefully, she back-paddled into the shadows. Her hands were shaking, her chest pounding. *Now what do I do?*

She stared at her spare camera in the canoe, then at the radio. She stared at the knives the men carried. She doubted they were using them to cut down the nets and rescue the gators.

Alisha gripped the paddle harder and retreated even farther. *To hell with pictures. I need reinforcements. I need Carson.*

CARSON'S RADIO CRACKLED. He recognized Alisha's voice calling his name even above the noise of the airboat.

"Where the hell are you?"

"Listen!" She sounded unusually agitated, and her next words explained why. "I've come across three, maybe four men playing slice and dice with gators on your land. You'd better write down these coordinates, because I'm only going to have time to tell you once. Over."

"Stand by." Carson gestured for Adoette to cut the engines. "Go ahead."

Alisha gave her location. Ray and Adoette leaned closer to hear.

"Are you sure of those? There's no trail there that I'm aware of."

"There is now, and it's not on my maps. It looks freshly cut."

Ray and Adoette exchanged a troubled glance.

"I know the general area. I'll find it. Are you in any danger?" Carson asked.

"I'll lie low. But you'd better get here quick. They've obviously done this before. They're not wasting any time."

Her voice grew fainter.

Carson rekeyed the mike and spoke into the radio again. "Hello, over?"

"Alisha?" Ray added.

"Don't use my name over the radio again! This is a common frequency."

Carson glared at Ray, who winced at his mistake.

"I'm Jane, as in Jane Doe, starting now. Just get reinforcements, and get here as soon as you—"

The transmission died abruptly.

"Ali—Jane? Over? *Over?*"

No answer. Carson tried more than once and failed repeatedly.

"What do you think happened?" Adoette whispered.

"I don't know. All ashore who's going ashore." His voice was harsh, abrupt.

"I'm in" was Ray's response.

"Me, too."

"Adoette, I think you should get off and head for your family's hammock," Carson said.

"No. I'm staying."

"There's no need—"

"Yes, there is. I stole her pack and made her run. And—" Adoette lifted her chin. "She wouldn't run out on *me* if our situations were reversed."

"No, she wouldn't." Carson gently moved Adoette away from the controls, but she refused to let him take her place. "Last chance, people," he said with a shrug.

Adoette answered by firing up the airboat. Ray reached for her shoulder, then for the grip-bars as the boat jerked forward.

"Carson...Ray...hang on."

ALISHA TRIED THE RADIO again and again. She turned it off for a few moments, then turned it on again.

The static sparked fresh, then faded away within seconds.

Dead batteries. Carson gave me more. They're in my—pack.

"Dammit, Adoette!" she whispered to herself. She could have screamed with frustration—if she'd dared.

Quietly, she placed the radio back in its waterproof case and put it down inside the canoe.

Now what? Her spare camera in its beat-up case, also in the bottom of the canoe, seemed to beckon her.

Taking photos of an escaping airboat going in the opposite direction was easy, she thought wryly. Especially when a ranger with a gun was standing right beside her. But now? Going close enough to take pictures—by herself, with no back up? Not a smart move.

Her high-power telephoto lens was with her Nikon. There was a smaller lens with this one, but it wouldn't do the job from here. Telephoto lenses needed lots of light to register film images. She was hidden away in the darkest area she could find.

Thoughts of failure haunted her. She could see herself knocking on her mother's door, asking for her old room back. Checking out of the hospital and spending the rest of her life in her childhood bed— she could picture it all too clearly. *Because I didn't have the guts to take a few shots! What a great piece for the evening news—Alisha Jamison returns home to hide under her blanket.*

Tears filled her eyes. *Such a baby! No one forced you to do this work. You chose it, so you do it. You might as well take a chance and get ready to face your demons. You want to live, don't you? You want to be independent, don't you? So do this, and don't get caught. Just take one roll.*

Alisha reached for her camera. *I can do this. I can. I can.*

Despite her pep talk, she shivered. Every part of her trembled except for her hands—hands that had taken thousands of photos. She went through the routine automatically.

Pick your lens. Store the cap. Screw on the lens. Check for film. Adjust the ASA-ISO. Crank the aperture to infinity. Place fresh film in your pocket. Click off the shutter lock. Place the camera strap around your neck.

Easy. She'd done it so many times. The next part was harder. *Pick up the oar. Row the canoe close to the poachers. Don't get too close or they'll hear the shutter.*

This time her hands did shake. But she picked up the oar. She had to get the sun behind her for the best shot. Make sure the sun's reflection off the lens didn't give away her position. She mentally framed the photo before approaching. *Don't rush in without a plan. Plan your escape route. Don't let this be another Africa. You got too close that time, too soon—and they caught you.*

Sweat rolled down her face. But Alisha refused to dwell on anything except doing her job…and staying safe.

The breeze wafted a smell of fresh carrion to her nostrils. Alisha snorted. She could never get used to that smell. In a way it was worse than rotting carrion because it still smelled of uncongealed blood—the life force. She remembered smelling her own blood, the odor forever imprinted on her memory.

Bastards, all of you. Low in the canoe, she positioned the wooden craft. Raising her camera to her eyes, she began to shoot the death of the alligators, frame by frame, machete slash by machete slash.

She shot a whole roll of film.

She shot another roll, then another. By the end of the third roll, the light was fading, the gators were dead and the men busied themselves washing off in the bloody waters. Alisha herself felt bloodless. She left the camera dangling around her neck and stealthily paddled away, using twilight as her cover.

Someone has to stop this carnage. Someone…has to help me. I can't do it alone. Carson…

Alisha didn't stop paddling until dawn. Then she found the nearest hammock, pulled the canoe into the densest brush and collapsed into a deep sleep in the bottom of the boat, her camera still around her neck.

CARSON AND THE OTHERS found the newly cleared, carefully concealed water trailhead—and the poachers' slaughter site—two hours after sunset. Carson, Ray and Adoette inspected what was once life, now scattered over the torn plants and sullied hammock. The nest site had been torn open by predators, broken eggs the only evidence of what would have been the next generation. Pieces of rope still dangled from the trees; discarded fast-food wrappings and empty beer cans littered the shore area, a testimony to the boldness of the poachers.

Carson used his flashlight to study the obscenity all around them. "I'd say they left before sunset," he said. "Ray, you take the boat and circle the island. You've got your gun. Is it loaded?"

"You bet."

"Adoette, you and I will look for Alisha."

The hammock was small. Even on foot, they could find no trace of Alisha. Carson radioed Ray, the couple reboarded the boat and searched the surrounding hammocks. Nothing. It was Carson himself who finally called off the search.

"It's getting dark. We might as well set up camp and start again in the morning."

"One good thing," Ray said, tying the airboat securely to a hardwood tree.

Carson didn't have the strength to follow up on his remark. There was nothing good about any of this.

"These poachers might be using our land, but I'm sure they aren't Seminoles."

"You were right, Carson," Adoette said. "At the very least, we'd clean up after ourselves. The carnage we've found on this hammock…"

"What about the other hammocks you and Ray searched?" Carson countered. "Were they left like this?"

"No, but some of our people cleaned up the mess," Ray said. "Which is why I was so confused in the first place. Why we hid from you. And why—"

"Alisha went dashing off with my canoe."

"But—"

"Don't you see?" Carson's tone was angry, urgent. "You two acted guilty. She won't trust us now, and she won't want us to find her. But the poachers might."

"She…she's dressed in my clothes," Adoette reminded him. "And she has your canoe—a wood canoe. That ought to give her some protection."

"Alisha doesn't speak Seminole. She doesn't have a gun or an airboat. Do you know how much protection native clothes and dark hair will give her? About as much as it gave my father!"

Adoette turned away and buried her face in her hands. Carson swallowed hard. He put an arm around her shoulders.

"Adoette, I'm sorry," he murmured. "This isn't

your fault. She chose to leave. We'll find her in the morning.''

"Sure we will," Ray said heartily.

Adoette lowered her hands. "I'm not a child. Don't treat me like one. Part of this *is* my fault.'' She stood and fired up the airboat.

"Where are you going?" Carson asked.

"Back to that hammock to clean it up.''

"In the dark? With only a flashlight?''

"I won't be able to sleep. Will you?''

CHAPTER ELEVEN

Day five—Alisha's hammock

HEAT, MOSQUITOES, THIRST and the hardness of the canoe against her back woke Alisha in the early morning. She groaned at the stiffness in her muscles, then silenced herself as yesterday's memories came flooding back. Her silence was unnecessary; eventually the sights and sounds of wildlife told Alisha she was alone.

She took the canoe to an area of water fairly clear of algae and weeds. A stirring oar showed it to be free of snakes, gators and leeches, as well. Alisha slipped out of her clothes and sank into the shallow water wearing just her bikini and Adoette's beads. She thrust her whole head underneath to wet her hair and face, and to wash away the smell of death. Most of Deborah's black dye washed away, too.

"Lord, that's better," she said, sighing, feeling more like her old self. The next order of business was to wash her dirty clothing. First, she dried her hands on the skirt, carefully removed all her exposed film, including yesterday's precious evidence, and placed it carefully in the dry bottom of the canoe.

Then she went back into the water, scrubbing the skirt and shirt between her hands until satisfied they were as clean as she could get them.

Putting on boots and bug spray, then drying her laundry came next. She spread her only outfit on some tree branches to dry, making sure it was far enough inland not to attract any attention. By now, her stomach was growling.

Alisha rummaged in the beached canoe for her supplies.

"Some of your fish and fruit would taste good right about now, Carson," she said aloud, biting into a piece of beef jerky and shaking some trail mix into her hand. "And coffee. A hot, strong cup with lots of sugar. Plus my pack and my own clothes. I don't need a disguise anymore. I found the poachers, Carson. They didn't find me."

Great. Now I'm talking to myself.

She sat beside her beached canoe, the sun drying her as she ate. The rolls of film seemed too vulnerable left on the canoe's seat. Alisha stared at the Ziploc bag that held the jerky, then shoved the jerky in with the trail mix.

"I'll just store the film in the bag...there! That ought to do until I get my pack." She chewed thoughtfully on the mix, reviewing her situation.

I've got to protect this film. And myself. I don't want to canoe out in the open. Too many poachers.

Reaching for her map, she paused. There was no-where to go, except back to Carson. She wasn't sure if she could trust Adoette or Ray, but all her instincts said she could trust Carson. And he *was* a park ranger. If he'd heard her coordinates correctly, he had to be at the poachers' last location. She knew the poachers weren't. So…

She put away her breakfast and retrieved her film—three rolls taken of the poachers, and one of the netted gator and Adoette's escaping airboat. The first-aid kit was still in the canoe, along with a convenient length of bandage.

"No, too white…" she murmured. Alisha ran the gauze bandage through some mud until it was good and brown. With the bag of film in one hand and the brown strip in the other, she returned to her laundry and the inside of the hammock to hide her "insurance."

"I know I can find this hammock again," she thought aloud, "but where's the best place to put it? All these trees start to look alike after a while." Alisha sniffed the air, suddenly noticing the smell of vanilla that emanated from a huge overhead cluster of orchids.

"Eureka."

She climbed the tree, found a narrow crook in a branch and placed the sealed bag with film there. She wrapped the muddy bandage around it, both securing and concealing its location. The orchids' bright colors were a perfect distraction from the brown lump, which was high enough to be mistaken for rough bark.

"Aren't you clever, Ms. Jamison," she complimented herself. "No one's going to steal it now."

Later, dressed in Adoette's clothes again, her hair braided, she began paddling back. She no longer felt so clever. Her hands ached, and her body was stiff and sore. Most of all, she was worried. *What if Carson's not there?* She swiped at the sweat on her forehead and continued paddling. What else could she do?

Alisha continued her path to the poachers' killing ground. The sun amid the cypress strands was a welcome sight after the horrors of the night before. She paid careful attention to her maps and the few guideposts attached to trees. *No way am I getting lost again....* After seeing a few other canoes boldly out in the open, manned by blessedly normal people, Alisha kicked off her boots, stowed the paddle and poled the canoe the rest of the way.

It felt good to stand, good to be among those who waved and called out a Seminole greeting. She waved back, the colored skirt wafting around her ankles, Adoette's beads thickly clustered around her neck.

It's beautiful here, she thought. *Just beautiful. I wonder...do Seminoles approve of mixed marriages? Surely they do; history seems to bear that out....*

Too bad Carson wasn't looking for a wife—at least until the poachers were found. *But I have evidence now. We can identify them.* Her spirits drooped as she remembered that Carson had mentioned children. Women with transplants, on antirejection drugs, weren't aren't allowed to get pregnant, ever. The drugs were toxic, often deadly to fetuses. But if she discontinued the drugs, her body might reject the new heart and lungs.

In fact, doctors strongly urged permanent, surgical forms of birth control for those on the transplant list. Alisha hadn't taken that final step yet, but she knew she had no business thinking about a husband without knowing if she'd even be alive this time next year.

And what made her so sure Carson would want to be that husband, anyway? How well did she really know him? It'd only been a few days. *I do know him. I know him in all the ways that matter.* She knew his decency, his honor and compassion. And she knew there was an attraction between them.

Well, never mind that now.

"Carson, you'd better be waiting for me," she puffed between poling strokes, the extra exertion making her wish she had her inhaler.

It was close to noon when she reached the cluster of hammocks she'd visited the day before. Cautiously, she put away the pole and paddled again, making herself less visible. Her caution wasn't needed for long. She could see Adoette's airboat, hear the men's voices from the beach. In a few minutes, Carson hailed her, waving his hand in the air.

Thank God her reasoning had been correct....

She paddled her way to the shallows near the tied airboat. The men pulled her canoe onto land so she could keep her feet dry as she disembarked.

"Long time, no see, Carson," Alisha greeted him. She smelled the warm fish cooked with fruit. Her stomach growled, her mouth happy to pass up the jerky and trail mix she'd lived on for the past two days. "Mmm. Food."

"Ray, you and Adoette get Alisha some lunch and bring us her gear. She and I need to talk."

Ray nodded. Carson held out his hand for Alisha to get out. She set down the paddle, gathered up her skirt in one hand and extended her other for his help.

"You okay?" he asked as she stepped onto shore.

Her breathing was ragged and audible. "I will be. I just need my inhaler. Otherwise, I'm fine."

"Glad to hear it." He waited until she was firmly on land before he dropped her hand. "Now tell me— *what* did you think you were doing, running out like that?"

She ignored his question. "The poachers—did you catch them?" she asked urgently.

"No. We only arrived in time to clean up. Which we did—not knowing if you were dead or alive. Not a pleasant feeling."

"I'm sorry, Carson. But I did what I had to do."

"Running away? Why?"

He's really upset. She met his gaze squarely. "Do you really want me to spell it out?"

"I wanted you to call! We lost your transmission and then we had no idea where you were."

"My radio's batteries were dead. The replacements are in the pack. I figured you'd show up here, though. I'd *hoped* with the airboat you'd have enough time and speed to catch the poachers."

"We didn't. All I could do was radio Deborah to notify the tribal council and be on the lookout. They're not locals, but they're probably still on our land. Not NPS land."

Ray returned with a plate of food, and Adoette brought her pack.

"They're not?" Alisha's voice mirrored her surprise. It was a moment before she saw the pack, checked on her camera and Camcorder and pulled out her inhaler.

"Who did *you* see, Alisha?" Carson asked.

"Wait." She took two deep puffs of medicine and held her breath for the requisite seconds. She exhaled, then stashed the inhaler and reached for the plate. "Thanks, Ray. Oh, that feels better."

"You want to eat first and talk later?" Carson asked. "You sound terrible."

"No, I'd rather talk first. This stuff leaves an awful taste in my mouth for a few minutes." She stared longingly at the food, though, as she continued. "I'm sure the poachers I saw weren't Seminole, just like you said. They were dressed in regular clothes, and I doubt they were any more Seminole than I am. I used a telephoto lens, and I was close enough to hear all four of them. They worked fast—and they all spoke English.''

A hard, driving fear flickered in Carson's eyes. ''You were that close?''

''How else was I supposed to take my photos? The telephoto lens was in my backpack, along with my main camera.'' She looked at the others pointedly. ''For all I knew, Adoette and Ray here could have been the poachers themselves.''

Adoette ducked her head. Ray shifted uneasily.

''What about earlier?'' Alisha said. ''When you raided our camp?''

''You probably know that was us in the airboat near the gator you freed,'' Adoette admitted.

''I don't understand. Why the act?''

''Because Ray and I assumed only our people would know about local gator nests. That's why we took your film. We didn't want you to know Seminoles were involved.''

''Which they aren't. But these two never thought to come to me,'' Carson said harshly. ''Or rely on the years of information my father and I gathered. Once they told me about the newly blazed water trails, I knew we were dealing with trespassers.''

''You should have come clean.'' The metallic taste in her mouth fading, Alisha finally started in on her food. ''Seems to me we're just as much in the dark as ever. We still have poachers. I'd recognize them again, but we don't know who they are.''

''I guess not,'' Adoette said.

Alisha relished the moist fish and juicy fruit after the dry trail mix. "But I still don't understand why you wouldn't tell Carson what was going on."

"Because I can't be trusted, obviously. By *anyone*." Carson pivoted on the ball of his foot and left for the privacy of the hammock.

"What did *I* say?"

"It's not you. It's us," Adoette told her.

"You were trying to protect him, weren't you? From what?"

Ray sighed. "We were afraid he might go off the deep end if he thought one of our people killed my uncle."

Alisha stared at them both. "Do you realize how much you've hampered this investigation? I left because you made me suspicious of him! No wonder he prefers to work alone." Alisha set down her plate, appetite gone, and hurried after Carson.

She found him down the shore, beneath a thick strand of cypress hanging over the water's edge.

"My turn to ask," she said. "You okay?"

"Tell me exactly what you saw, what you've figured out. I have to know my prey, or this whole expedition is pointless."

She sat down beside him. "Going by hard evidence, we're looking for an organized group of at least four men. I have photos of poachers on three rolls of film—and photos of Ray and Adoette on another."

"We don't have a way of developing the film.

We'll have to go back to the ranger station for that, which means we'll lose time.''

"But...what about the campgrounds?'' Alisha asked, surprised.

"They don't even have mail service, let alone film service.''

"Oh. I just assumed—''

"This isn't Disney World, Alisha. And I could lose the poachers if I leave the area.''

Alisha shrugged. "So now what do we do?'' she asked.

"Well, first...you owe me an apology. And I intend to collect.''

Carson lowered his mouth to hers.

Startled, Alisha allowed him the kiss. "What was that for?'' she asked when he was through.

"You owed me for stealing my canoe.''

"You kiss me because I'm a thief, yet you won't make love to me when I ask? Carson, I'm confused,'' she said, still in his arms.

"So am I. You seem to be a woman full of contradictions.'' He kissed her again, quickly, on the cheek. "Besides, I was worried about you.''

"Yeah, well, don't do it again. Worry, I mean.'' She grinned at him slyly. "The kissing I don't mind.''

"I'll make a note.'' Gently he released her.

"Good. Look, I'm going to change back into my own clothes.'' She gave a light shrug, "If we weren't about to leave, I'd ask Adoette to untie these beads.''

Then she smiled, despite herself. "We've got the apology taken care of, so—like I asked before—what's next?"

"For starters, get your film developed." He studied her carefully. "Where is it?"

"It's safe," she said, feeling more than slightly embarrassed. "I stashed it on a hammock. I was, uh, a bit paranoid at the time."

"We'll have to retrieve it."

She nodded. "Have you radioed in for help?"

"Only carefully worded requests to Adoette's family."

"What about the rangers?"

"They've got no authority here. Even if permission was granted for them to come in, it wouldn't be safe. And it might well chase the poachers away. They're probably monitoring our radio bands. I know I would."

"Good thing my batteries died, then," she said lightly. *I hope it was before Ray said my name over the air.*

"No, it *wasn't* a good thing. You might've provided me with the biggest lead I've had yet. But you'll follow my orders from now on, Ali. When this is over, I want everyone in one piece—including you."

"Can't argue with that." She gestured toward the airboat. "Come on, they're waiting."

They both began the soggy hike back.

As Alisha made her way through the uneven terrain, she said, "You know, I don't understand why alligator farms haven't put the poachers out of business. The reptiles there are raised for commercial slaughter. For research, too."

"You ever seen a gator farm?"

"I know about the one in St. Augustine."

"I'm not talking about the legitimate places where research is done, like in St. Augustine," Carson said. "I'm talking about for-profit-only gator farms. Those not open to the general public."

"What are they like?" she asked warily.

"The condition of the reptiles is a disgrace. In some of the less-reputable places, hundreds are crammed into ponds and mud holes that would ordinarily support only a handful. Hides are torn and damaged—as are eyes, limbs and tails during the bi-weekly feeding sessions."

"And these...damaged creatures—what happens to them?"

"They're commercially unacceptable, so they're killed and fed to the breeding stock. Plus, the stacking and packing of the uninjured gators causes so much hide friction that the alligators' surface textures—part of their camouflage—are sanded down. True collectors don't want that when they can buy a poached alligator with beautiful, natural markings. The result is...poaching."

"If the collectors would stop purchasing," Alisha said slowly, "they'd put the poachers out of business. It's a vicious cycle. And in this country, there's no excuse for it.''

"In my book, the collectors are as bad as the poachers. They should all be fed to the gators,'' Carson replied.

"A bit drastic, though I agree with the sentiment. I'll settle for turning them over to the authorities—and taking away their guns.''

"Guns?'' Carson's eyes narrowed. "Is that what our poachers used on the gators?''

"No, they only carried the guns. They murdered with the machetes....'' An involuntary shiver, a remembered night in Africa, with machetes slicing her own body, overtook her. Her eyes closed, then opened at the feel of Carson's arm around her waist.

"They used machetes on you, didn't they?''

Alisha lifted one shoulder. "Now you know why my sympathies are with the alligators.''

Carson pulled her back against his chest, folded his arms around her waist and hugged her close.

Alisha leaned into his strength and drew on his comfort. "Answer one question for me,'' she said. "Is sympathy the only reason you'll put your arms around a woman? Or have you decided I'm simply not your type?''

"No, and that was two questions.'' He released her, but his hand found hers and clasped it. Half walking, half wading, they continued. "In any event, I know you don't want too much sympathy,'' he said.

"And you don't need it. You have a tough hide—like the gators."

"Not like them. My family's relieved this is my last job. They're afraid I'll turn into another Dian Fossey. Maybe I'm a coward, but I don't want to die for the cause."

"That doesn't make you a coward. *Living* for a cause makes more sense. Your book could do a lot of good."

"The book's not even written yet, so let's get back to the poachers, okay? What's—"

Carson pulled on her hand, stopping her as a dark snake wove through the waters. Alisha froze.

"Water moccasin?"

"No, it's a banded water snake."

"What bands? It looks all black."

"The older snakes are duller and have darker bands—harder to see in the water. Don't worry—you're safe."

"It's tough to tell the difference between the ones that are poisonous and the ones that aren't."

"Not with animals. Only with people."

I can't argue with that.

Ray had coffee and the rest of the fruit waiting when they returned. Alisha and Carson joined him and Adoette on the airboat.

"Well?" Ray asked. "Have you decided what to do next?"

"I want the women to leave and—"

"What?" Alisha said indignantly. *This is the re-*

ward I get for letting a handsome man kiss me? "I don't remember telling you I wanted to quit."

"I didn't say quit," Carson emphasized. "We need that film developed. The four of us will head back to whatever hammock you hid it at. From there, we'll motor you to safe waters. You and Adoette will take the canoe, and Adoette will guide you to the nearest ranger station. They'll develop the film and try to identify the poachers."

"It's not a bad plan, but you could have consulted me first," Alisha grumbled, annoyed and yet relieved to be pulled out of action. "Where will you and Ray be?"

"Back looking for the poachers."

Alisha shook her head. As afraid as she was of poachers, she was even more afraid of *not* finding them. *Dammit, I want these men in jail! And I want to stay with Carson!* Maybe sympathy was all he could offer her, but she was feeling much more than sympathy for him....

"I have a better idea," she said. "I go where you go."

"No."

"Yes. For one thing, it's my story—and you invited me along. Besides, my shoulders hurt from poling that canoe! There's no way I'm getting back in it again."

"My way makes the most sense," Carson insisted.

"I want your word that I stay with you or—"

"Or what?"

Alisha crossed her arms. "Or I don't tell you where I hid the film."

Adoette gasped, her hand covering her mouth. Ray added his arguments to Carson's. "Come on, Alisha, my cousin's right. You shouldn't be out here any more than Adoette should."

"Why? Because we're women?" Adoette demanded.

Well! I didn't think Adoette was going to jump into the middle of this.

"No, because I have a gun and you don't," Carson said. "Because I'm prepared to use it—as Ray is."

Alisha smiled, a mirthless grin that didn't reach her eyes. "Ever heard the saying 'the pen is mightier than the sword'? As for shooting, I think my camera's already done more damage than your bullets could."

"Ladies, listen to Carson," Ray urged. "That camera wasn't much protection in Africa, was it, Alisha? As for you, Adoette, what can *you* do? Subdue the bad guys with cloth from your loom?"

Adoette thrust out a hand and shoved hard. Ray landed in the water with a resounding splash. Water dripped down his face as he yelled in Seminole to Adoette. She replied in kind.

This whole expedition is like a Keystone Kops movie, Alisha thought incredulously.

"Adoette, you know better! Throw the man a line," Carson ordered.

Adoette crossed her arms, echoing Alisha's posture. "It's only a few feet deep here. He can walk."

Carson glared. "I thought we were all on the same side."

"My feelings exactly," Alisha answered. "I've got a lot at stake here." *As much as anyone on this boat—even Carson.*

"Me, too!" Adoette insisted. "I'm not bailing out, Carson."

Carson threw Ray a line and hauled him in, dripping wet.

"You've got leeches," Adoette said calmly. The sluglike bodies stuck to both his bare arms. That set Ray's temper off again.

"Since no one wants to leave, can I make a suggestion, Carson?" Alisha asked. "Ray and Adoette can retrieve the film and have it developed. You and I can stay paired out in the field. This way there's a gun for each boat, each couple."

Ray frowned, while Adoette looked hurt, her expression reproachful.

"Sorry, Adoette. I really do appreciate all your help so far." Alisha didn't add the rest—that she was afraid Adoette lacked the toughness to do what might have to be done.

"You're not in charge of this expedition, Alisha," Adoette argued.

"No, but I am," Carson said. "And Alisha's right. It'll be safer if you stick with Ray."

Adoette protested, Ray protested, but Carson stood firm.

Alisha pulled out her map and pointed to the hammock she'd visited.

"Look for the largest cluster of vanilla orchids," she said. "You can't miss them—just follow your nose."

"It's settled," Carson said with finality. "Alisha and I stay with the canoe. You two leave in the airboat."

"What then?" Ray asked.

"Go home. We'll fill you in later."

"Come on, Adoette. It seems we're not needed anymore."

Ray was resigned, but Adoette definitely wasn't. "Can't I stay and help?" she asked Alisha directly. *"Please?"*

"Doing this, you *are* helping. Even I didn't jump into a nest full of poachers on my first assignment."

"No, but I jumped into these leeches," Ray complained, dipping his finger into the airboat's oil stock. "With a bit of assistance from my friends... Thanks for nothing, Adoette. Give me slot machines and card tables any day." He smeared the attached leeches with a coating of oil, watched them fall off and one by one, kicked them back into the water with his boot. "I hate the great outdoors" was his goodbye, followed by Adoette's "I'll get the beads later, Alisha."

Within minutes Carson and Alisha were back in

the canoe in their usual places, Alisha sitting with the paddle, Carson standing with the pole.

"Easy on the wake, Adoette," Carson warned.

"Hey, who's the best airboat operator this side of the Gulf?" Adoette started the engine and carefully maneuvered away from the canoe. "Good luck, you two."

Alisha waved. *We're gonna need it.* She and Carson watched as the airboat coasted over the glassy surface of the water, their wake a series of large, rippling vees.

"Now," Carson said when it was quiet again, "we head back to the poachers' last location and go from there."

ADOETTE EXPERTLY PILOTED the airboat through the waters. Ray periodically checked the maps, but Adoette considered it simply a precaution. Big Cypress was her home—where she'd grown up. She might still be an apprentice at the looms, but she had plenty of experience when it came to airboats and navigation. She was happiest doing what she did best—which wasn't weaving. As always, it felt good to be on the water, and she couldn't stop herself from smiling at the sheer pleasure of it.

Ray left his spot near the supplies to stand next to her. "What are you grinning about?" He swatted a large bug that seemed determined to keep pace with the airboat.

"Nothing. Everything." She gestured around her. "Isn't it beautiful?"

"Yeah, I love leeches and mosquitoes. And let's not forget the poachers and gator guts."

Adoette felt sadness mingled with her contentment. "Do you really hate it so much, Ray?"

"God, yes. The whole place reeks, and all I do is sweat and scratch."

"But...there's so much more to it than just heat and insects."

"There's not. Give me the casino any day. I want to be around people who smell of perfume instead of bug spray and sweat."

Adoette ignored the pain his words caused, and lifted her chin. "I'll pass. I prefer my men *not* to smell of perfume."

"That's after-shave. And I want my children to have more choices in life than raising cattle, weaving stupid skirts or—don't take this personally, Adoette—playing taxi-boat driver to tourists."

"I won't—as long as you add working in tourist casinos to your list of limiting jobs for a Seminole child."

"Don't throw that heritage bull at me, Adoette. The purpose of tribal law is to guarantee all members their freedom. I'm not a traitor just because I don't speak Seminole twenty-four hours a day, or want my future wife to deliver my child in the swamp muck."

"Birthing is a perfectly natural process!" Adoette

shot back. "And for your information, it was good enough for my mother."

"Lucky for you two nothing went wrong. But me, I believe in hospitals. If the mother of my child hadn't been so stupid—so damned traditional—she and my son would both be alive today."

Shocked, Adoette dropped her speed, cutting the boat's noise by a good half.

"I never knew! You—you were married?"

"No, I wasn't married," he said quietly. "But she and I were in love. Two teenage Romeo and Juliet types," he said, reverting to his angry sarcasm. "I was sixteen when my father died. My girlfriend—Susannah—was trying to comfort me, one thing led to another…and surprise, surprise."

"She got pregnant?"

"Yeah." He closed his eyes. "It was just that one time—that we made love—but once was all it took. We planned to get married. Before we could make the arrangements she miscarried. And died—all because of this place. Carson's father managed to get our tribal healer, but she needed surgery, and…" He shook his head. "Part of her placenta didn't detach itself from the uterine wall. She bled to death. A painful way to die. I know. I was there."

"Oh, Ray, I'm so *sorry*."

"Me, too. So save your lectures on the beauty of nature. I decided a long time ago that swamp life wasn't for me. People come, people go. I preferred to go."

"You're here now."

"Of course I am! Carson's father became *my* father after that. He gave me guidance, advice, respect—and he understood why I had to leave. So, yes, now I'm here. Because of him. And I'm damn tired of hearing how great Carson is—noble Carson. Ranger Carson. The good son, doing his duty. Well, he's been looking for his father's killer for almost a year, and what's it got him? Nothing. I always come running when he asks, but at least I've tried to have a normal life. I've dated women. I'm open to marriage. I've helped look for my uncle's killers. Yet everyone thinks *I'm* the black sheep for not worshipping the almighty land. You know what I think? Carson's the loser, not me."

"Ray, I never thought you were a loser! And neither is Carson."

"Hey, I didn't really mean that." He shrugged. "You might as well know, Adoette. Once we find the poachers, I'm outta here for good. Catching the man who killed my uncle is the only thing that's kept me in Florida. Once that happens, I'm off to Las Vegas. A good casino manager can always get a job there."

Adoette felt tears slip down her cheeks. "I'd miss you," she said sadly.

"Don't," he said. "These waters run in your blood. Be smart, Adoette. Find some local boy to be your hero."

Too late, she thought. *I already have...*

CHAPTER TWELVE

Day five—noon
Carson's canoe

CARSON MAINTAINED WATCH as he poled his way through the waters.

"Do you think Adoette and Ray are at the ranger station by now?" Alisha asked. Time was hard to judge in the Everglades. Yesterday's darkness had forced them to bunk down before reaching their destination, and most of the morning was already gone.

"Maybe, if that film wasn't hard to retrieve and they didn't need to stop for fuel."

"I wonder why Ray volunteered to come along in the first place. He doesn't like being out in the boonies. His words, not mine."

"Family loyalty. He *is* my cousin."

"No, I think there's more to it than that. He really hates it here. Could you tell me why—if it isn't too personal?"

Carson continued poling. "Ray lost his father when he was a kid—in his teens. My own father took over, acting as a father for Ray. Until he died."

"Poor Ray."

"Something else that not many people know—he also lost a high school sweetheart and their child. She miscarried and hemorrhaged." Carson took another long stroke with the pole. "Ray's got more than his share of bad memories here. Couldn't wait to leave. I'm surprised he's still in Florida."

"No wonder he hates the Everglades! And Adoette's had to pay the price, as well."

"What price?"

"She's in love with him, Carson! Surely you've noticed?"

"Oh, that. She'll get over it. As soon as she meets someone more…appropriate."

"First loves make quite an impression. Did Ray get over his? Did your aunt? Or your mother? You don't know much about love, do you?"

Carson stopped poling. He sat down, stowed the pole and reached for the second oar. In tandem the two began paddling. "Do you?"

"Maybe. If I'm not being too nosy, has there been anyone special in your life?" Alisha asked.

"I've had some casual relationships. One or two I had hopes for, but they didn't work out." He paddled twice, then added, "A woman never really fit into this life. Surely you understand that—you have the same problem."

"Yes. Still, it would be nice to spend time with a man who's more than a friend or partner. Or a hired porter. Or a guide whose language I don't speak. Once I get my life back on track, maybe."

"After the transplant?"

"Assuming I survive," she said bluntly. "If I do, I'll buy myself a little place with a big yard and a nice view. I'll get a dog, hope for a date on the occasional weekend and write my book. I figure a chapter on each of my assignments. I've kept a journal."

"Any deep dark secrets hidden in there?"

"Hardly. But my life's been fairly interesting. My partner—Josh—has convinced a publisher that it'll make good reading. And although I don't relish the idea—maybe even a movie. He's rarely wrong."

"A movie—"

"Maybe," Alisha broke in.

"A movie maybe, a book and a dog. What kind of dog?"

"I don't know—something from the local animal shelter. A dog I can rescue. Not too big, not too small. Just a friendly little puppy."

"Then what?"

"Catch up on all the things I missed. Visit with nieces and nephews. Shopping with Mom, holidays at my brothers'. Rent all the good movies I never got to see. Do some volunteer work, maybe visit schools to talk about conservation, if I'm able. Just normal everyday stuff, I guess."

"Alone?"

Carson waited expectantly. Alisha drew in a deep breath. *It's now or never. You don't have the luxury of time.*

"When I propositioned Prince Charming, I got

turned down. Just my luck, falling head over heels in only a few days—and on my last assignment.''

Carson lifted his head. "I thought—"

"It was just sex? Nope. Unfortunately, my timing stinks. Prince Charming is looking for a killer, not a lover. And if he ever finds his killer, he'll want an heir to the throne. But female transplants aren't allowed to get pregnant.'' She shrugged with pretended nonchalance. "I guess my feet just don't fit the glass slipper this time.''

"I'm hardly a Prince Charming," he said. "Like I told you, this ain't Disney World. But, Alisha—'' Carson took her hand. "I'm sor—''

"Don't. You know I'm not interested in pity. But I had to tell you. I've never told a man I loved him, and who knows if I'll have the opportunity again?''

"Alisha, I don't know what to say."

Alisha smiled and gently pulled her hand free. "Don't say anything. I'm a big girl. And I won't be alone. I'll have Willow.''

"Willow?"

She smiled. "My dog. That's going to be her name.''

"Not very exotic," he said gruffly. "For a woman who's been everywhere.''

"Well, that's okay," she said. "My retirement's going to be in a calm, peaceful neighborhood. Very ordinary.''

"Which neighborhood would that be?"

"Home in Chicago. Don't worry, I don't hold any

wild hopes of you showing up for a visit. On account of your job, and all.'' *Liar. Of course you do.* ''But Carson, you ought to think about finding *someone.*''

Too bad it can't be me.

They both turned their attention back to their paddling.

''About the poachers? Look at it this way,'' Alisha said suddenly. ''At least we don't have to worry about Ray and Adoette anymore.''

ADOETTE CHECKED the gas gauge on her airboat and frowned.

''What's wrong?'' Ray asked immediately.

''We're low on fuel. Because of all that backtracking we did, plus towing the canoe earlier. We're practically running on fumes.''

''So, we go retrieve the film, gas up at the nearest campground and head for the ranger station before dark.''

''I'd rather get the gas first. If we motor out to Alisha's hammock now, the pumps could be closed by the time we dock. It's almost five. Who knows how long it'll take us to find that film? Alisha said she hid it in a tree, and you know how many there are.''

Ray checked his own watch, then the position of the sun in the sky. ''If we miss the fuel man, we'll probably miss getting to the ranger station tonight, too.''

Adoette bit her lip. ''I guess we could gas up, have

dinner at the campground and go back for the film in the morning.''

"Sure, why not? We can only do so much in one day.''

"I don't like leaving that film out overnight.''

"We don't have a choice. We'll get the film to Carson's boss first thing tomorrow morning. Now, stop fussing and crank up the speed. I want a hamburger and fries served on real dishes. Get me there before sunset, and I'll even buy you dessert.''

Adoette opened the throttle a bit. Despite Ray's enthusiasm, she was still worried. Too many uncertainties...

CARSON AND ALISHA searched more cypress swamp trails for traces of the poachers. "This is leading us nowhere,'' Alisha complained. "They could be miles away by now, especially if they're using their airboat.''

"Not necessarily. Some of these cypress groves are too narrow to be negotiated by airboat. Are you getting tired?''

"Frustrated is more like it. No wonder it's taken you so long to find these people. There's a hiding place at every turn.'' Alisha stopped paddling so she could swivel around to face him. "You know, the more I think about it, the more I wonder if we're going about this all wrong. Maybe we shouldn't be looking in the deepest, darkest jungle. These people could be hiding in plain sight. You know, like in that Poe story 'The Purloined Letter.'"

"Where, though?"

"Someplace they have access to the rest of the world. I mean, they can't just be carrying hides out on their backs. They have to be someplace with connections to the outside. Like…the campgrounds?"

Carson stopped his paddling. "No."

"Why not?"

"Too obvious."

"I don't think so. I'll bet Everglades campgrounds are primitive enough for a poacher to hide skins. But modern enough for supplies to be packed in and out."

"I would have noticed. Alisha, the campgrounds are on public land, and other rangers frequent the facilities. Plus, patrolling rangers like me make regular spot checks there. No one's come across any evidence of poachers."

"Yes, but they have to purchase fuel *somewhere*. Did you stake out all the gas pumps at every campground at the same time?"

"Alisha, if someone with a boating license and park-use permit shows up at the pumps, how are we to tell if he's a poacher or not? We do careful ID and paperwork checks, but our poachers are careful men. We don't even know if they're using gas-powered craft exclusively. They're poaching with canoes, as well, according to what you saw. Your ideas are good, but trust me, this ground's already been covered.''

Alisha paused, reviewing the many years she'd spent tracking poachers. ''I remember in Africa...the elephant poachers needed fuel, too. Only it was for jeeps instead of boats. And like here, there were only so many places they could go. They weren't caught that way, though. They had forged papers and ID.''

''As our poachers probably do. Is there a point to this?'' Carson asked, impatiently picking up his paddle again.

''In Africa,'' she said slowly, ''the poachers somehow used their forged papers to shut down a fuel station out in the bush. They passed themselves off as government ecologists and closed the station on some trumped-up environmental violations. Meanwhile, they used it to supply themselves with gas. They were so bold, so obvious, that no one suspected a thing.''

''It's not *that* likely—but we should look into it. Why didn't you bring this up before?''

''I asked at the ranger station the day before we started out. The head ranger told me all campgrounds were open and had been for some time. I just assumed...''

''That was five days ago. Damn. It's probably a long shot, but I'll check with my boss and see if any campgrounds were closed this past week.'' Carson reached for his radio.

ADOETTE MANEUVERED the airboat through the thick growth that always surrounded any kind of shoreline in the land-scarce swamps.

"Uh-oh."

"What?" Ray asked.

She slowed the boat. "We're going to have trouble getting to the fuel docks from here. Look." Adoette pointed starboard. Off in the distance, a large black bear waded through a slough, then stopped to claw in the water.

"Can't we just go around him?"

Adoette studied the width of the slough and shook her head. "The canal's too narrow, and that bear's almost as big as our boat." Her hand dropped to the controls, stopping their progress completely. "This close to shore, he's after crawfish. We'll have to wait."

Ray rolled his eyes. "I am *never* going to get a decent meal at this rate."

"Would you stop complaining?"

"Like I have nothing better to do than watch some stupid—" Ray's voice broke off.

"What?"

"Pass me the binoculars."

She did. "What is it?"

Ray lifted the glasses to his face. "That's not crawfish he's eating. That's gator."

"Hatchlings? But from where, the campground? No female would nest there—"

"Not hatchlings. Looks like it's the remains of a bigger creature."

"An adult?"

Ray lowered the glasses, his expression puzzled. "No bear would come so close to a campground unless the trash or food was abundant. Look how bold he is! Even our boat isn't scaring him off."

"So?"

"I don't like it." Ray lifted the glasses again. "And look! There's a new sign posted saying the campground is closed. But it doesn't *look* empty. Something's not right."

"Yeah, like you're hungry and the bear's keeping you from dinner. No problem. I'll just go around the back of the hammock to get to the fuel docks. We can still gas up, even if the campground's full." Adoette reached for the boat's controls again.

"No, don't!"

She stopped, watching as Ray picked up his radio and keyed the mike for Carson. At the same moment, Adoette heard another airboat.

"Hey, we've got company," she said excitedly.

"Adoette, get us out of here!" Ray said. "Before they see us! Carson, it's Ray, do you read me? The campground's full of dead gator. It's the campground closest to Jane Doe's hammock, Carson. Over!"

Adoette paled. She studied the width of the slough near the bear. Behind her were not one, but two airboats, coming on fast.

"Quick, before they see you, over the side!" she urged.

Ray understood the situation immediately. "I'm not leaving you!"

"You're the stronger swimmer. I'll stay with the boat." She started the engine, even as the radio crackled with Carson's voice. Adoette grabbed the radio. "Carson, we need reinforcements! The poachers are here. We're splitting up!"

"Splitting up? No!" Ray protested.

"We have a better chance that way! They've already heard my boat, but they haven't seen you."

"I'm not leaving!"

Lightning-quick, Adoette grabbed his hand-radio, then planted her foot squarely on Ray's chest and shoved him overboard, binoculars and all. Ray came up sputtering.

"Would you stop pushing me overboard?"

"Swim, you fool!" She bagged the radio in its watertight case and threw it after him. "Hide it someplace and come back for it later!"

"God, Adoette—"

"Get away from the boat!"

"Wait! One thing!" he shouted.

She waited, her eyes not on him but on the approaching airboats.

"If either one of us is caught, tell the poachers Carson has the film!"

Her gaze swept down to him. "But…he doesn't. It's still on the hammock!"

"Doesn't matter! That's the only bargaining tool we've got. Tell them Carson will exchange the film for our safety—or we're all dead...."

Adoette's face was grim as she revved up the airboat. "They've got to catch me first. Now swim!"

She watched Ray swim away from the boat, glanced at the airboats behind her, then at the bear in front of her. The bear seemed less of a danger than the two approaching craft. She piloted toward the shore, revving the engine long and loud to try to frighten him off. The bear wasn't budging from his feast. He lifted a chin dripping with water, lumbered around and held his position. It wasn't until she was almost upon him that he moved to the side.

Adoette continued frantically through the open slough area. Her eyes flicked to her gas gauge. *I can't outrun these men for long. Maybe I can bluff my way out.* She deliberately slowed her speed, then turned around to see the two airboats go through the same maneuvering with the bear. Adoette gave the lead airboat a friendly wave and went on toward the fuel docks.

Maybe they'll let me fill up and go. Even if they don't, I've got to buy Ray some time.

Sweat ran down the sides of her face and dripped onto her chest. Without its beads, her neck felt naked, vulnerable. Just like the rest of her.

The campground docks were now visible. Adoette docked her craft, then reached into a pocket for cash to fill up the tank. She pretended nonchalance as the other airboats, both manned by grim-faced men, pulled up. One craft moved in front of her, one angled in beside her, effectively trapping her against the wooden pier.

"Hi," she said in English. "That was one hungry bear, yes?"

One of the men drew a gun and pointed it straight at her. Adoette held tight to the boat controls. Two men, neither of them local, boarded her boat. One grabbed her boat keys; the other grabbed her arm.

"Does this mean the gas pumps are closed for the day?" she asked.

One of the men gave her an ugly grin. "Little lady, you just said a mouthful."

MUTTERING A CURSE, CARSON reattached the radio to his waist. He looked down from his poling position to see Alisha, her expression as worried as his own.

"My God, Carson, they've got Adoette!" Ray said over the radio. "I saw it all! What now?"

"We pick you up and wait for reinforcements. Over."

Ray switched to Seminole. "We're miles from help! Reinforcements aren't going to get here any time soon. They can't do anything for us. We will have to get the film—it's the only bargaining tool we have. Over."

"I know that!" Carson said sharply.

"You and...Jane get the film," Ray said. "We

didn't have a chance. I'll lie low. I'm safe for now.
I don't know if our transmissions are being moni-
tored or not, so I don't want to stay on too long. I'll
get in touch later, okay? And meanwhile I'll try ne-
gotiating with the kidnappers if I have the chance.''

"Are you insane?" Carson radioed back.

"No. But I am on the scene. You aren't. And
Carson? The campground has a closed notice posted.
We don't have to worry about civilians getting hurt.
Just get the film. I'll be in touch. Over and out.''

Carson turned off the radio. Alisha's face was
white.

"This is all my fault. I should have told you about
those poachers in Africa—how they closed the fuel
station—much earlier. I mean, if it was done once,
it could be done again. But I didn't know—''

"It's not your fault. Alisha, I need that film.
Now.''

Alisha didn't hesitate for a second. "Let's go.''

He didn't say what he knew they were both thinking. *What if these poachers are the same men?*

ADOETTE'S CAPTOR DRAGGED her to the only permanent building at the campsite, a small, two-room
cinder-block structure. One room was used as the
camping store for food and supplies, the other as an
office. It was into the latter that she was pushed.

She shivered despite the heat. She'd been left
alone with one seated man. From behind the old,
warped desk, he gestured toward the chair opposite

him. Adoette sat down, taking in his features. He wasn't a local—definitely wasn't Seminole. But he certainly was in command.

"We have a problem, miss."

Adoette tried to hide her nervousness. "All I want is gas for my boat. Let me get it and I'll be on my way."

The man shook his head. He was much older than she was, Adoette noticed. There was a gun at his waist and a dangerous set to his expression.

"Ordinarily, that's exactly what I'd do. But my men are overzealous at times. I'm afraid we're beyond the point of sending you on your way. I apologize."

"For...for what?"

"Your death. Let me assure you, it will be quick and painless. We're civilized people."

Adoette fought for her voice as he started to reach for the phone on his desk.

"Kill me," she whispered, "and all the photos Alisha Jamison took of your whole operation—including your face—make tonight's news."

His hand froze.

"I work for Alisha," Adoette continued. "She knows where I am. If I don't rendezvous with her on time—"

The man swore. Adoette jumped as his hand slammed onto the desk, knocking the phone off the hook. Two armed men rushed in at the noise.

"Watch her. But don't hurt her—"

Adoette nearly slid out of her chair with relief.

"—yet."

CHAPTER THIRTEEN

Day five
Alisha's hammock

ALISHA TRAMPED THROUGH the now-familiar ground of the hammock. Her footsteps grew slower and slower as she approached the target tree with its fragrant vanilla orchids, Carson at her side. She had to face the future she'd lose once she lost the film. Probably no book deal. And therefore no retirement fund. And not even the satisfaction of seeing these bastards caught.

"I hope Adoette's all right," she said to Carson. "I should never have let her come along."

"I told you—none of this is your fault."

"She's such an innocent, Carson. What chance does she have against cutthroat killers?" Her pace slowed to a crawl.

"I know you're upset."

"Of course I'm upset! They'll let her live only long enough for someone to deliver the film."

"Don't say that."

She came to a complete stop. "Then they'll kill her *and* the delivery person."

Alisha couldn't go any farther. She couldn't advance toward the base of the tree with its precious film.

"Alisha? Ali?"

Waterfowl cried out warnings and flew to safety.

She hesitated. "Carson, you know the film is yours. But I'm more and more convinced that this is the same poaching ring. Be prepared... These men are completely ruthless. There's no chance for Adoette whether I give them the film or not."

"You can't be sure of that. Any of it."

"Yes, but they're probably..." Her voice trailed off and tears sprang to her eyes. She was suddenly overwhelmed at the thought of Adoette with the poachers. "It won't matter if I give them two rolls, no rolls, or all four rolls. They'll kill her. I hope I'm wrong."

"I hope you are, too," Carson said wearily.

FROM HIS HIDING PLACE among the cypress roots, Ray watched the campground through his binoculars. There'd been no boat traffic in or out since he'd seen Adoette dragged to the campground's single building. He hadn't seen any human traffic, either. Adoette must still be inside the building—alive, he hoped.

Damn it, Carson, where are you? Ray checked his waterproof watch, cursing the heat, the bugs and the muddy water that rose up his waist. He'd made sure the radio was safe, wedged above the waterline in a tree. *We've got to contact these men. But first we need the film. Unless…*

Unless Adoette was right, and Carson had a thing for Alisha Jamison. What if she'd planned on keeping the film all along for her precious career? What if Carson let her? What if they both figured Adoette didn't have a chance?

What if he lost another woman to the swamps he hated?

Come on, Carson. What's taking so long? Adoette needs us!

CARSON LISTENED to Alisha's words. Never had he felt so helpless, so hopeless. What she said made perfect sense. The moment they turned over the film, whatever advantage they had was gone. Adoette would die.

"You're right, of course," he said. But the relief on her face lasted only seconds. "We have to do *something* for Adoette."

"I don't know what—except stall them as long as possible before we give them the film."

Carson thought. "You have what—four rolls of film?"

She nodded.

"Then we'll only give them half the film. We'll bluff—tell them we have two rolls. We use one roll to ransom Adoette, and tell them they get the other when Adoette and the delivery person are back— alive."

Alisha honestly wanted to believe him. He seemed in control, confident, ready for action—just the opposite of the way she felt. "Do you think that'll work?"

"Half the film stays safe either way," Carson said. "It's worth a shot."

"So, who gets to play delivery person, you or me?"

"First—where's the film?"

She pointed; he followed the direction of her finger. It took a few seconds before he spotted the package, wrapped up in its muddy gauze.

"Wait here," he ordered. He passed her the radio hanging on his belt and started upward. "Everyone's seen these poachers but me. This time—" he reached the cluster of vanilla orchids and stretched his fingers out toward the film. "—I go."

As planned by radio, Alisha, Carson and Ray rendezvoused at a hammock a mere fifteen minutes from the campground. The canoe was safely hidden, as were its occupants. Their voices were hushed and low—except for Ray's.

"How much longer are we going to wait?" he demanded. "I say we go in, get Adoette and get out. You've got the film!"

"That's not enough," Carson said. "And keep your voice down. I've been in touch with the ranger station and the tribal council. The council has given permission for both the Fish and Game Department and the FBI to assist us. They'll get in touch with the state police, too.''

"I'm sure the poachers know that! These people aren't going to sit around waiting to get caught.''

"No, but we have to wait for their next move. They have Adoette. They're calling the shots. The police have the campground's phone number, and my radio's on and open. There's nothing else we can do for now.''

"Sooner or later we're going to have to go in there!" Ray insisted.

"Better if it's later,'' Alisha said. "The more help we get, the better the chances for Adoette…and the film for getting to—''

"The film, the film, is that all you can talk about, that damned film?'' Ray broke in. "There's a woman's *life* at stake here! God, Carson, how you ever hooked up with such a cold-hearted bitch is beyond me!''

Alisha blanched. She staggered backward a few steps, then turned abruptly and left both men.

"Good riddance," Ray spat out.

Carson grabbed his cousin's shirt, almost yanking the smaller man off his feet.

"Hey, what's the matter?''

"Shut up and listen. There are two women's futures at stake here. Adoette's *and* Alisha's.''

"What are you talking about?'' Ray pushed free of Carson's grasp.

By the time Carson was finished, Ray had turned almost as pale as Alisha.

"She needs a *transplant?* Why the hell didn't you tell me!"

"I only just found out myself."

Ray exhaled, the breath hissing between his teeth. "This whole mess is a no-win situation. The poachers have Adoette and the firepower. All we have is a few rolls of film to buy us time."

"With luck, we'll get reinforcements before we hear from the kidnappers," Carson said.

"Reinforcements have to come in by water. It'll take forever, and you know it." Ray pivoted, watching Alisha as she made her way to the hidden canoe, then past it to the vegetation beyond, becoming hidden herself in the process. He looked from Alisha to Carson, then swore.

"I should go apologize," he said.

Carson's hand on his shoulder stopped him. "Leave her alone. I'll go in a minute."

The men broke apart. Carson hunkered down; Ray chose a half-rotted stump to support his weight. They stared at their radios—Carson's on, Ray's off, to conserve batteries—and then at each other. Carson spoke first. "We'll get Adoette back in one piece."

"Who's arguing? Am I arguing?"

"No, but I've seen you under pressure before. You usually handle it better than this."

"Women," he snorted. "Nothing but trouble. You know what Adoette did? She made me jump off the boat and covered my escape. I wanted it the other way around, so she shoved me in the water—''

''That's Adoette.''

''I don't think so. Alisha Jamison's been quite an influence on her.''

''*You're* the big influence on her, Ray. Adoette loves you.'' Carson had tried to deny it, to discount it, but he no longer could. ''She'd do anything for you.''

''Yeah, well, I don't remember asking her to risk her neck. I tried to discourage her on the boat.'' Ray ran his fingers through his hair. ''I swear, I have the worst luck with women. The worst. I always fall for the wrong ones and—''

Carson glanced up. ''You're in love with Adoette, aren't you?''

''I— Yeah, I guess I am. God help me, it just sort of happened. There's only one thing worse than swamps. And that's swamp women.''

Ray looked into the distance again, Alisha's head barely visible through the vegetation. ''What about Alisha?''

Carson followed his gaze. ''What about her?''

''Adoette said you two were sharing a hammock. Fun or serious?''

''She had a nightmare, that's all it—'' *Serious,* he suddenly realized. *I don't want to live without that woman.* ''Dead serious. Not that it's any of your damn business.''

Ray shrugged. "Didn't say it was. Just making conversation."

A pause. Then Carson said, "She's an incredible woman. She goes after what she wants."

"She wants you?"

"That's what she said. I turned her down. Told her I was off relationships until I found the poachers."

"I take it back. Alisha's not the cold-hearted one. You are."

"I don't see *you* doing the boyfriend thing with Adoette."

"That's different! She's a traditional Seminole maiden, for God's sake. And as healthy as a horse. But ignoring the honesty of a dying woman? I don't know, Carson..." He shook his head. "Hey, I thought I was a screwup with women. I'm positively noble next to you."

"Go to hell."

Ray laughed, a bitter, hollow sound. "Carson, I'm already there. We both are. Only I've at least tried to climb out."

"I know the Everglades are your vision of hell— but no one's keeping you here."

"Wrong. You are."

"*What?*"

"You and your damned crusade. Your year-long wallow in revenge—like a gator in mud. I would've left Florida last summer, except your father was my father, too, in every way that counts. Until you let him rest in peace, I can't leave.''

''What the hell are you saying?''

''I've accepted his loss, although I'm not sure you have. I also share his sense of family. So I'm stuck doing for you what your father did for me. Watching over you.''

''No one's asking you to.''

''Then make it easier for me! Come to your senses!''

''What are you saying?'' Carson asked again. He rose to his feet.

So did Ray. ''You've lost it, man. And if throwing away a dying woman's love is any indication, you're heading downhill fast.''

''You don't know if it's love. Hell, I don't know if it is. We meet a week ago. Not even a week!''

''She doesn't strike me as the promiscuous type. She's a lady, just like Adoette. While you're as heartless as a gator-gutting poacher.''

Carson's clenched fist sailed through the air. It connected hard with Ray's jaw, knocking him off balance but not off his feet. Carson braced for Ray's retaliation. It never came. His anger abated at the hurt in Ray's eyes.

''Ray—I'm—''

''What? Sorry?'' Ray rubbed his jaw. ''I'm not. That punch just ended my faithful-relative gig. When this is over, Carson, I'm through with you for good.

You're on your own—which is what you've always wanted, anyway.'' He started stomping away.

''Where are you going?''

''To find Alisha.''

ALISHA HEARD THE SOUND of footsteps. To her surprise, it was Ray who appeared, not Carson. Immediately she was on her feet.

''You've heard from the kidnappers? Is Adoette—?''

''Nothing like that. Just thought I'd check up on you. Carson told me about your—uh, medical problems.''

''He did, huh?'' Alisha studied Ray's face and swollen lip. ''Looks like that's not all he did.''

''Yeah, well, I never know when to shut up. Are you all right?''

''About as good as you.'' She withdrew a bandanna from her pocket, wet it with her canteen and passed it to him. ''Here. Try this.''

''Thanks.'' Ray held the cloth up to his face, wincing just a bit. They both sat down; Alisha had managed to find a dry patch of ground.

''I don't know what to do for Adoette,'' Alisha admitted. ''I hate waiting.''

''Yeah—me, too.''

''This is all my fault. I should never have come here.''

''The Everglades seems to inspire that feeling in a lot of people. Except Adoette and Carson.''

"Do you really think she'll be okay?"

Ray didn't answer at first. "Who knows? I wish I could hear her voice. The poachers have made no attempt to reach us or the police—not since the initial phone contact, which was hours ago."

"That bothers me." Alisha raised her head. "I think we need to get over there and find out what's going on."

"I'm with you." Ray tossed the bandanna back to Alisha, then extended his hand to pull her up. To her surprise, he didn't release her once she was standing.

"Are you in love with Carson?" he asked.

Alisha's mouth parted. "I beg your pardon?"

"Because if you are, get him out of here. Get him out of these damn swamps before whatever heart he has left dies forever. Revenge and loneliness is eating him alive."

Alisha searched for words. "Ray, we don't have that kind of relationship. I—we've barely met. I made a few tentative overtures, he—well…"

"Carson won't listen to me. Maybe he'll listen to you. Don't underestimate yourself."

She made no promises. "Let's find Adoette first."

LOCKED INSIDE the windowless cinder-block office, Adoette tried to stop shivering and failed. The phone had been removed. Her frantic search for a weapon had proved fruitless. The one time she'd tried pounding on the door, a guard had shown up—with a gun and a vicious warning.

No radio. No phone. No window. *No film.* Where was the posse? Surely someone should be there by now. *What's going to happen to me?* Adoette's hand reached for her almost-bare throat. Funny, she'd never noticed how comforting the touch, the sound, the weight of her life-beads were. All she had for comfort now was her single birth-strand, some frantic prayers and her thoughts of the only man she'd ever loved.

I'm going to die. I can't believe it. And I'm going to die without loving Ray even once. Ray, my heart, where are you?

The door was thrown open. Adoette jumped. The hand at her neck jerked, breaking her remaining strand. Hundreds of birth beads spilled to the floor, bouncing in fits and starts, then lay static around her feet. She stared at them in horror. Only the long string with a few tangled beads still caught on it remained about her throat.

Her captor saw it all. "I usually don't believe in omens. In this case, however..." His voice trailed off.

"You—you didn't get the film?"

"Sweetheart, I didn't even ask. Alisha Jamison would never release it to me. If it even exists." His smile frightened her even more than the gun did.

"But it does!" Adoette insisted. "She took the photos herself! I can even show you the hammock where she was." Adoette hurried to the map on the wall and pointed. "See? You were here! Right here!"

The smile faded from the man's face. "That bitch has probably notified every authority from here to kingdom come. I should have used a gun on her myself back in Africa."

Adoette gasped.

"Oh, yes, Ms. Jamison and I go a long way back. Elephant tusks, it was. One of my men decided hacking her to pieces would be more entertaining than the bullet in the head I'd ordered. Turns out she's a hard woman to kill. She'll never let me walk away, not for a roll of film."

"You're wrong! She will! Just ask her!"

"I know better than to give that woman an inch. I have other plans. You and I are leaving. It's time we abandoned ship."

"I—why do you need *me*?"

"You're my insurance policy, little lady."

He reached out his free hand to take hers. Adoette stepped back, the beads crunching under her feet. She slipped and fell forward on her knees, the string with a few beads left tangling in her long hair. "But—there won't be room for me on your boat," she stalled. "Not with all your men."

"You mean all those witnesses?" The man smiled again. "I'm afraid you're all that's left."

He pointed the gun straight at her head. "Get up."

Adoette shuddered and let him take her wrist.

"Wise woman. Let's go. It'll be dark soon."

He pulled her to her feet, the beads sticking to the sweat on her palms.

I'm a dead woman unless I do something quick, she thought. *What would Alisha do?*

RAY AND ALISHA CAME UPON Carson dragging the canoe out of its hiding place.

"News?" Ray asked, his eyes meeting Carson's.

"No. We're pulling out."

Ray grabbed one side of the canoe and helped carry it to the water. "Good. I'm through with waiting, too. Have you seen anyone leave the island?"

"Nope. Cops in the helicopters haven't, either. But once it's dark…" Carson's lips thinned as both men dropped the canoe into the water. Ray held it to the shore with the pole.

"Hey, wait for me!" Alisha hurried after them, glad she no longer wore a skirt to hamper her progress. *I was so stupid. As if a disguise could keep anyone safe from killers.*

"You stay here," Carson ordered. He reached into his pocket and withdrew all four rolls of film. "With these."

Ray's sharp intake of breath was audible. So was Alisha's.

"You're…giving me *all* the film? But Adoette needs two rolls! You said so yourself!"

Alisha saw Carson glance at Ray, who nodded.

"Adoette was going to tell her captors about the

film. If they wanted to make a trade, they would have contacted us long before now.''

She felt her knees buckle with relief, even as she saw the pain in the men's eyes. Carson's was bad enough, but Ray's was like a raw wound. She couldn't look at him. Her fingers curled around the film.

''I'm coming along.'' There was no real choice. ''I'll hold onto the film in case the poachers change their minds.''

Ray's eyes filled with hope, but not Carson's.

''No,'' he said.

''Yes.''

''Give me the film,'' Carson spoke through clenched teeth.

Alisha forced herself to answer calmly. ''It doesn't matter who carries it, Carson. Unless you plan on hog-tying me, I'm coming along. Sorry.'' She defiantly shoved the film into her shirt pocket and climbed into the canoe. ''You're wasting time, gentlemen.''

''Come on, Carson,'' Ray said, gesturing to his cousin. ''And you turned this woman down?'' he added in an undertone. ''If I wasn't so worried about Adoette, I'd kiss her right here and now.''

''Don't even *think* about it.''

Carson grabbed one side of the canoe, Ray did the same, and they shoved off. Seconds later both were inside, sitting at either end, Alisha safe in the middle.

Each took up a paddle. They began equally powerful strokes in a long-practiced rhythm.

Alisha couldn't have paddled even if her efforts had been needed. Without a camera to hold, her hands were shaking too badly.

CHAPTER FOURTEEN

Day five
Poachers' hammock

CARSON'S CANOE GLIDED softly through the water, the paddles almost noiseless.

"We don't want to alarm them," he'd said earlier. "We'll go in at the most heavily vegetated area, away from the docks."

That had been the plan. But as they approached the island, they saw no life, even from a distance. Alisha used the binoculars to scan the shore. "Carson, there isn't anyone at the docks. The airboats aren't guarded, and there's no one watching the pumps. The whole place looks deserted."

"Even the bear's gone. I don't like this, Carson," Ray said. "Where's the police helicopter, anyway?"

"Nowhere in sight," she said. "Maybe they went to refuel?"

"And maybe whoever has Adoette made their getaway in the meantime," Ray said, adding a string of curses.

In the end, Carson entered via the boat docks, after all. Alisha did the paddling as the men drew their guns. Her paddle struck a submerged object and disrupted the smooth rhythm of the canoe.

"What the—" She didn't finish her sentence. The motionless body of a poacher, holster and gun still strapped to his waist, rose to the surface. She instinctively jerked back, almost losing her paddle in the water.

Ray reached for the man's shirt and flipped him right side up. "No one I know," he said. "You?"

Carson shook his head, his lips in a thin line.

"I don't suppose the posse rushed the island and didn't tell us?" Ray grabbed for a line as Alisha averted her head and paddled around the grotesque obstacle to finally reach the dock.

"No. I've had the radio on the whole time. Let's keep going. I've got a bad feeling about this."

Minutes later, they were cautiously trekking inland. Carson led the way, Ray brought up the rear, and an unarmed Alisha stayed in the middle. After another hundred or so feet, they found two more bodies. Carson crouched down to inspect them.

"Killed with one shot, and rigor mortis hasn't set in. These men haven't been dead long."

"Mutiny?" Ray asked.

"Or greed getting the best of someone." He rose, still wary. "Come on, let's find the main office."

From under cover, they moved carefully toward their goal. Their caution was wasted. The other three bodies they discovered were not about to challenge their presence.

"Lord almighty," Ray whispered. "These men were executed. I hope Adoette isn't—" He couldn't finish.

Alisha reached for his arm. "I didn't see her airboat at the docks," she reminded him. "Someone had to be driving it. If the kidnapper was driving, he would've taken his own boat, don't you think?"

"That's right!" There was renewed hope in his voice.

"Get on the radio, Ray," Carson said. "We need the authorities out here. And that damn helicopter, if we hope to find Adoette's boat."

Ray soon confirmed that the police helicopter had indeed left to refuel and would be returning within half an hour.

Alisha stared at the bodies around her. Heightened by her fears for Adoette, the gruesome sight twisted something inside her. Tears ran down her face.

"Adoette would want you to take pictures," Ray suggested in a broken voice. "Wouldn't she, Carson?"

"Go ahead, Alisha. It's safe enough."

The two men stood guard while she fumbled with the backpack she wore and withdrew her equipment. As always, once her camera was in her hands, her fingers stopped shaking. She worked rapidly, hating her subject matter but knowing this was necessary.

"That's it for now," she said. "Let's try the office."

"I'll go," Carson said. "Ray, you wait here."

"The hell I will! If Adoette's in there...I want to know."

"Stay," Carson urged.

"No. Get your camera ready, Alisha," Ray insisted. "If anything's happened to Adoette, I want this story all over the news."

The three were unchallenged as they arrived at the campground office. Despite Carson's pleas for discretion, Ray rushed the door and burst into the little store. Carson and Alisha were right behind him.

"Nothing!" Ray cried. He tried the office off to the side. "She's not here, either! But she was.... Look!" Ray gestured to the scattered beads on the dirty floor. "Dammit, where is she?"

"This whole campground's deserted," Carson said.

"I know why. Look at this sign—and the one we saw at the pier. Closed for Renovations. An easy way to have the campground all to yourself," Alisha observed. "It's the same poachers who did this in Africa—has to be the same group. Or the same mastermind, anyway. Obviously all the staff are gone—bought into the renovations story."

Ray slumped against a wall, the hope draining from his face. "You'd think they'd leave a ransom note or something. What are we supposed to do now?"

There was no answer. Alisha stepped behind the store's counter to examine the tools kept under the glass. "I wish I could develop the film here—but you were right, Carson. There's no film service."

"You running low?"

"On still film, yeah. But maybe I can get my Camcorder working again. I have plenty of videotape—I just haven't been able to use the thing since the switch broke and jammed."

"Can you repair it?" Carson asked.

"Maybe, if I can dig out enough of the broken plastic. I should take some photos of the, uh, other body we first saw—the one floating at the dock. And the others.... It might help the police identify any poachers still alive."

"Ray, you game?" Carson asked. "Why don't you go take those pictures?"

"I'm not a photographer!"

"But I need to work on my Camcorder," Alisha said. "Unless you know how to do that."

"Nope. Oh, all right, I'll haul out the floater at the dock and take his picture." Ray held out his hand for the camera. "Only don't expect anything more than a point and click."

"That's all the police will need. There should be enough film left. Just use the auto-focus and you'll be all set." She passed him the camera and showed him the appropriate buttons. "Okay?"

"No, it's not okay. Nothing about this place is okay." Ray took the camera and left.

"I'm going to search the office. Here." Carson placed his gun on the counter separating them. "In case you see or hear anything suspicious. Use it if you have to. And yell. I'll come running."

She nodded. "Although it doesn't look like we're going to see anything." Alisha eyed the gun, left it on the counter, then got to work on the video recorder, using the basic tools she'd found. *If the switch isn't broken, I might be in luck.* The Camcorder was one she'd worked on before. She began to dismantle the switch, then carefully picked out the broken plastic. *Looks like the switch is just jammed. Let's hope it still works.* Keeping an eye on the entrance, she successfully removed the rest of the broken plastic and was about to test the camera when she heard Carson call.

"Alisha, I've found something!"

"What?" She quickly shoved the tools back in the case, gingerly picked up the gun to return to Carson, and hurried out from the behind the counter.

"This." He pointed to the blinking light on the office's answering machine.

"Did you listen to it?"

"Yes…but I want you to." He pressed the play button. "Here goes."

"Hello, Alisha." The voice she heard instantly made her breath catch, her stomach churn. "We meet again. Tell the cops I have the young woman named Adoette. She's going to be my constant companion until I'm safely away from the hounds you've set on me. I'll kill her if anyone gets in my way. You, better than anyone, should know I mean business."

The answering machine clicked off. Her hand covered her mouth as she swallowed hard.

"You know this man?" Carson asked.

"Not by name. But..." She remembered her attacker in Africa, the machete strokes, and the authoritative voice chastising the other man for not shooting her. She'd been left alone, left for dead, by his command.

"It's the man who ordered my death in Africa. I'd know his voice anywhere. If Adoette's in his hands..." She shivered. "He'll never let her go, Carson. She's a witness! He kill her, like he killed his own men."

Carson picked up the phone. "I'll relay this information to the authorities. This bastard hasn't had time to leave the swamps. We can set up roadblocks and notify the airports. I'd better call Adoette's family, too," he said grimly.

"That might stop him, but it won't help Adoette. We've got to find her *now*."

Carson had just finished his calls when Ray entered the office, camera at his side. "What about Adoette? You have news?"

"Yes." Carson played the answering machine for his cousin. "It gets worse," he said when the tape finished.

"How can it get any worse?"

"The man who has Adoette is the same man who ordered my death in Africa," Alisha said.

"He's in Florida? Are you sure?"

"Trust me, I'm sure. It appears his poaching interests are international. He's got this campground closed, just like he got one of the gas stations fraudulently closed back in Africa."

Ray grabbed the phone. Carson stopped him.

"I've already notified the authorities," Carson said. "And Adoette's family."

"Now what? We can't just let him kill her!"

"We won't. We'll split up and go after him."

"How will you know where he is?" Alisha asked. The three left the office of one accord and entered the main room. Alisha passed Carson the gun, then he and Ray consulted the waterways map Ray pulled off the office wall.

"Our man only has a few choices," Carson said. "He'll either head south to link up with the Tamiami Trail or the Tamiami Canal. Or he'll head north to Alligator Alley. They're the only paved east-west roads through the Everglades. He'll either steal a vehicle or he's got one stashed and waiting."

"Alligator Alley?" Alisha echoed.

"Interstate 75. It's a toll road that links up to Naples in the west and Fort Lauderdale in the east," Carson said.

"The Tamiami links up with Naples, too, but it ends in Miami on the east," Ray said. "He's probably planning to lose himself in one of the larger cities."

"I'd guess Miami or Fort Lauderdale. Both have airports," Carson said.

"Miami has international flights." Alisha played with the video recorder switch, then set it on playback, hoping her repairs had been successful. "Wouldn't he go to Miami if he wants to leave the country?"

"Maybe, but Fort Lauderdale's closer," Carson said. "Plus it's easier to exit onto the road without being seen. The Tamiami has more visitor centers and ranger stations—more checkpoints. It'd also be easier to hide Adoette from the authorities in the waterways near Alligator Alley."

"That's where I'm headed, then," Ray announced. "You can take the Tamiami, Carson. Alisha can stay here with her cameras and wait for the police."

"Oh, no, I'm not," Alisha said. The Camcorder operated perfectly, despite the cracked plastic casing. "I'll review this tape and then I'll be ready to leave with Carson. This playback will only take me a few minutes."

Carson didn't argue. "I'll top off the gas tanks on the airboats. There's a couple we can use. Ray, call in our plans, then I'll meet both of you down at the docks."

Ray used the phone in the office, then returned to lean on the counter as Alisha worked. "So...this poacher kingpin is bad news. What kind of chance do you think Adoette has?"

"As long as he's on the run, he'll hold on to her. Once he sees a clear path to escape, though... I mean, look what happened to me—and Carson's father.''

"Not what I wanted to hear," Ray said, "but thanks for being honest. And thanks for offering to trade your film for Adoette."

"The film didn't do Adoette much good, though I wish it had." She talked as she studied her viewfinder, watching her original video footage of the netted gator, and then Ray and Alisha's airboat. *If only I had this fixed when I discovered the poachers! I could have got audio and video instead of just stills.*

"It took a lot of guts," Ray said. "I won't forget that. I'll make sure Adoette knows, too, when we find her."

"Alive and well," she added.

"We should go," Ray said impatiently. "Is this going to take much longer?"

"Not if you write the note for the police while I finish watching this. Let them know where all the bodies are—and that I have film and videotape of the poachers. I refuse to leave it sitting around here until I know—" She gasped at the sudden revelation in the viewfinder.

"What's wrong?" Ray asked.

"I found…something."

"Then tell me, I'll scribble it down in the note, and then let's go!"

"I don't know if we should say anything about this to the authorities."

"What?"

Carefully Alisha rewound the tape, then started it again as she passed the Camcorder to Ray. "Look through here. I took this on the hammock when Carson freed the trapped female gator. You and Adoette should be visible in the airboat speeding away."

"I see. But wait—there's one other person in the frame...."

"I know."

Ray stared at it, then passed her back the camera. "It can't be," he said.

"The camera doesn't lie. And I don't have time to show it to you again." She fast-forwarded the tape to the end of the recording, ready for the next taping session.

"But what am I supposed to do about the video-tape?" he asked, still shocked as to the extra person's identity.

"You tell me. Talk to Carson. For now, we go after Adoette."

Grimly, Ray led the way back to the docks. They were about to begin the search for Adoette.

CHAPTER FIFTEEN

Day five—late afternoon

ALISHA HELD ON TO the hand bar of the airboat, her binoculars hanging loose around her neck.

"Which way are we going?" she asked, trying to locate their position on her map. *This place is so large, with so many hidden water trails.... How will we ever find Adoette?*

"Easterly. There's only so many trails an airboat can take."

"But how will you know which one to try?" Alisha lifted the binoculars for a moment. Their weight was pushing the beads into the sensitive skin of her neck.

"Airboats often leave some traces, mostly muddied water and broken surface vegetation. Look for those. Once we find the initial route, it'll be easy to follow. If Adoette's driving, maybe she left us a trail."

Search they did—unsuccessfully.

"I don't see *anything!*" Alisha cried an hour later. "Carson, if we continue tracking up and down like this, looking for traces, we'll muddy the trail so much we'll never find them.''

Her gaze swept toward the western horizon. Already the sun was low in the sky.

"Either Adoette didn't have a chance to mark her passage, or the poacher's piloting the boat,'' Carson said.

"Damn, damn, damn.'' Alisha rubbed at her neck, then lifted the binoculars strap. *Adoette missing, with a murderer...* "Carson, we have to find her soon!''

"I know.'' Carson slowed the airboat, stopped.

Alisha tensed. "What's wrong?''

"Fork in the road. We haven't tried here.'' He gestured ahead. The open water split into two sections, one toward thick areas of cypress, the other a water trail with fewer trees.

"Which way?''

"I don't know. We've stirred the waters so much....''

Alisha took the opportunity to reach for the watertight ammo case. "I'll stash the film in here,'' she said. "Make sure Josh gets these if anything happens to me.''

Carson cut the engine. "Nothing's going to happen to you.''

"Yeah, well, that's what I thought in Africa.''

He turned to face her. "I swear, Alisha, this will turn out okay.''

"I don't believe in fairy tales. Adoette is missing. We'll be lucky if we see her alive,'' she said bluntly.

"Your father's killer is still free, we can't track the man who ordered my death—and they might not even be the same person."

"*What are you talking about?* Of course they are! They must be...."

"I, uh, found out something else—something I taped."

"You managed to fix the Camcorder?"

She nodded. "I played back the tape when you were gassing up the boats."

"Tell me."

"I can't, not yet. Ray's going to check it out. I don't know all the facts." She watched as Carson's gaze swept back and forth between the two water trails. "We don't know anything for certain, do we? Choosing which way to go—it's guesswork."

"I know that when this is over, I want us to spend more time together," he said quietly.

"Let's wait and see how this goes first." She paused, not looking at him. "If anything happens to Adoette, the slim odds of us having a future go down to zero. You'd never forgive me."

"Alisha, I—"

"Don't" was her harsh reply. "I'm not looking for a charity romance."

Carson took her arm. "You said you loved me."

"I do. But I just can't see a future, Carson. Not for us—and maybe not for me." She leaned over and gave him a quick kiss on the cheek. "Thank you, though. For everything."

He gathered her into his arms then, and kissed her long, hard, with a trace of desperation. They drew apart, eyes downcast.

What a hell of a time for me to fall in love! "Look, Carson, let's forget about us and concentrate on finding Adoette." Alisha picked up the discarded binoculars and handed them to him. "Pick a trail."

"I just don't know…" She'd never heard such anguish in his voice before. "Between us and the poachers, this whole area has been canvassed by far too much boat traffic. It's impossible to tell anything here."

"Take your time. I trust you." She watched him studying the two trails again. As she waited, she noticed that she'd left the ammo box unlocked. *As long as we're stopped, I might as well add these,* she thought, unpacking her camera gear and stashing it safely. *And these, too.* She reached behind her neck to unfasten the beads. *Adoette will want them back— if we find her. Dear Lord, please help us find her…. If Carson and I can't live happily ever after, at least let Ray and Adoette have a shot at it.*

One by one, Alisha carefully untied the life-strands that belonged to Adoette. Birthday-strands, celebration-strands, the strand Adoette was given the day she became a woman… One by one, they went into the ammo box. Finally, only a single strand was left around Alisha's neck, its tight knot and the humidity making it impossible to remove. She picked at the knot, but it stubbornly refused to budge, and in the process of trying, she broke a fingernail down to the quick.

At her "Ouch!" Carson whirled around.

"What's wrong?"

She ruefully studied her bleeding finger. "Just busted a nail when I was taking off Adoette's beads. I didn't have time to do it earlier."

He stared at her. "The beads..." Carson lifted the remaining strand and quickly untied it. He stared at it like a man possessed.

"What?"

"Adoette's beads! The color! I thought I saw—"

He shoved the beads back at her and cranked up the airboat. He piloted toward the trail that led to the denser stands of cypress. "There!" He pointed toward a patch of floating vegetation. "Look!"

On top of the vivid Everglades green was a contrasting splash of blue—the blue of three Seminole life-beads with the necklace string still attached, tied and looped around a cypress "knee."

"Adoette, you clever girl!"

"Wait! Let me get it. It's from her birth-strand."

Carson held out his hand and she took it. With trust in his grip, she leaned over the water and retrieved the three-beaded strand for Adoette.

"Got it!"

Carson hauled her in. She passed him the loop; he studied it, then placed it reverently inside his shirt pocket.

"Thank you for that sweet inspiration—both of

you. We've got a chance here, after all.'' Carson faced her, tangible hope expressed on his face. ''Get on the radio to Ray. Tell him where we are and ask him to call in the information. Then hold on. We're in for a wild ride.''

Carson took one last look at the map and they were off, the fan of the airboat blowing at top speed. Alisha kept her head down because cypress branches were everywhere. She held the binoculars to her eyes, gaze sharp for their quarry.

Carson slowed again at the next juncture in the watery trail. Now that they were on the right path, he could easily identify damage to vegetation—damage that might be significant. He peered in both directions, then swung the boat to the left and proceeded at an even faster pace.

''Do you think he'll hear us coming?'' she yelled to him.

''Can't be helped. We have to catch them before sunset.''

''What about Adoette?''

''She's safe for now. She's the only bargaining chip he has. This is the only way.'' He continued his rapid progress, the airboat jumping and bumping along its course. ''Why not get your camera out?''

''You might need my help. Just get Adoette back—I'll take a photo of our kidnapper in handcuffs. That's the only shot I need.''

''Keep your head down!'' Carson warned her as

they again tore through a patch of overhanging vegetation.

A cry caught her ears. She immediately looked to Carson for confirmation. "Panther?"

He listened without slowing the boat.

"There it is again!" Alisha said, goose bumps racing down her neck at the inhuman shriek.

"Something's disturbing the cat. That could be our man!"

Carson pulled out the gun and passed it to her. "Here, take this. I need two hands to steer."

She obeyed, making sure the safety was still on.

"If you have to, can you drive one of these?" he asked.

"You bet. I've been watching you and Adoette."

He nodded. "Then get ready. Because there they are."

Alisha saw the faint outline of an airboat in the distance. Two people were visible.

"Hang on!" he ordered. He pushed the speed to maximum. Within minutes they were closer. Alisha could now see Adoette clearly.

They were closer yet.

"We've almost caught up!" she yelled.

"Give me the gun and take the controls."

She was just about to do so when suddenly the kidnapper shoved Adoette into the water. "Carson, slow down! Grab Adoette!"

Carson immediately swung the boat in the direction of Adoette. The water wasn't the usual six-inch depth here, but was much deeper. Adoette had to tread water. Carson slowed the boat to cruising speed, then stopped it altogether and let it float toward her.

"Are you hurt? Need help?"

Adoette held up her fingers in a silent "okay," then yelled, "He's trying to buy himself time!"

Alisha held tight to the handrail, leaned over and took Adoette's wrist. Within seconds Adoette was on the airboat, her arms around Carson as they embraced, water dripping on all three of them.

"I knew you'd find me," Adoette said, breathless. "I knew you'd see my birth-strand."

"Thank Alisha," Carson said. "Without her, I wouldn't have."

"Thanks for making me wear my birth-strand!" Adoette hugged Alisha, too. "Don't let him get away, Carson!"

"Is he armed?"

"Yes, but he's the only one. He killed all his men," Adoette said, shivering. "He was going to kill me, too. We have to stop him!"

"You women want off first?" he asked. "I'll leave you a radio."

"Not me. I want that bastard behind bars, and you'll need a pilot." Adoette took her place at the controls. "No one can captain an airboat like me."

Carson gently took his gun from Alisha. "You want off?" he asked again. "There's no reason you have to stay."

"I'm here for the whole show. I'm staying!"

"It's settled, then." Adoette reached for the tiller. "Hold on to your rail, Alisha. Carson, watch your gun. Gators and birds, out of my way. Today it's gonna be a bumpy ride."

Alisha clutched the hand bar tightly as Adoette accelerated to the boat's top speed.

She watched Carson, drawing on his strength. As if aware of the scrutiny, he flicked her a quick glance. Their eyes met, and she gave him a slight smile.

She stared at the man ahead, the man who'd killed so ruthlessly, so easily.

"Get close enough so I can hail him," Carson called out to Adoette.

"I will, but be careful!"

"He can't shoot and drive. Just catch up! Ladies, heads down!"

"You, too, Carson," both women said.

He nodded once, then his attention was back on the airboat in front of them. The poacher's desperation fueled his escape run, but Adoette's skill and familiarity with the area made her faster, despite the extra weight of two passengers. She gained easily—and then they were right behind him.

The poacher didn't waste time turning around to take aim. He simply shifted sideways, pointed his gun and started shooting with his near arm while driving with the other.

Adoette and Alisha crouched as low as they could.

Carson, however, fired a warning shot above the man's head. "Pull over!" he shouted.

The poacher's answer was to accelerate even more.

"Aim for the engine!" Adoette yelled. "Don't hit the fan blade! We'll get ricocheting shrapnel all over."

Carson aimed, pulled the trigger—and the gun misfired. "Son of a—"

"What?" Alisha asked.

"The ammo's wet!" He flicked the safety back on and shoved it into her hand. "Reload for me out of the ammo box if you can. Adoette, get me close enough to jump!"

"But Carson…"

"Do it! He's not getting away this time."

Adoette nodded. Her hair streamed in the wind as she coaxed every possible ounce of speed from the airboat. The poacher tried to avoid her with a sharp turn and almost overbalanced, half the hull clearing the water as it tipped. That was all the time Adoette needed. She cut across his wake and was alongside the boat before he'd regained control.

The poacher grasped the situation immediately—and then everything happened at once. Carson jumped onto the other airboat as the poacher pointed his gun. Adoette swerved to spoil his aim. Alisha saw the gun's trajectory swing from Carson to Adoette.

Alisha jumped for Adoette, intending to knock her aside. At that instant the gun went off. Alisha jerked forward as the bullet slammed into her back. She fell against Adoette, who caught her just as Carson tackled the poacher.

The boats crashed into each other, and four bodies flew through the air, the two women falling in one direction, the men in another.

Alisha felt herself sink into the deeper waters of the Everglades. The bullet's path burned painfully, from its entry wound in her back to where it had lodged, somewhere in the vicinity of her damaged lung. She couldn't breathe, nor could she float; the impact of the shot had knocked her airless.

I'm going to die, she thought. *That killer's done me in after all—and I don't even know his name.* Her chest burned with raw pain and lack of air. She felt herself sink to the bottom, the mud and vegetation alien against her shocked skin. *Carson, where are you? Are you safe? Is Adoette?*

That thought sent a surge of adrenaline through her veins. *I can't die without knowing they're okay!* She couldn't lift her arm to swim, but the base bed of the slough was firm beneath her. *It's not that deep. I may be underwater, but the surface can't be far above.* She bent her knees and pushed off as hard as she could.

As soon as her head broke the surface of the water, she sucked in air. Immediately she screamed at the pain and started to sink again. She reached up, reached for life, and a hand caught hers.

It was Carson's. She'd recognize that firm, strong

grip anywhere. He swam with her as Adoette swam over to intercept and assist. Carson grabbed one of Alisha's arms, Adoette the other. They paddled a face-up Alisha to the nearest hammock. Staring into the sun, she felt solid ground beneath her back. She registered the beautiful riot of orchid colors. She registered Carson's hands as he gently rolled her over to her stomach, heard Adoette's gasp as he lifted her shirt.

He ripped off his own, folded it and quickly positioned it over the wound. He placed Adoette's hand on the pad.

"Direct pressure, Adoette," he ordered. "Don't let go."

Alisha barely recognized his voice. Cheek-down in the mud, she turned her head to see the man she loved. "Get him!" she whispered, his face a more beautiful sight to her than the orchids above.

"Hush, now. No talking." His hand stroked her wet hair. "Adoette, I'm going back to the boats. I'll see if I can dive for the radio—call for help. It's in the ammo case. It should still be dry."

Alisha managed to lift her head. "Forget about me. Get the poacher!"

"You need a medi-chopper. We've got to get you out of here," Adoette said. Shocked, Alisha realized Adoette was crying.

"I'll be dead before then." She meant every word. She closed her eyes and laid her face back down in the mud.

There was a moment of silence, with nothing but the sound of Alisha's heavy breathing. Carson's hand stopped stroking her head.

"You stay alive," he commanded. *"Promise me."*

"Just get him."

"Only if you promise to fight."

She couldn't open her eyes, but she could whisper. "Poacher first, radio second?"

"Damn it, Alisha!"

"Swear."

"I swear. You?"

"Yes." The word was a ragged sigh.

"Keep the pressure on," she heard him say to Adoette. "I'll be as fast as I can."

Alisha felt him touch her cheek, his fingers warm against her chilled skin, then he was gone.

CARSON RAN TO THE WATER'S edge. He pulled off his boots and socks, placed the knife he always carried in his boot inside his waistband, and waded in as quickly as possible. He felt the heat of the Everglades' water enfold him. His own hot fury seeped through his veins until he felt as though he'd become part of the swamps himself.

The poacher's boat—Adoette's—was completely overturned in the water, the engine off, flooded by the slough. Carson's airboat lay on its side. The wreckage of the boat beneath it kept it from overturning. The higher engine, the one part of Carson's boat still dry, continued to run.

Carson swam toward the wreckage. He had no intention of honoring his word to Alisha about disregarding her condition. For the first time in his life, he was about to break a promise. *I have to retrieve the ammunition box!* Inside it was everything crucial—the radio, the first-aid kit, Alisha's four rolls of film, the cameras and Adoette's beads. The box he could find. *I know where it is.*

There was no trace of the poacher.

First things first. Like a medi-chopper.

Alisha's white face, her desperate words and the hole in her back frightened him like nothing had since his father's death.

Don't die, Alisha. Don't you dare die! I love you. I just need the time to convince you.

Carson continued to swim. Once he reached the airboats, he climbed aboard Adoette's and shut off the boat's ignition. The crash had torn the safety grill right off her boat. Carson had no intention of slipping into raw fan blades while looking for the radio.

Please, box, be here, be here...

A sudden scream—perhaps the panther he'd heard earlier—caught his attention. On the opposite side of the two-boat wreck was a hammock—and on that hammock was the poacher. His attention was divided between Carson and the panther. The panther screamed again and leapt from a lower cypress to a higher one at the poacher's intrusion.

The two men briefly locked eyes. Carson saw that the poacher no longer had a gun, but he, too, carried a knife. His own hand dropped to his waistband, checking to make sure his weapon was still there.

"Give yourself up." Carson didn't yell. His voice carried easily across the water. "I've got the only airboat. You'll never make it outta here without one."

"I'll take my chances."

"If I have to come after you, I will."

"Since I don't see a gun, I won't come without a fight. Seems we have a standoff, ranger."

"Only until we get some reinforcements."

The poacher actually smiled. "Who? The girl I threw overboard? Or the one I finally killed?"

Carson reined in his fury. "That girl deliberately left a trail for us to follow. And Alisha Jamison is alive and kicking." *Please, God, may that be true.*

The poacher scowled. "I shot the bitch."

"She's a tough woman to kill. Doesn't give up. Neither do I." Carson found the ammo box he was searching for. He opened it, retrieved the radio and locked it again, taking care that Alisha's film and cameras remained dry. He lifted the radio high in the air. "Reinforcements are on the way. I can take you in now or later. In either case, your killing days are over."

For the first time, the poacher's bravado failed him.

Carson smiled grimly and made a show of keying the mike. The poacher jumped into the water and began swimming for the boats. The smile left

Carson's face as he logged on, requested his ranger station and waited for a response.

All the while, the poacher swam closer.

"Come on, come on!" Carson begged.

No response. *I should have been more cautious. I should never have rubbed his nose in defeat! Damn my pride!* His pride had made him spurn the advances of a woman he admired, was already loving. His pride now might cost him the radio. And Alisha's life...

He keyed the mike again. "Ward to any ranger station. Ward to any ranger station. Come in, over."

The poacher was halfway to the boats. Carson left the radio free but tied it to a handrail for safety. His stomach churned with fear for them all.

"Adoette!" Carson yelled.

"What?"

"The radio's on the boat, but I'm not getting a response! The poacher's in the water. I've got to restrain him before I try the radio again."

"Be careful!" he heard Adoette yell back.

"Alisha?"

"Still breathing!"

The poacher had covered two-thirds of the distance already. Carson chanced keying the mike one last time. Nothing.

I failed to capture this man last summer. I've got to now—for Alisha and for Adoette.

Carson remained on the boat, his position higher and more advantageous. With one hand he held his knife, with the other he continued to unsuccessfully key the radio.

Three strokes, two, then the poacher was at the side of the boat. Carson tried one last time for a peaceable surrender.

"Give it up, mister. Your name and yourself."

"My alias is Leery this week, and that's all you're getting." Leery suddenly yanked on the hull of the crushed boat beneath Adoette's. Both boats rocked in the water. Off balance, Carson grabbed a handrail and made sure the radio stayed secure. He watched from his higher airboat as the poacher quickly scrambled aboard the lower boat.

Leery then climbed onto the higher boat, making straight for Carson and the radio. Carson pretended to counter with a kick toward Leery's face. Leery slashed with his knife, exactly as Carson had known he would. Carson kicked at Leery's right hand, but didn't have the pleasure of seeing his knife fall into the water. Both boats shivered as Leery fell backward into the water, knife still tightly grasped.

Leery's splash was followed by a second splash from the shore.

Carson lifted his head, at first worried that Adoette was joining him. A rugged reptilian shape ducked under the water and gave him his answer.

"Gators in the water, Leery!" he called out. "Throw down your knife and I'll let you come aboard!"

HER OWN RANGER

Leery's head swiveled around. "Liar! I don't see anything!"

"I tell you, I saw a gator! Was there a nest on your hammock? Did you disturb it?"

For the first time, Leery seemed worried. "I climbed on top of one to scout you out, but only for a minute...."

"Throw down your knife and I'll let you aboard," Carson said again.

Leery's bravado returned. "I'm not falling for that old ruse. The only place I'll throw my knife is in your chest!"

Once more, Leery attempted to reach Carson and the radio via the lower airboat. Carson watched the open jaws of a female gator clear the water with a powerful burst of tail power just as the poacher climbed aboard. The gator missed him by inches.

"Well... You weren't bluffing, after all."

"Drop the knife," Carson repeated.

"Not yet. First tell me why you've hounded me for so long. This isn't ranger land."

"You're a cold-blooded killer."

"Of animals only."

"And what about your men back at the campground?"

"That wasn't my affair. They were arguing about money, and the shooting started. I finished what they began. They're just criminals to you. Why the vendetta?"

"You kill the innocent, too. What about Alisha Jamison?"

"Technically she isn't dead, so that doesn't count."

"What about my father?"

"Who?"

Carson's rage built. Leery was stalling, preventing him from using the radio. "A Seminole—a retired ranger. You murdered him last summer."

"Don't recall." He grinned evilly. "Don't consider myself a murderer. Though I might have to make an exception for you."

Leery advanced toward Carson, blade glinting in the fierce sun. Carson waited, the radio swinging freely by its strap at every step. He didn't ask any more questions. He thought of Alisha, bleeding and in need of help. The time for talking was past.

This is a fight to the death.

Leery took another step upward. The boats began to shudder.

"Stay put! You'll overbalance us both!"

Leery's answer was to take one last step.

"We'll both lose our foot—" Carson couldn't finish his sentence.

With a screech of metal, the two boats separated, each passenger hanging on to a rail. Carson's airboat slammed upright into the water. Leery's airboat fell sideways, toward the nesting beach, the full extent of the hull's gaping hole now visible. A fair distance now separated the boats, a distance that grew as their momentum continued to push them in opposite directions.

"You're sinking! Get clear, man!"

"I'm not about to jump into gator water!"

"The boat will drag you down into it, anyway. It's deep here! Swim to me!"

Leery needed no further urging. Within seconds, he was away from the sinking airboat, swimming as fast as possible toward Carson, his knife tightly clasped in one hand.

Carson watched the waters. Whether Leery was a murderer or not, his own duty was unmistakable. He planned to warn Leery of any possible gator attack.

It was not to be. Leery refused to release his double-bladed knife, which made his swimming awkward, clumsy. When the gator strike came, it was silent, the surface motionless. Leery was pulled straight down into the water. He came up just once, sputtering and screaming, his weaponless hands flailing at the water.

"Help!"

Carson reached for the gun he usually carried, then remembered he'd left it with Alisha when it failed to fire. He reached for his knife to toss to Leery, but Leery was dragged underwater again before Carson could complete the action.

Carson watched the waters between the two airboats turn a dark, ugly red. Only then did he reach for the radio. As he keyed the mike and heard the ranger station finally reply, he gazed at the hammock across the water.

The female alligator finally emerged and triumphantly encircled her egg mound—the footprints of her victim still visible on the top.

CHAPTER SIXTEEN

Miami, Florida
Hospital

THE MEDI-CHOPPER HOVERED above the hospital's landing pad, then gently touched down. Alisha opened her eyes, moaning. Strangers moved around, lifting her, speaking to her, checking IV lines and vital signs. She couldn't register anything clearly.

In a pain-filled haze, she heard Carson's voice.

"Hang in there, sweetheart. We're at the hospital."

Sweetheart? Hospital? She didn't remember leaving the Everglades, and she certainly didn't remember Carson ever calling her sweetheart.

"Carson?" she whispered through the oxygen mask on her face.

"Right here." She felt him squeeze her hand.

"Adoette…"

"She's fine. So's Ray. The poacher's been…dealt with."

Alisha sighed and closed her eyes.

"Alisha? Ali!"

Carson moved aside as the staff unloaded Alisha's

stretcher, transported it on a hospital gurney and rolled her into the emergency unit. Carson followed, until he was told, "Sir, you'll have to stay here and do the paperwork."

"Does she have allergies? Is she on any medications?" the desk clerk asked him.

"She's on meds, but I don't know which. She keeps some in her wristband," he remembered. Alisha's pack was at the bottom of the Everglades.

"I'll have the nurses check. Birth date? Next of kin? Home address?"

"I don't know." *I only just met her—but I know the things that matter. Like her courage. Her generosity with that damn film. How much I love her. And need her.*

The clerk took in Carson's still-damp ranger uniform. "We have to report all bullet wounds to the state police. You're the presiding official on this case?"

"Yes." Carson reached for the pen and signed his name, then added Josh's name, and his phone number at Ray's hotel.

"This man knows Ms. Jamison's particulars—birth date, medications and so on. He can also contact the next of kin in Chicago. You have a phone I can use? I'll call him myself."

"That would be a help," the clerk said. "Come around the desk. You can use the staff phone."

Ten minutes later, Carson sat down again, Alisha's paperwork completed in his neat block printing and passed to the clerk. Josh was on his way to the hospital.

"If you want to wait in the staff lounge until the police show up…" the clerk suggested. "Anyone in uniform is welcome. And the coffee beats the vending machine's."

"Thanks."

Carson joined the other professionals in the lounge—EMTs, doctors, nurses, firemen and one of the helicopter crew members. Carson recognized her as the pilot.

"You waiting for paperwork and medical supplies, too?" she asked Carson.

"Just paperwork, and to make sure she's okay."

"I've never lost one in flight yet." The blonde filled a coffee cup for Carson and brought it to him. "Here."

"Thanks." Carson stared at it. "Do you…do you think she'll be all right?"

"I'm not a doctor, but she seemed like a fighter to me."

The pilot hooked a chocolate doughnut with her finger and held it up to Carson. He shook his head, and she took a bite of it herself before filling her own cup.

"Well, I'm off to fuel up. It's a gas-guzzler into the Everglades and back. Got my fingers crossed for her."

"Thanks," he said for the second time. "She needs it. She was supposed to go on the transplant list before she was—'' His voice broke off and he shook his head. *Shot.*

''Rough...'' The pilot hesitated. ''Friend of yours?''

''Yeah.'' His voice was harsh. *Too bad I didn't realize it earlier. What if Alisha dies...?*

''More than a friend, huh?'' she said sympathetically. ''Isn't there anyone to sit with you?''

''No. The other two are still out in the field. One of them's without a boat, too. I was the only extra allowed on the chopper.''

''Hmm. Give me their coordinates.''

The pilot set down her coffee and unfinished doughnut and wrote down the information. ''Let me see what I can do.''

Carson's thoughts returned to Alisha as the pilot left. Time seemed to stand still. Before an hour had passed the blond woman was back with Ray and Adoette. Carson thanked her warmly.

''Hey, it was nothing. Lucky for you it's a slow day. My boss bent the rules since you're a uniform. Good luck to your friend,'' she said, retrieving her cup and getting some fresh coffee. ''Things'll turn out okay.''

''Will they?'' Adoette asked as soon as the pilot was gone. ''How's Alisha?''

''Still in surgery. I haven't heard anything since we arrived.''

''I'll go check,'' Ray volunteered. ''Adoette got the film to the police, Carson. Thought you should know.'' His hand rested on Adoette's shoulder, and he lightly brushed his lips across her cheek.

"Looks like one good thing came out of this mess,'' Carson observed.

Adoette moved closer to Carson and took his hand. "Yeah, well—I'd trade anything to have Alisha safe and sound for you.''

Carson lifted his head. "Adoette, you're the most unselfish woman I know.''

"You're wrong. Alisha is. She took that bullet for me.'' Her eyes filled with tears. "She deliberately kept me safe.''

"Oh, God, I hope she pulls through.''

"She will. She's an incredible woman.'' Adoette hesitated. "I have to tell you something else. It's about Ray.''

"Ray?'' he echoed.

"Yes. When Alisha fixed her Camcorder, she showed him some video on the viewfinder. It showed someone else at the scene.''

"What scene?''

"The netted gator's hammock.'' Adoette squeezed his hand. "Would you quit repeating everything and listen? This isn't going to be easy. I need you to come with me.''

"No. I won't leave the hospital.''

"We're just going outside to the parking lot. Listen—your ballistics report is back. It's…odd. Not what we expected. They're faxing it here, and Ray's gone to pick it up. We won't be long, okay?''

Adoette rose to her feet and tugged at his arm. "Come on."

Carson followed Adoette through the hectic hubbub that was the emergency room and walked outside into the parking lot. There, the heavy scent of Florida's green, lush landscape filled his nostrils, the thick humidity of the summer air wrapping itself around him.

Adoette led the way, stopping at Josh's rental car. Deborah sat inside. She immediately exited, Alisha's Camcorder around her neck, to give Carson a big hug.

"Any news?" was her first question.

"Nothing. Ray's in there."

"Josh went inside, too."

Adoette took Deborah's place inside the car. Deborah and Carson walked a little distance off for privacy. Carson glanced at his watch, his gaze traveling frequently to the emergency-room doors.

"What's this about? I want to get back inside."

"I know. But first turn this on playback and look carefully."

Deborah held out the Camcorder for Carson to study. He did so, lifting it to his eyes. After a moment, he said, "Is that…you, Deborah?"

"Yes."

"What were you doing there?"

"Watching you. Worrying. Alisha took this video and gave it to Ray for safekeeping. She told Ray, and Ray came to me.'' Deborah switched to Seminole. ''She'd figured it out, you know.''

''Figured what out?''

''When she saw me on the video, Alisha thought…I might know something about your father's death. She couldn't think of any other reason for my being there.''

Carson suddenly remembered Leery's words, recalled the ''odd'' ballistics report Adoette had mentioned and felt an ominous sense of certainty. ''Dad wasn't killed by poachers, was he?''

''You know?''

''Only that much. Who killed him?''

Deborah took both Carson's hands in her own. The afternoon breeze played with her skirt as she looked into his eyes.

''It was an accident, Carson—a case of mistaken identity. It should never have happened.''

''Who killed my father?'' Carson repeated.

Deborah didn't answer right away. ''You know, Carson, your mother was always afraid in the Everglades. Afraid of everything. Including poachers. I always used to carry a rifle. Last summer, the day your father died, we were at the border—looking for you. It was raining, and we'd seen some dead gators. Mary had asked me to bring my gun…. Your mother was nervous, Carson. She mistook you and your father for intruders. And I foolishly believed her. I'm a good shot—like you. I always hit my target.''

Carson dropped Deborah's hands and backed away from her. "You killed my father?"

"By accident, Carson. Only by accident! How could I know your mother's paranoia was so great she couldn't recognize her own husband and son in the rain? That her fear would make me sight the rifle—and ruin all our lives."

Carson staggered backward, almost tripping over the concrete parking curb in his agitation. "Why didn't she *tell* me? Why didn't you?"

"I wanted to, but she wouldn't let me! She took full blame for the accident. Said she'd already lost her husband. She was afraid of losing her son, too."

"So Mom ran to Ray last summer. Letting me believe poachers had killed Dad."

Deborah stared up at him. "I wanted to tell you the truth. Your mother forbade it. If it wasn't for Alisha, I'd never have spoken up."

"So you wait until someone else nearly dies?" Carson spat out.

"For a whole year your mother and I have lived with guilt and pain. You don't know how hard it's been, facing you every day and knowing—" Deborah's voice broke. "When Alisha showed up, I panicked. I was watching you—and her."

Carson ran shaking fingers through his hair. "What could you possibly hope to accomplish?"

"We thought we were protecting you, Carson."

"You mean protecting yourselves."

"Carson, you took the death of your father so

hard—we were so worried about you. And I'll admit it, we were afraid you'd push away the only family you had left—your mother and me. Guilty as we were, we did what we thought was best for you.''

''Well, you were wrong.''

''Yes. But now, Alisha's set us all free…''

Carson couldn't believe what he was hearing. ''Let's hope the price of our freedom isn't her life,'' he said coldly.

He shoved the Camcorder back into Deborah's hands and headed back to the emergency room, tears on both their faces.

IN THE POST-SURGICAL recovery room, Alisha was experiencing a strange kind of self-awareness. She wasn't really conscious. Nor was she in some drug-induced state. What she felt was a mental and spiritual awareness of her own mortality. She was very near death, even closer than she'd been in Africa, and she knew it.

This time there was no pain, no fear, just a great weariness pressing down on her. Her body felt empty with loneliness, her heart tired. There was no foreseeable happy future.

She'd done her best. Those poachers would no longer ravage the Everglades or any other place. Her own attackers would never hurt her again. Adoette and Ray were safe. Carson would soon know that Deborah had probably been involved with his father's death. But he was strong; he'd be fine. Carson didn't need her. No one did. There was nothing else to live for. She believed that her life, which had once held purpose, had attained its goal. Her body was useless, tired. It was time to move on.

The way was clear. All she had to do was wish her departure, and Alisha Jamison would be free. But something was holding her back. A voice disturbed the weary, emotionless being she'd become.

"Alisha, it's Carson. Can you hear me? Can you feel me? I'm holding your hand."

She felt her fingers being squeezed. She didn't return the pressure. It was too much effort.

"Alisha? Come on, you've got to stay with me, sweetheart. *Please.* Open your eyes and look at me. I'm right here. Right here."

She recoiled at the pain in his voice. It bothered her, that raw agony. It seemed so much worse than the physical pain she was suffering. She couldn't handle it. She couldn't handle anything. She wanted to rest.

His voice continued. "Alisha, I love you. Listen to me. I love you. Fight back, baby. Just open your eyes so I know you've heard me. I love you, okay?"

She felt his love mingled with her pain and his. It flooded into her being, brought her emotions to life as his fingers squeezed hers even more tightly. She felt his other hand gently stroke her cheek, forehead, hair. A war raged within her. She had to make her choice, and she had to make it *now*.

"I love you, Alisha. Please don't leave me alone."

With those words, Alisha made the choice. Carson's suffering—and her own loneliness—must be eased. With a sigh, she opened her eyes for the briefest of seconds.

"No," she mouthed. Alisha delighted in his brilliant smile.

"I'll stay right here," he promised. "I'll be here when you wake up. Always. Always, Alisha. You understand?"

She smiled and closed her eyes again.

CARSON'S HAND STILL HELD hers when she awoke in Intensive Care. Pain made her gasp, and suddenly doctors and nurses and shots and IVs were her whole world. Surprisingly, she was able to bear it all. When the scene cleared, only Carson and a woman in white remained at her bedside.

"Well, Ms. Jamison, how are you feeling?" the doctor asked.

"Awful." Her voice sounded faint but clear.

"I know. You've had surgery. Do you remember what happened?"

"Yeah." *A bullet in the back.*

"We removed a bullet from your left lung…and something else." The doctor reached into her pocket and withdrew a sealed plastic bag. "See this? It's a piece of ivory that was lodged in one of your ribs. Mr. Ward here thinks it's from an earlier attack."

"The hasp…" she whispered. The man who'd attacked her had a machete with an ivory hasp.

Carson took the bag from the surgeon and held it in front of Alisha so she could see it. "It seems *this* caused all your lung infections."

The doctor confirmed it. "Because this was bone trapped in bone, it didn't show up on your X-rays. But as a foreign body cutting into the pleural cavity, the ivory caused the scarring on your lung. When we removed the bullet, we found the ivory, removed it, cleaned up your rib and the scarring and drained as much of the infection as possible. Right now, we have you on a heavy dose of antibiotics."

"The doc here says you'll be back on your feet in no time—maybe two to three weeks," Carson said.

Alisha managed a weak smile.

The doctor's pager went off. "You want to tell her the rest?" she asked.

Carson nodded.

"I'll check on you later, Ms. Jamison. As soon as Mr. Ward finishes, you get some sleep."

"Okay." She was so tired, all she wanted to do was sleep. For Carson's sake, she forced herself to stay awake. She saw that he still held the bag with the ivory. "Please—take it away," she begged.

Carson immediately shoved the bag into his pocket and pulled his chair closer, all without releasing her hand.

"Ready for some good news? They've taken you off the transplant list."

What? Alisha couldn't take it in at first. "Off?" she whispered.

"Yep. Seems with that piece of tusk out of you, you'll recover nicely. Except for a few more scars, there'll be no long-term effects."

Oh, well, a few more scars won't matter.... But no transplant? Hope started to spread throughout her weakened body.

"Isn't that great news? In fact, you could get back to work in a few months."

I don't know about that. But getting off the transplant list, that is good news.

"Your mother and brothers are flying in from Chicago," Carson continued. "They've already heard. Josh says the book and movie people can't wait to talk to you. You know, it's ironic. If you hadn't tried to help Adoette..." He stopped, then started again. "I'm so glad you're okay. I love you, Alisha."

He really does.... If I hadn't helped Adoette, I wouldn't have been shot. They wouldn't have found the ivory. I wouldn't be getting well again. I wouldn't have a future. Carson wouldn't be here to say he loved me. I'm not a coward—I'm a woman with a future.

She gazed up into Carson's face. "Stay?" she asked.

He leaned over to kiss her forehead. "You bet."

CHAPTER SEVENTEEN

Three weeks later
Miami Hospital

"I CAN'T BELIEVE YOU'RE being discharged tomorrow!" Josh said with satisfaction.

Dressed in her own bathrobe instead of the usual hospital gown, Alisha brushed her hair in front of the mirror. She was back on her feet and moving fairly easily.

"You look great, kiddo," Josh said, watching her.

"I feel great." It was the truth. There was some discomfort left around the surgery incision, but that was to be expected. The weighty tightness she'd once felt in her lungs was gone. She could breathe without pain or effort. Her recovery had been complete.

"So, what's next?"

"Hmmm?" Alisha finished with her hair and reached for the lip gloss. She intended to be dressed in time for her usual lunchtime visitor, Carson.

"Don't play coy with me, Al. This is your business partner talking. You're getting out tomorrow. Where are we going, what are we doing, how are we doing it? You can't lie around in bed forever."

"I know."

"So…what about the book and movie deal?"

Alisha bit her lip. "I really don't want a movie about me. It's too—"

"Lucrative?"

She flushed at his sarcasm, then lifted her chin. "It's too personal. I don't want some gorgeous Hollywood actress wearing phony scars and pretending to be me. Besides, I'm not a writer."

"Sure, you are."

"I research and document my work, yes, but you're the writer. The focus of my life has always been photography. I only considered doing an autobiographical book because I needed money—and because I thought my career was over. Since it's not…"

"It's time to get back to work. My point exactly. We'll write the book and movie script together."

Alisha shook her head. "As they say in Hollywood—I'll pass."

"Dammit, I knew it! It's that park ranger, isn't it?"

"Afraid so." Alisha picked up her sweatpants and top, her daily outfit once she'd been moved from intensive care to a regular private room on the post-op ward. She stepped behind the screen to change. "You're the one who always said I needed a man in my life."

"I don't see any diamond on your finger," Josh argued.

"I'm not after diamonds. I'm after stability—which is something I can't get if I'm spreading my personal life all over the bookstores. I know Carson wouldn't like that. And I wouldn't, either." Dressed, she came out from behind the screen and sat back down on the bed. "It's time to reorganize the business."

"No book? No movie deal?"

"Definitely no movie deal. Maybe the book later—but more of an educational publication, not a sensational biography. The story I turned in on the poachers is probably the last piece the two of us will do together."

Despite her pronouncement, Josh grinned. "It's one hell of a story."

"It ought to be—thanks to you. You held a tape recorder to my mouth and assembled the shots I wanted. And wrote the whole thing without my help." She kissed him lightly on the cheek. "Thanks."

"Humph. Don't ask me to do that again. Talk about confusing! The poachers didn't kill Carson's father—the aunt did it."

"Accidentally, because of Carson's mother. Both have been cleared of any wrongdoing."

"Yes, but what a thing to live with... I feel for them both."

"Me, too. Thank God Carson's forgiven them. And thanks for leaving that part out of the article."

"Hey, I have some tact! Besides, I was saving the juicy parts for the movie."

"I know you're joking—but keep in mind it'll never happen. His family has suffered enough without Hollywood and the public sharing their tragedy."

"I suppose." Josh sighed. "Alisha Jamison in love. Who would have thought? I'm happy for you, Al. I really am. But what am I supposed to do for a partner now?"

"Josh, I didn't say anything about dissolving our partnership or never working together again. I just said I was giving up globe-trotting for a while. I need to rest up, recuperate."

"While you're smelling the roses, what am I supposed to do?"

"We'll figure that out later. Maybe even rest up yourself," Alisha suggested.

Josh actually seemed to consider her idea. "I have a few bucks saved. I could spend some time working on a screenplay I've been thinking about." He frowned. "But I'd rest easier if I knew there was someone looking after you."

"That would be me." Carson entered the room.

Josh rose to his feet. "That's my cue," he said. "I'm out of here."

ALISHA WATCHED AS CARSON sat down on the chair next to her bed and held out his arms. She immediately sat on his lap, his arms around her waist, hers around his neck. She couldn't get enough of their closeness.

"Have you decided where you'll recuperate?" he asked.

"Not in Chicago. Mom and my brothers tried to get me to come home, but...I can't. I hate living in the city. I asked them to find me an apartment locally, but they're bound and determined to drag me back." Alisha bit her lip. "I don't want to go."

"That's part of the reason I'm here. The tribe's authorized you VIP status at the casino hotel. Room, board, everything is gratis until you're back to full steam. The casino's also authorized you to run any tab you need for personal items."

"Really?"

Carson nodded. "Ray took care of the whole thing."

"It—it wouldn't be for long...." she said, overwhelmed by her sudden good fortune. "I'll be getting paid for the poacher article."

"The council also took care of something else. Here. This is for you."

He handed her an envelope. Alisha opened it and withdrew a statement. Her fingers shook. "Paid in full?"

"Yes. You don't have to worry about the hospital bill."

"I—this is incredible. Thank you."

"No, we're the ones who're thanking *you*. If it

wasn't for you, I'd still be out there looking for poachers. We'd still have killers on our land.''

"I'm grateful. Please tell them I'm glad I could help.'' Alisha carefully folded the statement and replaced it in the envelope, which she put on the bedside stand. He drew her arms around his neck again. "So what are your plans?'' she asked.

He shrugged. "I've resigned from the rangers.''

"Oh, Carson, no! Not because of me.''

"It's okay. Twenty years is long enough. I'll help out the tribal officials if there's trouble, but I doubt there will be. Maybe I'll go into conservation efforts myself. I thought I could go after orchid poachers, for starters.''

"That's an interesting idea.''

"Have you ever heard of the Seminole's Green Corn Dance?'' The expression on his face, and his abrupt change of subject, puzzled her.

"Umm, not really.''

"As you know, the Seminole people take a very flexible approach to life. We adapt to new situations by adapting our culture and customs to fit them. But we still have a few hard-core traditions remaining from the old days.''

"And one of them's the Green Corn Dance?''

"Yes. It lasts about a week. The dance itself is a purification ceremony. Corn Mother is the traditional spirit of farming, and the ceremony begins when the corn reaches the roasting-ear stage in late June or July. When that happens, all our old fires are extinguished. New wood is laid out, and four perfect ears of green corn are placed on top. After the corn's blessed, the sacred fire is lit. All other fires in the village are rekindled. When the corn ears have completely burned out, the festivities end and a new Seminole year begins.''

Alisha nodded.

''Because we're putting aside old troubles and celebrating life, it ensures the well-being of the tribe for the next year. My mother and Deborah will both be attending this year. It's time for our whole family to be cleansed of the tragedies and the lies from the past.''

''Sounds like a good custom.''

''I thought you might like to join me this year.''

''But—I'm not Seminole.''

''You're considered a friend of the tribe.''

''But if it's a religious ceremony... I wouldn't want to intrude, Carson.''

''It's not all solemnity and blessings. We play, we dance, and we also hold a court of justice.''

''Court?''

''Yes, where we settle disagreements, repay debts, dissolve relationships, and begin them. Especially begin them.''

''Oh?'' Hope began to build within her.

''The Green Corn Dance is the traditional time of year for new beginnings.'' He took her hands in his.

''I could use a new beginning. And I haven't

danced for a long, long time,'' she said. *I wouldn't mind laying to rest old nightmares, either.*

''Then you'll come with me?''

''Yes.'' She felt some of the tension leave his body.

''We haven't known each other long, but maybe we could work together on orchid poaching?'' he said casually.

She knew he was choosing his words carefully, not trying to pin her down. True, they *hadn't* known each other long, but Alisha didn't make him wait to answer the question they both knew was in her heart.

''Yes, but only as your wife. If you don't mind marrying a woman you've only known a month, and most of that as a hospital patient.''

He gathered her into his arms. ''I don't mind a bit.''

OUTSIDE IN THE PARKING LOT, Adoette climbed into Ray's car. Ray hurried around to close her door for her, something he'd started doing since the kidnapping.

''So Alisha's really going to be okay?'' Ray asked as Adoette clicked her seat belt. ''She goes home tomorrow?''

''That's what the doctor said.''

''Well, that'll be one weight off Carson's mind. He's had a tough time of it lately.'' Ray shook his head. ''First Alisha, then learning about my mother killing his father…''

"Are you okay with that, Ray? I mean, your uncle was your second father, and your mother—"

"I'm okay with a lot of things, Adoette. I'm done with the old baggage. I hope Carson won't carry his around, either."

"He isn't the type. And even if he was, he's got Alisha now. She's pretty sensible."

"Carson's barely left her side during the past three weeks." Ray started his car and drove them out toward the main road. "I like your new look," he said suddenly.

Adoette touched the beads at her neck. "I never thought I'd miss these so much." She wore the traditional beads and Seminole blouse; she also wore jeans, boots, and had left her hair long, fastened in one thick braid. She'd gone back for the beads from her birth-strand, still on the floor of the campground office, and restrung them, then replaced the strand around her neck.

"The combination of old and new suits you," he said thoughtfully.

"Especially the old. If Alisha hadn't made me wear my birth-strand, who knows if Carson could have tracked me down?"

Ray reached for her hand and continued to hold it as they drove. "Forget about those two for a minute. Let's talk about you. Are you sure you want to do this?"

"Join the rangers? Yes. It's something I've thought about for a long time. I love my home, Ray.

I want it safe, and I do just about everything the rangers do, anyway, except carry a gun. And after what happened to me, I won't have a problem with that, either. Since Carson's leaving the rangers— well, it seems like the right time. Carson took his father's place keeping the borders safe. Now it's my turn to take his."

"You never seemed too excited to be working the looms," Ray said.

"No. I never really wanted to weave. I have the skill but not the passion for weaving. I just wanted to be near you."

"Still feel that way?" Ray asked.

"Does it matter? You're moving to Las Vegas." Adoette tried to pull her hand away, but Ray held on.

"The tribal casino's good enough for me, Adoette. I can't very well drag a rookie ranger away from her new job, can I?"

"Not that I'd ever let you drag me anywhere," Adoette replied on a shaky note. She stopped trying to pull her hand away.

"There's something in the glove compartment for you…if you'll accept it."

"Oh?" Adoette opened the compartment with her free hand. Inside was a jeweler's box. Adoette opened it and found a blue bead-strand. It was fashioned not of the usual Seminole materials, but out of the finest turquoise. Adoette gasped.

"Is this—"

"A bride-strand? Yes, if you'll have me." He ignored the light before him as it changed from red to green. "I know you could do better, Adoette. But I respect you. Trust you. I promise to be the best husband and father a woman could ask for—if you'll give me the chance."

Her answer was given in actions instead of words. She lifted the strand from the box and placed it around her neck with the other strands. He tied it for her, despite the honking horns behind him.

"Looks good," he said in a gruff voice, returning his hands to the steering wheel and driving forward. "Goes with your jeans."

Adoette smiled. "I love you, too, Ray."

CHAPTER EIGHTEEN

One year later—Green Corn Dance
Ward family hammock

ALISHA WATCHED the night-dancing from Carson's old bachelor chickee while nursing her son. Month-old William Ferris Jamison-Ward, named after the great Seminole chief Billy Bowlegs and Carson's father, greedily drank his fill, undisturbed by the sounds of gaiety.

Alisha smiled down at the child in her arms. "Finish up, son," she said softly. "Our family is waiting."

Ray and Adoette, now a full-time park ranger, were among those down at the campfires. Both had matured since that terrible time the previous summer, and planned to be married this Green Corn Dance.

Alisha remembered her own wedding to Carson during the last Green Corn Dance. Her mother and brothers had been present, as were Deborah and Carson's mother. Both women had begun the process of coming to peace with the past.

Josh had also come to celebrate Alisha's wedding, and he was here tonight, as well. He'd moved back to Florida, and continued to work as Alisha's business partner.

Alisha had sold another documentary, although it wasn't the poacher story originally planned. Thanks to Josh's efforts, her work with Carson on endangered orchids and their poaching had been favorably received by both the scientific world and television audiences. With Josh again working on their behalf, husband and wife were now researching and filming the life of the Everglades' banded snails. As Alisha frequently reminded her viewers and readers, all of nature was interconnected, and even such innocent-looking species as orchids and snails held important places in the survival of the Everglades' ecosystem.

Billy stirred in her arms and noisily started feeding again.

"Patience, little one," she scolded fondly. "You're just like your father."

"Neither of us can get enough of you." Carson came up behind her and wrapped his arms around his wife and child.

Alisha leaned her head back onto his chest. "He's always hungry."

"Again, like me."

Carson kissed her cheek, then her lips. Their lovemaking had been everything Alisha knew it could be. The doctors had cured her body, but Carson's strength had brought her peace and put to rest the last of her nightmares. Together, the two of them were happier than either could have imagined.

Carson watched her feed his son. "My God, Alisha, you are so beautiful."

Incredible. He really sees me that way. I am so lucky.

They sat together in contented silence as the baby finished nursing, then nuzzled against her scarred breast. Finally, he sighed and settled down to nap.

"If he keeps this up, he'll be on cereal by the time he's five months old," Alisha predicted. "I'm feeding him every few hours as it is."

"Nothing wrong with a healthy baby…and a healthy mother," Carson said. "Here, let me take him."

Carson was the most devoted of fathers. He and Ray had relocated to a more private hammock and built two chickees and two comfortable cinder-block houses, complete with generators and modern amenities. Carson and Alisha worked at blending the old and the new; Ray and Adoette, as newlyweds, would do the same.

Alisha fastened her nursing bra. "Carson, he'll never learn to walk if you carry him everywhere. I swear, his feet haven't touched the ground yet!"

"As long as he can swim, that's fine with me." Carson kissed her cheek again, then kissed the fine down on his son's head. "I'll rock him awhile, then put him to bed if you want to go back to the dancing."

"I'll wait for you. Maybe I'll go for a walk."

"Want a flashlight?"

"No, it's a full moon. I'll be fine." She rose and made for the water, far from the campfires, where the quiet of the Everglades could surround her.

A singular noise—one she now recognized— caught her attention. She walked quietly toward a large nesting site, the mound pregnant with hatching eggs. The tiny gators chirruped for their mother, centuries of instinct urging them to call.

A splash of water on the shoreline heralded a textured head. A female alligator rose from the depths to encircle the mound. Alisha watched as the mother dug into the mound with gentle strokes, the massive claws delicately feeling for, and assisting, new life. One by one she retrieved the hatching eggs with her teeth, helped the gators emerge for their first breath of Everglades air.

The wind shifted.

The mother stopped, catching a whiff of human— Alisha's scent—on the night air.

"It's okay," Alisha whispered. "I won't hurt your babies."

After a moment, the mother returned to her task. She loaded the new alligators on her back, her face, even inside her mouth, and carefully stepped into the water. The babies floundered only an instant—then instinct took over. Tiny legs and tails moved in a graceful ripple, and the offspring made their first swim, all under the watchful gaze of the mother.

"Take good care of your family," Alisha whispered to her. "It's time for me to go back and do the same."

If I hadn't risked it all, I wouldn't have any of this.

After one last glance, Alisha turned. The night air of the Everglades, like Carson's touch, whispered of magic...and surrounded her with love.

Heart of the West

A brand-new Harlequin continuity series
begins in July 1999
with

Husband for Hire
by
Susan Wiggs

*Beautician Twyla McCabe was Dear Abby
with a blow-dryer, listening to everyone else's
troubles. But now her well-meaning customers
have gone too far. No way was she attending
the Hell Creek High School Reunion with Rob
Carter, M.D. Who would believe a woman
who dyed hair for a living could be engaged
to such a hunk?*

Here's a preview!

CHAPTER ONE

"THIS ISN'T FOR the masquerade. This is for me."

"What's for you?"

"This."

Rob didn't move fast, but with a straightforward deliberation she found oddly thrilling. He gripped Twyla by the upper arms and pulled her to him, covering her mouth with his.

Dear God, a kiss. She couldn't remember the last time a man had kissed her. And what a kiss. It was everything a kiss should be—sweet, flavored with strawberries and wine and driven by an underlying passion that she felt surging up through him, creating an answering need in her. She rested her hands on his shoulders and let her mouth soften, open. He felt wonderful beneath her hands, his muscles firm, his skin warm, his mouth... She just wanted to drown in him, drown in the passion. If he was faking his ardor, he was damned good. When he stopped kissing her, she stepped back. Her disbelieving fingers went to her mouth, lightly touching her moist, swollen lips.

"That...wasn't in the notes," she objected weakly.

"I like to ad–lib every once in a while."

"I need to sit down." Walking backward, never taking her eyes off him, she groped behind her and found the Adirondack-style porch swing. *Get a grip,* she told herself. *It was only a kiss.*

"I think," he said mildly, "it's time you told me just why you were so reluctant to come back here for the reunion."

"And why I had to bring a fake fiancé as a shield?"

Very casually, he draped his arm along the back of the porch swing. "I'm all ears, Twyla. Why'd I have to practically hog-tie you to get you back here?"

HARLEQUIN®
SUPERROMANCE®

From July to September 1999—three special
Superromance® novels about people whose
New Millennium resolution is

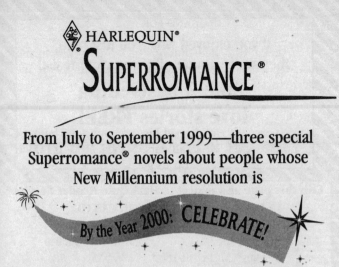

By the Year 2000: CELEBRATE!

JULY 1999—*A Cop's Good Name* by Linda Markowiak
Joe Latham's only hope of saving his badge and his reputation is
to persuade lawyer Maggie Hannan to take his case. Only Maggie—
his ex-wife—knows him well enough to believe him.

AUGUST 1999—*Mr. Miracle* by Carolyn McSparren
Scotsman Jamey McLachlan's come to Tennessee to keep the
promise he made to his stepfather. But Victoria Jamerson stands
between him and his goal, and hurting Vic is the last thing he wants
to do.

SEPTEMBER 1999—*Talk to Me* by Jan Freed
To save her grandmother's business, Kara Taylor has to co-host a
TV show with her ex about the differing points of view between men
and women. A topic Kara and Travis know plenty about.

By the end of the year,
everyone will have something to celebrate!

HARLEQUIN®
Makes any time special ™